THE MAN WHO COULD NOT SLEEP

and Other Mysteries

Michael

EDITED AND INTRODUCED
BY JOHN COOPER

ROBERT HALE · LONDON

ISBN 978-0-7090-9156-1

Robert Hale Limited
Clerkenwell House
Clerkenwell Green
London EC1R 0HT

www.halebooks.com

2 4 6 8 10 9 7 5 3 1

Typeset in Sabon
Printed in Great Britain by the MPG Books Group,
Bodmin and King's Lynn

THE MAN WHO COULD NOT SLEEP

and Other Mysteries

CONTENTS

INTRODUCTION

Ｎone of the plays or synopses of plays presented in this book has ever been published before. They provide further testimony to the talent of that prodigious storyteller, Michael Francis Gilbert (1912-2006).

The present volume celebrates Michael Gilbert's skill as a playwright. The plays included were written between 1955 and 1970. Each synopsis, written in the 1950s, was created for a play which actually never came to fruition.

In 1947, Gilbert joined the Lincoln's Inn law firm of Trower, Still and Keeling. He was made a partner in 1952 and retired in 1983. His legal knowledge is used to great effect in much of his work.

Michael Gilbert wrote 30 novels and 185 short stories. The stories have all been collected in 14 volumes. His novels and stories are always believable, elegant and entertaining. He was a master of a variety of styles, equally at home writing police procedural, espionage, thrillers and classic detection. Some of his outstanding crime novels are 'Smallbone Deceased' (1950), 'Death Has Deep Roots' (1951), 'Death In Captivity' (1952, U.S. title, 'The Danger Within'), 'The Crack In The Teacup' (1966), 'The Night Of The Twelfth' (1976), 'Death Of A Favourite Girl' (1980, U.S., 'The Killing Of Katie Steelstock') and 'The Black Seraphim' (1983, U.S. 1984).

Gilbert became a member of The Detection Club in 1949 and subsequently wrote a story for two of their anthologies, 'Verdict of Thirteen' (1979) and 'The Man Who...' (1992). In 1953, Michael Gilbert was one of the founder members of the Crime Writers' Association and in 1994 he was presented with its highest award, the Cartier Diamond Dagger, for an outstanding contribution to the genre of crime fiction. Michael Gilbert was appointed C.B.E. in 1980. The Swedish Academy of Detection appointed him Grand Master in 1981 and The Mystery Writers of America, Grand Master in 1987.

Michael Gilbert created several popular series characters for his novels and short stories. These include the two policemen Patrick Petrella and Chief Inspector (later Chief Superintendent) Hazelrigg, the two ruthless MI6 agents Mr Daniel Joseph Calder and Mr Samuel Behrens, and Henry Bohun.

Henry Montacute Bohun (pronounced Boon) is a solicitor and partner in the Lincoln's Inn firm of Horniman, Birley and Craine. He made his debut on the printed page in Michael Gilbert's first published short story, 'Weekend at Wapentake', which appeared in Good Housekeeping, 16 October 1948. This story involves murder, a lost manuscript and more deaths.

Bohun is a bachelor and, as Gilbert states in his introduction to 'The Man Who Hated Banks', (1997), 'Bohun's detective activities arose by chance. Since he suffered from a form of parainsomnia which never allowed him more than two hours sleep each night, and sometimes none at all, this left him with a lot of time on his hands which he spent, as another man might puzzle over an unsolved clue in The Times crossword puzzle, in thinking out answers to the problems which he encountered either from his growing friendship with Inspector Hazelrigg, or from his job as a solicitor.'

The tall, middle-aged Henry Bohun has a 'plain, serious rather white face' and lives in the London he loves above the Rising Sun Restaurant off Chancery Lane. Before becoming a qualified solicitor, he spent three years serving in the war, part of that time as a Second Lieutenant in North Africa and Italy. At various times, Bohun studied for two years at medical school, trained for eighteen months as an actuary in New York and, before the war, he worked for an oil firm.

Henry Bohun appears in nine stories (see Appendix A) and the novel 'Smallbone Deceased'. His various investigations involve unravelling a case of poisoning at a birthday party for a five year old in 1896, using the Highest Common Factor in mathematics to elucidate a mystery concerning anonymous letters and solving the death in a train compartment of someone sitting opposite him. Other cases include problems of missing wills, stolen funds, the danger of playing practical jokes and the uncovering of a traitor who is about to betray British agents.

In the novel 'Smallbone Deceased', the body of Marcus Smallbone is found in the office of Horniman, Birley and Craine inside a hermetically sealed deed box thus shattering the law firm's tranquil atmosphere. Written with great style and wit, the police investigation as well as the day to day happenings in a solicitor's office are dealt with realistically. This is a very clever detective story with much of the detection done by Henry Bohun who, at the time, is a newly qualified solicitor in his first job. It is therefore not surprising that 'Smallbone Deceased' was included by Julian Symons in 'The Hundred Best Crime Stories' (1959) and in H.R.F. Keating's 'Crime and Mystery The 100 Best Books' (1987).

It is Bohun's parainsomnia, which has plagued him for thirty years, that gives the series of six radio episodes their overall title 'The Man Who Could Not Sleep'. The six part serial was broadcast on the Light Programme between 21 July 1955 and 25 August 1955. Bohun discovers that he is the sole executor of the will of an Oxford acquaintance, Rupert Tangee. This leads to his involvement with double agents, British Intelligence, a foreign espionage organisation, secret hideouts and several deaths. The part of Henry Bohun was played by William Fox.

The wily Mr Rumbold, senior partner of solicitors Markby, Wragg and Rumbold, appears in the unperformed play 'The Price of Knowledge'. Additionally, he is in four of Gilbert's short stories, two novels 'The Doors Open' (1949) and 'Death Has Deep Roots' (1951) and the synopsis 'My Aunt She Died A Month Ago'.

Mr Rumbold's son, Noel Anthony Pontarlier Rumbold, a junior partner in his father's firm, plays an important part in 'The Game Called Justice', published for the first time in this volume. Nap Rumbold also appears in a single short story, 'Prize of Santenac' and the two novels 'The Doors Open' and 'Death Has Deep Roots'.

The final series character to appear in this book is Hargest Macrea Q.C. who wears 'a monocle of peculiar distortion and its application had more than once unnerved a recalcitrant witness. In addition, he possessed a truculent intellect and a reasonable memory.' He features in the novel 'Death Has Deep Roots', four short stories, the synopsis 'The Game Called Justice' and the play 'Unnatural Causes'.

This collection includes two hitherto unpublished synopses for proposed plays. In 'My Aunt She Died A Month Ago', an author realises that the deaths of some of his relations may not have been accidental. 'The Game Called Justice' involves a footballer accused of murder, with Nap Rumbold looking for evidence as to who the true murderer is.

During the late fifties and into the early sixties, Michael Gilbert had four plays on the stage in London's West End. Three of the plays were thrillers, whilst one, 'Windfall', was a comedy.

'A Clean Kill', an ingenious murder thriller, was Gilbert's first play for the stage. It opened on the 15 December 1959 at the Criterion Theatre, directed by Alistair Sim, and ran for 142 performances. Incidentally, this was no mean achievement as Agatha Christie's 'Go Back For Murder' ran for only 31 performances in 1960.

'A Clean Kill' involves the discovery of a revolutionary cleaning fluid by research chemist Charles Reese and his attractive assistant Ann. His wife, who is the co-director of the firm, becomes difficult and refuses to allow the product to go on sale. She is later found poisoned. Whodunit? The cast included Peter Copley, Hugh Latimer and Rachel Roberts.

Among other thriller plays running in 1960, two were by Agatha Christie, 'The Unexpected Guest' which lasted for 614 performances, and 'The Mousetrap', which incredibly is still running after 58 years.

'The Bargain' is a murder thriller written on comedy lines and was performed for approximately four months from 19 January 1961 at the St. Martin's Theatre. Alistair Sim was again the director and also took the lead role of the staid family solicitor George Selwyn. The solicitor acquires a miniature by his favourite artist through private treaty but discovers that the painting is stolen property. He is then blackmailed, held prisoner, escapes but then one of his employees is found murdered. The cast also included George Cole, Helen Christie and Peter Copley.

'The Shot In Question' was the shot of morphine which brings about the death in a car accident of a young girl who has everything to live for. The disquieting aspect is that the girl has had an affair with a young doctor whose patient she was before he married a nurse. Who has the greatest motive for dispatching the girl? The Duchess Theatre announced 'The Shot In Question' as a play of conjecture starring Andree Melly and John Carson. The play opened on 7 May 1963 but was withdrawn after only two weeks. Thrillers were apparently not in vogue in 1963.

Gilbert's fourth stage play, 'Windfall', a comedy was directed by Alistair Sim and opened at the Lyric Theatre on 2 July 1963. Sim also played the lead role of Alexander Lindsay, the housemaster of School House at Ramsfield, a public school. The school is in serious straits and is saved by a pupil's financial skills. His astute investments correct the unhappy state of affairs. The play ran for just 45 performances.

Michael Gilbert's three thrillers are still being presented by theatre groups. For example, 'The Shot In Question' was performed at Sidmouth, Devon in Summer 2009.

All four stage plays were published by Constable with paper covers.

The first book of Michael Gilbert's to be adapted for radio was his 1952 novel 'Death In Captivity'. The play was broadcast on the Home Service on 8 June 1953. Subsequently, six other novels were adapted for radio. (See Appendix B).

'Petrella' was a series of fifteen plays broadcast between 1976 and 2001 and based on the short stories. The policeman, Patrick Petrella, was played by Peter Gilmore in the first six episodes then by Philip Jackson for the remaining nine episodes. The final nine episodes were adapted by Michael Butt.

'Game Without Rules', a series in twenty parts on Radio 2, was aired in 1968. All of the plays feature the ruthless and efficient counter-intelligence agents Mr Daniel Joseph Calder and Mr Samuel Behrens and their controller, Mr Fortescue. Calder was played by Stephen Murray, Behrens by Peter Howell and Fortescue by Carleton Hobbs. Most of the plays were based on stories found in the three collections 'Game Without Rules', 1967 (U.S.), 1968 (U.K.), 'Mr Calder and Mr Behrens' 1982 and 'Even Murderers Take Holidays' 2007. Importantly, two of the plays 'Churchill's Men' and 'St. Ethelburga and the Angel of Death' were written especially for radio and were published in 'The Murder of Diana Devon and Other Mysteries' in 2009.

'Stay of Execution', broadcast in 1965 on the Light Programme, consisted of six untitled episodes featuring Barry Foster, Maurice Denham, Frederick Treves and John Westbrook who played Hargest Macrea Q.C. A collection of stories was published as 'Stay of Execution' in 1971. The final story in the collection was based on the play.

'Crime Report', a 1956 four part serial, was based on the short story 'The Murder of Diana Devon'. Superintendent Mahood was played by Hugh Burden and Detective Sergeant Leavis by Gerald Campion (of Billy Bunter fame).

Two of Gilbert's stage plays, 'A Clean Kill' and 'The Bargain', were also adapted for radio.

Michael Gilbert wrote six separate plays for the radio which were broadcast between 1956 and 1979. Amongst them, 'The Last Chapter' is concerned with wartime betrayal and featured Maurice Denham, James Bolam and Anna Cropper. The 'Black Light', in the play of the same name, is caused by a prismatic ray. Much happens during the course of the exciting action including four murders and one suicide. Colin Gordon and Edward Kelsey were amongst the cast. The 1979 play 'In The Nick Of Time' involves an escaped sex murderer. In 'You Must Take Things Easy', a wife gets her revenge on her very unpleasant husband after he accidentally kills someone. Stephen Murray plays the part of Dr Summerson, a pathologist, in 'Unnatural Causes'. He is called in by the police to find the cause of death in a case that maybe murder. This was programme No. I in the series 'Doctor at Law'. For the thirty minute play 'The Waterloo Table', Gilbert has returned to Melchester, the setting for 'Close Quarters', his first book, published in 1947. The Dean, assisted by Sergeant Brumfit, helps to settle an argument over the inheritance of the Waterloo table which affects some residents of the cathedral close.

Michael Gilbert also wrote a large amount of material for television, which included instalments of various crime series, over a period of twenty years. (See Appendix C).

Amongst these were six episodes in 1956 for 'The Crime of the Century' which featured Edward Chapman and William Lucas. One of Gilbert's biggest contributions to television was the series 'The Men From Room 13' which ran between 2 November 1959 and 22 July 1961. Gilbert devised the series and scripted the entire twenty five episodes based on Stanley Firmin's work 'Men In The Shadows'. The series was concerned with Scotland Yard's department of undercover detectives, the 'Ghost Squad'. In charge was Superintendent Halcro, played in the first series by John Welsh and in the second by Brian Wilde.

Other examples of Gilbert's television work are six episodes each for 'Wideawake' 1957, 'Fair Game' 1958, 'A.P. Herbert's Misleading Cases' 1971 and five episodes for 'The Mind of the Enemy' 1965. He also wrote single episodes for 'No Hiding Place' 1959, 'Zero One' 1963, 'The Third Man' 1965, 'The Man In Room 17' 1966 and 'Hadleigh' 1971.

In addition, Michael Gilbert wrote stand alone plays especially for television. 'The Body of a Girl' was his first, which was transmitted on 27 April 1958. A school girl is found murdered in the school gym. The suspects are a teacher who lodged with the mother of the girl, a young man and a farmer. The play bears no relation to the 1972 novel of the same name. 'Dangerous Ice', 14 August 1959, has nothing to do with bad weather but is concerned with diamonds and a plot to steal some. 'Trial Run', shown on 9 June 1963, poses the question whether Nico, a hairdresser, has murdered his wife.

In 1959, Gilbert adapted his short story 'The Blackmailer' (also known as 'Did You Say Blackmail?') for television. This very clever play entitled 'Blackmail Is So Difficult' starred Fay Compton as Miss Prince. In 1961 he then adapted his stage play 'A Clean Kill' for transmission.

'The Blackmailing of Mr S.' was written for the Armchair Mystery Theatre and broadcast on 26 July 1964 featuring Peter Butterworth, Peter Vaughan and John Le Mesurier. 'Scene of the Accident' was the Sunday Night Play for the B.B.C. on 30 April 1961. A Q.C. is killed by a car near his home and John Carson, playing an insurance company man, investigates.

It may come as a surprise to many readers of Michael Gilbert's novels and short stories that he was such a prolific contributor to the performing arts. His characters invariably sprang to life and his plots rarely failed to entertain the audience.

I would like to thank Barry Pike as well as the staff of the B.B.C. Written Archives for their help in providing information on the radio and television plays for this book.

John Cooper
Westcliff-on-Sea

'THE MAN WHO COULD NOT SLEEP'

CAST:

Henry Bohun	. . . .	William Fox
Miss Prince	. . . .	Anne McGrath
Anderson	. . . .	Rolf Lefebvre
Detective Sergeant	. . . .	Gordon Davies
Doctor	. . . .	Arthur Lawrence
Major Rooke	. . . .	T. St. John Barry
The Intruder	. . . .	Michael Finlayson
The Man (Albert Hinckley)	. . . .	Hamilton Dyce
Commander Rivett-Yarde	. . . .	Leslie Perrins
Train	. . . .	Bryan Kendrick
M. Horsnail	. . . .	Vernon Smythe
D/Sergeant Hibbs	. . . .	Arthur Lawrence
Mr Moss	. . . .	George Merritt
Mr Craine	. . . .	Peter Elliott
Jackson	. . . .	Rolf Lefebvre
Major Bagshawe	. . . .	John Boxer
Head Porter	. . . .	George Merritt
Superintendent Farmer	. . . .	Donald Bisset
Clarence Thresher	. . . .	Allan Jeayes
Miss Tappett	. . . .	Kathleen Helme
Mr Taylor	. . . .	Michael Finlayson
Archdeacon Laxater	. . . .	Owen Berry
Other parts	. . . .	Anne McGrath, Geoffrey Matthews
Clerk/Cloakroom attendant	. . . .	Rolf Lefebvre
Second solicitor/Clarence Thresher	. . . .	Allan Jeayes
Davis/Third solicitor	. . . .	Brian Haines
Second Porter	. . . .	Geoffrey Matthews
First solicitor	. . . .	Peter Howell
Fourth solicitor	. . . .	Hamilton Dyce
Fifth solicitor	. . . .	Bryan Kendrick
Constable/Voice	. . . .	Olaf Pooley
Messenger/Sergeant	. . . .	John Gabriel
Cipher expert/Constable	. . . .	Peter Claughton
Police Sergeant	. . . .	George Merritt

14

Higgins/Driver/Constable/Boris . . . . Geoffrey Matthews
Milo/Police Sergeant/Inspector . . . . Gordon Davies
Mrs McWhirter . . . . Olga Dickie
Hopper . . . . Rudolph Offenbach
First Lady . . . . Beth Boyd
Second Lady . . . . Belle Chrystall
Commander Shaugnessy . . . . Robert Mooney

Produced by Michael Bakewell

EPISODE 1. 'THE HAMPSTEAD FLAT'

Transmission: Light Programme
Thursday, 21st July 1955 8.00–8.30 pm

(MUSIC – HOLD UNDER ANNOUNCEMENT)

OPENING
ANNOUNCEMENT: We present William Fox in 'The Man Who Could Not Sleep', a serial-thriller in six parts by Michael Gilbert. Episode 1 – 'The Hampstead Flat'.

(MUSIC)

BOHUN: First things first. My name is Bohun. It's spelt B-O-H-U-N, but don't let that put you off. I'm the junior partner in the firm of Horniman Birley and Craine. We are solicitors, and we have been using the same offices in New Square, Lincoln's Inn for nearly two hundred and fifty years. Legal firms which have been going for a long time are remarkable institutions. They collect other things besides dust. I don't suppose that any of us, even old Horniman himself, really knew what *was* in our strong rooms. Jewel boxes; family bibles; packets of letters; portraits in oils; share certificates and papers, papers, papers. It was one such paper that started everything off; on the late afternoon of a fine day at the tail end of July. (Legal London goes to sleep in July and August. The Courts are shut, and the barristers are away, frolicking, in the South of France, or wherever barrister do frolic

15

nowadays. Only the solicitors, poor devils, must keep their noses to the grindstone ...)

(A KNOCK. DOOR OPENING. SOUND OF TEA CUPS)

BOHUN: Thank you, Miss Prince. Just put it down there.

MISS PRINCE: I've brought you an evening paper. We seem to be in a bit of a mess.

BOHUN: Oh, dear, what is it now?

MISS P: Two hundred and four for eight.

BOHUN: Curse those Australians.

(DOOR CLOSING. RUSTLE OF PAPERS)

BOHUN: Hey!

(BELL. FOLLOWED BY DOOR)

              Miss Prince. Look at that! No, nothing to do with the Test Match. In the Stop Press.

MISS P: (Reading – half to herself, half aloud) 'Early this afternoon – well-known broadcaster and journalist – Rupert Tangee – suddenly, at his Club.' Is he one of ours?

BOHUN: That's just what I wanted to ask you. The name rings a bell. But I don't think he's a client.

MISS P: It's not a common name, is it?

BOHUN: (Half 'narrator'. Half to himself) Rupert Tangee. Rupert – Tangee. Wait a minute. It was at the back of my mind. Rain. The quiet, persistent, rain of an autumn afternoon at Oxford. Myself, a very new undergraduate, holding a red and green golfing umbrella over the head of Rupert Tangee, who was standing, tall, thin and serious at the foot of the Martyrs Memorial addressing a select and, at that moment, a rather depressed band on the subject of Liberty. And how irritated he had been when I had incautiously shifted that umbrella and funnelled half a pint of rain water down the back of his neck! And afterwards, in his rooms; drying-out over his fire and eating muffins and talking. It was then that I had promised to act as his executor. A curious turn for a conversation between a young man of nineteen and another of twenty three. But I suspect that Death and Muffins go rather well together. The actual Will must have been made later, when he was going down – or after he had gone down. The original had been posted to me before the War, with a short note. I had brought it with me when I came to Hornimans, and it had lain in our safe ever since. One executor was to be his mother. Then there was a brother, I think – and myself.

(to Miss Prince) Miss Prince, would you have a look through the Wills Index in the strongroom?

MISS P: Very good, Mr Bohun.

BOHUN: Rupert Tangee. Well! A voice from the past. Who would have thought it? He was older than me, but he can't be more than forty five or forty six. Odd type. Did a bit at Broadcasting House, I seem to remember. Journalism. Lecturing.

(DOOR)

Oh, thank you very much, Miss Prince.

(CRACKLING OF A STIFF DOCUMENT)

Let's have a look. Oh, yes, of course. His mother <u>and</u> his brother and myself. Well, there's a chance that one of them's still alive and can act with me. I hope to goodness they are—

MISS P: I've just remembered.

BOHUN: Remembered what?

MISS P: Where I'd heard the name Rupert Tangee. He was on the wireless. On a quiz programme.

BOHUN: That's the chap. Let me have another look at that newspaper. 'At his Club'. Doesn't say which Club.

MISS P: You might ring up the Newspaper.

BOHUN: Good idea, Miss Prince. Fleet 1452.

(STARTS TO DIAL AND THE SOUND FADES OUT INTO AN OLD-FASHIONED TAXI HOOTER; NOISE OF BRAKES; TAXI DOOR OPENING AND SHUTTING)

TAXI DRIVER: That's it, sir. The Monument.

BOHUN: That one? It looks like a museum.

TAXI DRIVER: It's worse inside. Oh, thank you very much sir.

(NOISE OF TAXI DEPARTING WHICH DIMINISHES AS BOHUN GOES THROUGH THE IMPOSING, AND ALMOST NOISEPROOF, DOOR OF THE MONUMENT CLUB)

HALL PORTER:	Yes, sir?
BOHUN:	I was enquiring after one of your Members – I saw the name in the Evening Paper – Mr Tangee.
HALL PORTER:	Oh, yes sir. The Dead Man.
BOHUN:	Er – yes. That's the one.
HALL PORTER:	Perhaps you would like a word with Mr Anderson. He is looking after things in the Small Library. Please come this way, sir.

(OPENING AND SHUTTING OF DOORS)

BOHUN:	Mr Anderson?
ANDERSON:	Yes.
BOHUN:	I'm Bohun – Tangee's solicitor.
ANDERSON:	(Precise, and with a very slight hesitation between groups of words, here represented by 'h'rm') I am glad you have been able to get here – h'rm – at last. My name is – h'rm – Anderson.
BOHUN:	Splendid. You are – were a friend of Mr Tangee.
ANDERSON:	Hardly a friend. More – h'rm – an acquaintance.
BOHUN:	Do you happen to know if he left any relatives?
ANDERSON:	So far as I am aware – none. His mother, I recollect, died last year. His only brother was, I believe, killed in the – h'rm – last war.
BOHUN:	Oh dear.
ANDERSON:	Is there anything wrong?
BOHUN:	No, no. It's just that I had been hoping – but never mind.
ANDERSON:	I was not by any means in his confidence you understand. Merely a nodding acquaintance. We shared a common interest in – h'rm – dried egg.
BOHUN:	Dried egg?
ANDERSON:	Tangee was interested in its commercial development. He had promoted a small company for using dried egg in the manufacture of – h'rm – door handles. I have always been immersed in dried egg. I received the honour of the – h'rm – O.B.E. for my services to it in the late war.
BOHUN:	It must have constituted quite a bond between you.

ANDERSON:	That is so.
BOHUN:	I expect you can tell me what happened here this afternoon.
ANDERSON:	It was sudden. Absolutely sudden and unexpected. We were taking lunch together, as we sometimes did. In fact we had finished lunch and were commencing to drink our coffee. Rupert had just said to me 'Do they call this stuff coffee? Why, in France they wouldn't use it to – h'rm – disinfect drains' when – crash. The cup fell from his hand. He was – h'rm – dead.
BOHUN:	Had he ever shown any signs –?
ANDERSON:	None at all. I had noticed, once or twice, that he looked tired. Nothing more.
BOHUN:	He was rather a reserved sort of person?
ANDERSON:	Oh, very.
BOHUN:	I suppose a doctor has seen him.
ANDERSON:	Oh, certainly. Most fortunately his own doctor is a member of this Club. In fact, I think I hear—

(OUTER DOOR OPENING AND INDISTINCT VOICES)

—and that would be the Club Secretary, Major Rooke, with him.

(ROOM DOOR OPENS, AND A MILITARY VOICE SAYS 'QUITE SO, DOCTOR, QUITE SO'. SUBDUED INTRO-DUCTIONS ALL ROUND. THE DOCTOR IS A BRISK SCOT WHO EVIDENTLY KNOWS HIS JOB)

DOCTOR:	Good afternoon, gentlemen. A tired heart. Commonest phenomenon of modern life. As I was saying to my friend here. Can't explain it. Can't do much about it. As fast as medical science advances, life thinks out a counter-move.
BOHUN:	Do I gather, doctor, that you knew of this condition? Had he consulted you before?
DOCTOR:	Certainly. He first came to me – let me think – must be more than a year ago. I told him then that if he kept up his way of life, you know – public meetings – journalism – broadcasting – no proper holidays – he might drop down dead at any moment.
ANDERSON:	An unfortunately accurate – h'rm – prognostication, doctor.

DOCTOR:	We can't be wrong all the time, you know.
BOHUN:	And you've examined him, and are prepared to certify cause of death?
DOCTOR:	Certain. (Rather tartly) Who are you?
BOHUN:	I'm in the process of finding out. I think – if what I hear is correct – that I am his sole executor.
DOCTOR:	Oh, I see.

(PAPER BEING UNFOLDED)

BOHUN:	I looked out the Will as soon as I read of his death. There you are – last will – revoke all other wills – appoint my mother Louisa Tangee, my brother Robert William Tangee and my friend Henry Montacute Bohun. I understand—
ANDERSON:	Mrs Tangee is certainly – h'rm – deceased. I attended her cremation. His brother Robert, I understand, was killed in the war.
DOCTOR:	(Cheerful) That certainly seems to leave you in possession.
BOHUN:	You ought, I suppose, to satisfy yourself that I'm me – if you see what I mean. I don't carry cards, but you could easily ring up my office.
MAJOR ROOKE:	Speaking for myself – quite unnecessary – only too glad to hand over – ah – everything to you, sir.

(MURMURS OF ASSENT. IT IS CLEAR THAT
EVERYONE IS GLAD – ONLY TOO GLAD)

BOHUN:	Where has the body been placed?
MAJOR R:	Had to move it from the small coffee room – fact is – four of our oldest members always play bridge there after tea – would have been very disturbed.
BOHUN:	I quite understand – where—?
MAJOR R:	Had it laid in the game larder – quite reverently, of course.
BOHUN:	Well, then. If I could possibly have the use of your telephone for a few minutes. I had better instruct an undertaker. He will make all the necessary arrangements. I see the Will calls for cremation and scattering of ashes. Then there must be the usual announcements in the Press. You will be able to help me with the personal details, Anderson?

ANDERSON: Certainly, certainly. Only too pleased.

(THE VOICES RECEDE AS THEY DRAW OUT OF THE ROOM INTO THE PASSAGE)

DOCTOR: You won't want me again, Anderson.
BOHUN: Then I'd better secure his possessions. Loose cash and keys and papers and so on–

(FADE)
(IN THE SILENCE A WESTMINSTER CHIME CLOCK IS HEARD STRIKING SIX)

BOHUN: (As Narrator) This, I suppose, is the point at which almost any conventional solicitor would have called it a day and gone off home to supper and bed. I ought, however, to explain that so far as I am concerned, bed is a place I just don't hurry off to. Or if I go to bed, I don't go to sleep. Not for more than ninety minutes. The doctors, who know practically nothing about it, call it para-insomnia. One of them even had the impertinence to tell me that I was lucky to get ninety minutes. There's a man in Hungary who hasn't slept at all since the Treaty of Versailles. In fact, there is only one aspect of my case about which medical opinion seems agreed. And that is that one day I shall drop down dead without warning. I used to worry a bit about that, but with the passage of time I have grown quite hardened to it. I even find the idea attractive. It seems to put most of the affairs of this life into a very proper perspective. However, the long and short of it is that I seldom go to bed before five in the morning and that leaves a big piece of the night to fill in. An occasion like the present seemed a God-sent opportunity to get on with the job. There wasn't a great deal in Rupert Tangee's pockets. A wallet, with a few nicely engraved cards, which give me his address and telephone number. The return half of a third-class ticket to Chorminster in Essex. A couple of pound notes and some loose change. A small bunch of keys. One clean handkerchief. For a complicated, modern, man, it was a light haul. Nothing brought he into this world, and very little took he out of it. When I had finished, I accepted Major

Rooke's offer of a quick supper at the Club – Tangee's strictures on the coffee, by the way, were fully justified – and then started out for the address shown on the cards, No. 9 Heathway Villa, Hampstead. Whilst I had been eating, the sky had been getting steadily darker, and as I got out into the hall the storm burst. Not just a summer thunderstorm, but heavy, steady rain coming out of the massed black clouds, and looking as if it meant to go on. Taxis are always difficult at that time of night; when it rains they are quite unobtainable. I made up my mind to take the train to Hampstead Tube Station – not the Heath station, which would be a pretty God forsaken spot at that time of night, but the station at the top of Fitzjohns Avenue. I could ask my way from there. It took me about three quarters of an hour to get there and it was still raining when I arrived.

(SOUND OF LIFT GOING UP AND GATES OPENING)

PORTER:	Shocking weather, sir.
BOHUN:	Not the sort of thing you expect in summer.
PORTER:	Expect anything after last summer. You far to go?
BOHUN:	I was wondering if you could help me. A place called Heathway Villa.
PORTER:	Heard of it. Block of flats?
BOHUN:	A house converted into flats, I believe.
PORTER:	S'right. Tidy step from here. Lessee. Up Ivy Hill – fork left – that brings you to the Ponds – left again, then fork right.

(HIS VOICE FADES INTO THE SOUND OF FEET IN AN EMPTY STREET, OVERLAID WITH THE SOUND OF RAIN)

BOHUN:	I say, excuse me.
STRANGER:	Yes?
BOHUN:	Could you possibly direct me to Heathway Villa?
STRANGER:	(Evidently foreign) 'Eathway Villa? Of 'im I 'ave 'eard. You must go back.
BOHUN:	Back?
STRANGER:	Back. So. I point. Then to your right 'and. After that, at the forking of the roads, to your right 'and once again.

BOHUN:	Oh – I say. Thank you very much. But are you absolutely sure—
STRANGER:	'Eathway Villa. All know it. It is celebrated. The poor lady, she cut 'er lover's throat and placed 'im upon the kitchen stove. It was in the newspapers.
BOHUN:	No. I don't remember. Recently?
STRANGER:	Sixty years ago it was. But in 'Ampstead we do not forget.
BOHUN:	Oh, well. Thank you for your help. Horrible weather, isn't it?
STRANGER:	Rain. I love it. The sound of rain. There is nothing more beautiful. Rain, on an acre of cabbages....

(<u>HIS VOICE FADES. FOOTSTEPS RESUMED. UP STEPS,
AND A HEAVY DOOR OPENING AND CLOSING.
SOUND OF RAIN FADES</u>)

BOHUN:	(<u>Narrator</u>) Well, I got there at last. It was a relief just to be out of that rain. Heathway Villa was a solid old dark brick building, with a depressing looking front hall in which the gloom was emphasised rather than relieved by a single, blue painted, electric light bulb; either an economy measure on the landlords part, or a relic of the Black-Out. I got out my cigarette lighter, and by its flickering flame was able to make out that the basements flats were Nos. 1 and 2, the sub-basement No. 3, the ground floor Nos. 4 to 6 and the first floor Nos. 7 to 9. I looked no further. No. 9 was the one I wanted. There was no lift. It wasn't that sort of place at all. So I climbed the stairs, past the half-landing, and up again until I reckoned I was on the first floor. I felt my way along to the end of the T-shaped passage and there, in the one place I had *not* expected it, I did see a light. It was shining, bright and clear, *through the fanlight of No. 9.*

This struck me suddenly as being odd. If Tangee had left his flat to go to his club before lunch, he can hardly have left the light on. And as far as I knew, I had the only keys to the flat. Perhaps the porter had a master key, and had let himself in – always supposing there was a porter.

I stood for quite a long minute, in that dark passage, with my heart bumping, and at the end of that time, I felt no real doubt. There was some unauthorised person in the flat – more than one person. I found the keyhole, pushed in the key, and opened the door quietly. The light streamed out of a room at the end of the passage, and the people, whoever they were, were in that room. I could hear them distinctly now. Another thing – there was a telephone on the table, beside the lighted door. I tiptoed quietly up to it, lifted the receiver, and started to dial.

(NOISE OF DIALLING. YOU HEAR THE FIRST TWO 'DIALS' DISTINCTLY. THEN, AS THE THIRD ONE BEGINS, THERE IS A SHOUT, POUNDING STEPS, AND THE CRASH OF A TABLE GOING OVER)

OPERATOR: Emergency. Which service?

BOHUN: Police.

FIRST MAN: Konstant, the telephone!

SECOND MAN: Um (or some other indistinct noise of assent).

(FURTHER CRASH)

FIRST MAN: Now, what's all this? What are you doing?

BOHUN: (Breathlessly) Oddly enough, I was just going to ask you the same question. And I don't think your friend has done that telephone much good. They aren't meant to be dropped on the floor and stamped on.

FIRST MAN: Suppose we go back into the room. Konstant, the front door.

(SOUND OF THE FRONT DOOR BEING SHUT AND BOLTED)

BOHUN: Suits me. I say, have you been having a sort-out, or something?

FIRST MAN: We have been engaged in arranging Mr Tangee's papers for him.

BOHUN: You've certainly been arranging them all right. With his permission, I assume.

FIRST MAN: Of course.

BOHUN: (Noise as he kicks something metallic with his foot) Hullo! Why did you have to break open this deed box? If you're here with his permission, couldn't you have asked him for a loan of the key?

FIRST MAN: (An 'edge' in his voice) You ask too many questions. You should answer them, instead. How did *you* get into this flat?

BOHUN: In the normal, civilized way. By inserting the key in the lock and turning it.

FIRST MAN: And how did you get the key?

BOHUN: Mr Tangee gave it to me.

FIRST MAN: That's a lie. He's dead.

BOHUN: And how did you know that?

(SHORT PAUSE)

FIRST MAN: Did I not read an announcement in the papers?

BOHUN: I don't know. Did you?

FIRST MAN: (More confidently) Certainly I did. He died at his Club. After eating his lunch today. (Sharply) How then are his keys in the possession of a stranger a few hours later?

BOHUN: All right. It's a fair question. I'm a solicitor. My name is Bohun. I am named executor in Mr Tangee's Will. I have therefore the right and the duty of taking in charge all his property – including, incidentally, his private papers with which you seem to have been making so free.

FIRST MAN: I do not believe one single word of it.

BOHUN: Then you have a very simple remedy. There won't be anyone at my office at this hour, of course. But I don't suppose the Secretary of the Monument Club has gone to bed yet. Ring up the Club and ask for Major Rooke – oh – I forgot. Your friend has wrecked the only telephone. Very well. Let's knock up the next door flat and use theirs.

FIRST MAN: And what will Major Rooke tell us?

BOHUN: I shall speak to him and remind him of what happened at the Club this afternoon. I think we should be able to satisfy you between us.

FIRST MAN: And what if I refuse to do anything of the sort?

BOHUN: I shall be forced to conclude that my first idea was current.

FIRST MAN: And what was that idea?

BOHUN: That you have no right of any sort to be here; that you probably broke in. Why you should have done so, I can't

	think, except that you seem to be interested in the late Mr Tangee's personal papers.
FIRST MAN:	Yes?
BOHUN:	And that far from *my* having to give any explanation to *you*, it is *you* who should be doing some explaining to *me*.
FIRST MAN:	And suppose that I do not feel called upon to explain anything?
BOHUN:	(<u>Beginning to speak more slowly, with pauses between each sentence, as if he is listening for something</u>) It had occurred to me that you might not want to talk – to me. That is why it is so fortunate that (<u>looking at his watch</u>) four minutes should already have elapsed since I came into this flat.
FIRST MAN:	(<u>Sharply</u>) What do you mean?

<u>(IN THE FAR DISTANCE, A CAR)</u>

BOHUN:	I thought that perhaps you had not quite appreciated the situation. I completed dialling 999 and called the police *before* your big friend here succeeded in pulling the telephone out of the wall and stamping on it. That, of course, will have made some policeman scratch his head. (<u>More slowly still</u>) It will have taken them a little time to trace the call (<u>CAR NOISE MUCH NEARER</u>) but I rather think, that that must be them now.

<u>(A CAR SQUEAKS TO A HALT IN THE ROAD OUTSIDE)</u>

FIRST MAN:	Konstant!
BOHUN:	Leave me alone, you—

<u>(INDETERMINATE SORT OF NOISE – SOMEONE HITTING SOMEONE – TEARING OF CLOTH – TERMINATING IN A CRASH OF FURNITURE. THEN FOOTSTEPS RUNNING. THEN THE SLAM OF THE FRONT DOOR)</u>

BOHUN:	(<u>Groaning</u>) Ouch.

<u>(NEW VOICES FROM OUTSIDE THE FLAT. KNOCKING AT THE DOOR. HEAVY, AND REPEATED)</u>

BOHUN: All right, hold it. Don't break the door down. We've had enough dilapidation in this flat this evening. I'm coming.

(DOOR OPENS. NEW, AND OBVIOUSLY OFFICIAL VOICE SPEAKS)

D/SERGEANT: Now, what's going on here?

BOHUN: Thank goodness you've arrived. Mind that lamp. You didn't by any chance pass two men going out?

D/SERGEANT: We didn't pass anyone. Are you the gentleman who made the emergency call?

D/CONSTABLE: Just look at that telephone, Sergeant.

D/SERGEANT: Ah. Someone been tampering with Post Office property.

BOHUN: I shouldn't myself describe pulling a telephone out of the wall, dropping it on the floor and stamping on it as 'tampering' – but I expect you know best.

D/SERGEANT: Are you the owner of this flat, sir?

BOHUN: I suppose I am, in a way, yes.

D/SERGEANT: In a way? (D/Constable whispers something to the Sergeant that sounds like 'name on door') Are you Mr Tangee then?

BOHUN: No. My name's Bohun.

D/SERGEANT: The card outside the door says this flat belongs to a Mr Tangee.

BOHUN: Did belong. He's dead.

D/SERGEANT: What's that?

BOHUN: Oh, not on the premises. He died at his Club. This afternoon. I've got an evening paper somewhere.

(SOUND OF PAPER)

There. In the bottom left hand corner. Stop Press. Well known journalist and broadcaster.

D/SERGEANT: Ah, I see. That's him is it? Then who are you?

BOHUN: I'm his legal personal representative.

D/SERGEANT: (Baffled) legal—? You mean, you're a lawyer?

BOHUN: Well, as a matter of fact, that wasn't what I meant, but I am. I'm a solicitor. Horniman Birley and Craine, New Square, Lincoln's Inn.

D/SERGEANT: I see, sir. You're a solicitor. And you're Mr Tangee's legal-what-ever-it-was-you-said.

BOHUN: That's right. His executor, it's sometimes called.

D/SERGEANT:	Named in the Will?
BOHUN:	Named in the Will.
D/SERGEANT:	So you take charge of all his stuff now he's dead.
BOHUN:	That's the idea.
D/SERGEANT:	You'll excuse me asking I'm sure, but do you happen to have anything on you to prove all this?
BOHUN:	I've got the Will. Careful with it! It's got to go to Probate yet. The first Clause is the one. That's it. His mother and his brother are dead – and the other one's me.
D/SERGEANT:	I thought you said your name was Boon.
BOHUN:	So it is. B-o-h-u-n – Boon.
D/SERGEANT:	Ah. Like C-h-o-l- whatever comes next – Chumley.
BOHUN:	That's right. Just like Chumley. Now are you happy?
D/SERGEANT:	Just one other thing, sir. Would you have anything on you to show that *you* are Mr Boon?
BOHUN:	I don't carry cards round with me. I've probably got a letter. Yes. Here's a demand for Water Rates.
D/SERGEANT:	Very good, sir. That seems to be in order. Mr Tangee's dead and Mr Boon's his executor – and you're Mr Boon. Right?
BOHUN:	Right.
D/SERGEANT:	Only thing is – and I'm sure you'll excuse me mentioning it – but it seems an odd time of night to start dismantling the flat.
BOHUN:	Good heavens. I didn't do that! That was the two men.
D/SERGEANT:	Two men? Here?
D/CONSTABLE:	Never saw two men.
BOHUN:	I've no doubt they ducked into a doorway as you went past. It's dark enough. But they were here, all right. That's why I dialled 999. I came along here to start work – collecting papers, and so on – and when I arrived I saw a light on and found these two men in possession. They appeared to be doing exactly what I had come up to do myself – sorting out Tangee's papers – as you can see – all over the floor. I guessed they were up to no good, so I dialled for help. Then they attacked me and wrecked the telephone.
D/SERGEANT:	I see, sir. Can you describe them?
BOHUN:	The one who did all the talking was – was a – well, he's absolutely impossible to describe. You can see him by the hundred getting in and out of suburban trains. He's stoutish – I don't mean like Billy Bunter, but a bit full on the cheeks and chin and that extra inch or two round the

waist that you get if you sit on your bottom all day. Oh, and gold-rimmed glasses – slightly un-English that. Hair running away. Fat hands. Soft voice, well-dressed, but not oustandingly so.

D/SERGEANT: That's not too helpful is it? What about the other?

BOHUN: He really *was* something. He was dressed in a sort of rusty black suit, like an old fashioned man servant. White face, without a lot of expression in it. Dark hair – almost a crew-cut, but not quite. And big – I'm six foot. I'd say he was all of six inches taller than that, and broad in proportion. Hands like hams. I tell you, when we heard you coming just now, he picked me up, without any effort at all, and tossed me across the room. Luckily most of me landed on the sofa. That's when my face hit the lamp standard. It was like being handled by a crane.

D/SERGEANT: Sort of ape man.

BOHUN: If you can imagine a very respectable ape dressed up as a family retainer, yes.

D/SERGEANT: And you wouldn't have any idea what they might have been doing here?

BOHUN: Not a clue.

D/SERGEANT: There's nothing in Mr – Mr Tangee's – past to suggest any reason to you?

BOHUN: I'm afraid I don't know anything about his past, except the little bits I've read in the papers from time to time. He wasn't a man who called much attention to himself, I wouldn't think.

D/SERGEANT: A quiet sort of man.

BOHUN: That's it. A quiet sort of man.

D/SERGEANT: Well, perhaps our first guess was right and it was just a couple of sneak thieves. Sort of things they get up to. Artful. They read of a death in the papers and think that's a good opportunity to nip along and help themselves. And if you hadn't been right on the job, sir, that's just about what they would have done. And got away with it, nobody the wiser.

BOHUN: Could be. Only I should have thought they'd have gone for his silver, not his papers.

D/SERGEANT: You never know with that sort. You'll excuse me asking, but what are you planning to do?

BOHUN: Whilst I'm here, I might as well get on with what I came to do. I've got the night in front of me.

29

D/SERGEANT:	The night?
BOHUN:	Oh, I sleep rather badly.
D/SERGEANT:	Well, if that's your idea, sir, I'd better tip them off at the local station. Tell them to keep an eye on the place.
BOHUN:	It's very good of you. But I shouldn't think they'd come back tonight. By the way – before you go – just curiosity – nothing to do with what's been happening. I met an odd character on my way up here. He said something about a murder here.
D/SERGEANT:	Murder?
BOHUN:	Before your time. In fact, about sixty years ago.
D/CONSTABLE:	That's right, sir. Don't you remember, Sergeant? Cissie Barnes. Cut 'er paramour's throat. Tried at the Ol' Bailey. Hanged at Pentonville, January 15th, 1895.
D/SERGEANT:	(Repressively) You want to keep your mind on things that happen in front of your eyes, Coleclough. Not sixty years ago. That's the way to get promotion.

(FRONT DOOR OPENED)

Well, I'll wish you good night, sir.

(VOICES DIE AWAY DOWN THE CORRIDOR. THE VOICE OF THE SERGEANT IS HEARD IN THE DISTANCE)

D/SERGEANT:	(distant) You and Cissie Barnes.

(FRONT DOOR SHUTS)

BOHUN:	(Narrator) I thought I'd better start on the papers. There was quite a collection. I began by sorting them out. Letters in one pile. Printed pieces in another. Memoranda in a third. He seemed to have been a devil for memoranda!

(DURING THESE MUSINGS BY BOHUN THE FLAT IS QUITE SILENT EXCEPT FOR THE TURNING AND CRACKLING OF PAPER. IN THE INTERVALS OF SILENCE A SMALL CLOCK MAKES ITSELF HEARD, TICKING AWAY BUSILY IN THE BACKGROUND)

BOHUN:	(<u>still as Narrator</u>) There were a few that looked like diaries. Not diaries, Minute books. The Central League for Encouragement of Free Thought. It sounded desperately dull, but I stacked them all together.
FOREIGN VOICE:	(<u>on echo</u>) 'Eathway Villa. All know it. It is celebrated. The poor lady she cut 'er lover's throat, and placed 'im upon the kitchen stove.
BOHUN:	(as Narrator) On second thoughts, perhaps it wasn't the most cheerful place to have chosen to spend the night in. I kept my mind on the job.

(<u>RENEWED CRACKLINGS</u>)

Newspaper cuttings. Dozens of them. Some going back about ten years, some quite new.

D/CONSTABLE:	(<u>on echo</u>) Cissie Barnes. Cut 'er paramour's throat. Tried at the Ol' Bailey. Hanged at Pentonville. January 15th 1895.
BOHUN:	(as Narrator) Look here, if you can't keep your mind on what you're doing, you'd better pack up and call it a day. You'll start imagining things soon.

(<u>A BLOOD CURDLING SHRIEK FROM THE GARDEN OUTSIDE</u>)

Good lord! That's not imagination. What—

(<u>WINDOW OPENING</u>)

Oh! Cats! Can't you conduct your love affairs quietly?

(<u>RENEWED, BUT SOFTER GROWLS AND SPITTINGS</u>)

Just take your paramour a bit further off.

(<u>WINDOW SHUT</u>)

There you are, you see. Just nerves. A natural explanation for everything if you choose to look for it. Now what comes next? These look like household bills. No need to bother about them. A few more letters. Some of them quite recent. Ha. Here's one post-marked yesterday. He must have got it this morning. In fact, it must have been one of the last things he read. Odd sort of letter. No beginning and no end. What's all this.

(Mounting excitement in his voice) 'We should be much obliged if you would stay clear of your flat from lunch time until after supper.' Lunch time until after supper? That must refer to today. Well, he certainly carried out those instructions all right!

(IN THE BACKGROUND THERE HAS BEGUN A DISTINCT BUT MUFFLED TAPPING. TAP-TAP. TAP-TAP-TAP. AT THIS POINT BOHUN HIMSELF SEEMS TO HEAR IT FOR THE FIRST TIME)

What the—? More imagination. No. It's real all right. Seems to be coming from this inner room. Must be the bedroom. Careful now.

(OPENS DOOR QUICKLY)

Good lord. (Pause) Poor devil. Get the gag out first. He's nearly suffocated.

(GASPING SOUNDS AS OF SOMEONE DRAWING BADLY NEEDED BREATH)

Hold hard, sir. Don't wriggle. I'll soon have the rest off. Haven't got a knife. Never mind. Scissors on the dressing table. Soon have you cut loose. Hold still.

(SOUND OF SNIPPING)

THE MAN (Hickley):	They hit me. And tied me up. I've been here for hours. We've got to get out. Quick. Quick. Quick.

(MUSIC – FADE)

EPISODE 2

'THE EARLY HOURS OF THE MORNING'

<u>Transmission: Light Programme</u>
<u>Thursday, 28th July 1955 8.00–8.30 pm</u>

(<u>MUSIC – HOLD UNDER ANNOUNCEMENT</u>)

OPENING
ANNOUNCEMENT: We present William Fox in 'The Man Who Could Not Sleep', a serial-thriller in six parts by Michael Gilbert. Episode 2 – 'The Early Hours of the Morning'.

(<u>MUSIC</u>)

ANNOUNCER: Bohun, junior partner in a firm of Lincolns Inn solicitors, reads one afternoon in the stop press of the death of an Oxford acquaintance, Rupert Tangee, journalist; economist and broadcaster. He goes to Tangee's Club (where his body lies) then decides to put in an evening's work up at Tangee's flat in Hampstead, sorting through the dead man's papers. He does not grudge an evening – or even a night – to such a job since he suffers from a rare and acute form of insomnia. Arrived at the flat, he surprises two foreigners rifling Tangee's papers. Fortunately he succeeds in dialling 999 and the two men make off.   Bohun is ultimately left in possession of the flat. He finds Tangee's papers rather a curious collection, suggesting that Tangee might himself have been involved in subversive activities. Half way through his task, he hears a thumping noise from the bedroom, and discovers an unknown man, gagged and tied with strips of sheet.

BOHUN: That's better. Take it easy, now.

HICKLEY: (<u>Busy trying to get his breath back</u>)

BOHUN: Quicker if I cut it. There are too many knots.

(<u>SNIP</u>)

33

That's it.

(SNIP, SNIP)

Someone has wasted a whole sheet on you, I'd say. A very thorough job.

HICKLEY: (Voice very slightly common. By no means uneducated) We – must – get – away!

BOHUN: Stop worrying. The police are in the street, and the door's locked, and we're alone in the flat. At least, come to think of it, I suppose we are alone. Don't want any *more* shocks. I'd better have a quick. look.

(SOUND OF DOORS BEING OPENED AND SHUT)

No. Seems all clear. Unless anyone's hiding under the bed. No. Now then, sir, suppose we go and make ourselves comfortable and you tell me just what you were doing in Rupert Tangee's bedroom, and who tied you up, and gagged you so tight they nearly suffocated you.

HICKLEY: (More quietly) We must get out of here.

BOHUN: What are you afraid of?

HICKLEY: I can't explain. It would take too long.

BOHUN: Is it two men? One of them sort of soft and ordinary-looking and the other like King Kong in dress clothes?

HICKLEY: Yes. Those two – and others.

BOHUN: Was it them who tied you up?

HICKLEY: The big man, yes.

BOHUN: I sympathise with you. He threw *me* across the room – with one hand. What's his name, by the way?

HICKLEY: Konstant.

BOHUN: And the other chap?

HICKLEY: I know him as Mr Taylor. I don't think that is his real name.

BOHUN: Taylor'll do for the time being. Well, that precious pair left here about half an hour ago. Just before the police arrived. (Pause) Good heavens, man, what's wrong with you? Every time I mention the police you jump like a mountain goat. You're not afraid of the police too, are you?

HICKLEY: (He sounds as if he might burst into tears) I – I'm in a

BOHUN: very difficult position. I can't – I don't know what to do. The first thing to do is take a grip of yourself. Now I wonder—

(SOUND OF MOVING ROUND – CUPBOARD BEING OPENED)

I don't recollect that Tangee was a teetotaller. Ah! What's this? Is it? It is indeed. Scotch, too. Can you drink Scotch out of a tea cup. Mr—?

HICKLEY: Hickley. Albert Hickley.

BOHUN: Mr Hickley? You can? I think I'll join you. Don't be afraid of it. All Mr Tangee's goods have devolved upon me. We'll regard this one as an administrative expense! That's right. Now, as I was saying … That precious pair are lurking somewhere outside. In the dark and wet. We are inside in the light and warm, with a reasonably stout front door between us. So put any idea of leaving out of your head. We're much better off where we are.

HICKLEY: (The whisky and Bohun's confident manner are having an effect on him) I suppose so, yes.

BOHUN: Suppose we relax a bit, and tell each other our life stories. Mine is quite simple. I am Rupert Tangee's executor. As soon as I heard of his death I came up to take possession of his worldly goods. And I found Taylor and Konstant had beaten me to it. So I called the police, but they got away before the police arrived. Then I found you, tied up with strips of sheet and kicking like a gaffed salmon. Right. Your turn.

HICKLEY: So Tangee's dead, is he? Yes, that explains a lot.

BOHUN: Don't start in the middle. Start at the beginning.

HICKLEY: I'm not sure that I can—

BOHUN: Do you want me to help you?

(LONGISH PAUSE)

HICKLEY: Yes.

BOHUN: Then tell me the whole story. I'm a lawyer. Part of my job is keeping secrets. Only mind this. I'm not going to play at all unless you tell me everything.

(ANOTHER PAUSE)

35

HICKLEY:	I – you won't – you *swear*, you won't tell anyone? It's pretty bad, some of it.
BOHUN:	I hear bad things every day of my life. Is it criminal?
HICKLEY:	Yes.
BOHUN:	(<u>With deliberate brutality</u>) Treason?
HICKLEY:	I don't know. I suppose so. I've made a complete fool of myself. The only comfort is I can't have done much harm to anyone. Both sides knew about me, you see.
BOHUN:	Now don't go plunging into the middle again. Start at the beginning. Who are you. What's your job?
HICKLEY:	I'm a chemist. Not what you'd call a research chemist. A bit lower down the scale than that. My job is laboratory assistant – at Pond End.
BOHUN:	The guided missile place? Near Chelmsford, isn't it?
HICKLEY:	Yes. It's not the sort of job that puts you in the headlines, but I'm near enough to Cranthorpe and Beim and Carpenter to know what goes on. I work with Sir Edward Carpenter chiefly. I'm his head assistant.
BOHUN:	I see. Yes. And how did the other side get hold of you?
HICKLEY:	In the simplest, stupidest, cleverest way imaginable. You see, I live at Chorminster – that's in Essex—
BOHUN:	I know it well. I've an uncle who has a farmhouse at Barrowby-on-the-Marsh. That's only a few miles away.
HICKLEY:	It isn't a very exciting sort of neighbourhood. Nothing much to do in the evenings except go to the cinema – and they only change the film once a week out there. So I joined a Club – a sort of social and debating Club – the League for Encouragement of Free Thought. L-E-F-T, you see – 'Left'. It was mostly women. They were quite harmless. In fact one of them – a Miss Tappett – I even got quite friendly with.
BOHUN:	What did you do at those meetings?
HICKLEY:	Oh – we read papers, and had debates. One of the things we were keen on was Peace.
BOHUN:	Me too.
HICKLEY:	Sometimes we used to stage quite big discussions about that. No more war. Brotherhood of Nations. Whenever we had one of those, the Central Organisation – C-L-E-F-T – were sure to send down a speaker—
BOHUN:	And one speaker was Mr Tangee?
HICKLEY:	He came once or twice. I got to know him quite well – and – oh – one thing led to another – and—

36

BOHUN:	And you found that it wasn't quite as innocent as you'd imagined, and that you were expected to propagate the cause of peace by selling our secrets to the other side.
HICKLEY :	Well – yes. That's about it.
BOHUN:	How long ago? When did you start active espionage, I mean?
HICKLEY:	It started nearly three years ago. But I can't have been as clever as I thought because – six months ago – I got a telephone call—

(FADE. FADE UP TELEPHONE)

	Yes. What is it?
RIVETT-YARDE:	Mr Albert Hickley?
HICKLEY:	That's me. I'm afraid I haven't the pleasure—
RIVETT-YARDE:	This is Rivett-Yarde. Commander Rivett-Yarde, I have made arrangements for you to come and see me tomorrow morning. Eleven o'clock sharp.
HICKLEY:	Really – I don't know – I'm very busy.
RIVETT-YARDE:	Professor Carpenter has been informed and agrees.
HICKLEY:	Oh. Can you tell me what it is all about?
RIVETT-YARDE:	Certainly. When I see you.
HICKLEY:	Where do I go—?
RIVETT-YARDE:	The Foreign Office. Ask for me by name.

(FADE) (FADE UP)

HICKLEY:	And so I did. He was a very – er – a very forceful personality. He put it to me quite bluntly. They had been watching me for months and they had it all. Recordings of telephone conversations. There was even a photograph of me handing a packet of papers to a man I used to meet near the British Museum. It had been taken from the back of a newspaper van. It was a very good photograph indeed. When I saw it I just gave up and told him the whole story – and waited for the handcuffs to be brought out.
BOHUN:	But I gather that they weren't.
HICKLEY:	No. He made me a proposition. If I'd go on pretending to work for the other side, but actually work for our people, then – well, he didn't promise anything, but the implication was that the past might be forgiven and forgotten. Particularly if I got results.

BOHUN:	What did he want you to do?
HICKLEY:	Pass on information. Most of it true. But some of it rather remarkably not so.
BOHUN:	I see. What then?
HICKLEY:	Well, I'm afraid I must have been just about as inefficient as a double agent as I was as a single one. At least, that's the only conclusion I can come to.
BOHUN:	They tumbled to you?
HICKLEY:	I think they must have done. Because they invited me to come on a one-way journey. Across the Iron Curtain. They said that there was always a warm welcome for competent scientists in the People Democracies.
BOHUN:	I bet. And did you fall for it?
HICKLEY:	I didn't know whether to believe it or not. So I went to see Rivett-Yarde—

(FADE. FADE UP)

RIVETT-YARDE:	Excellent! Excellent! A splendid opportunity.
HICKLEY:	I'm not sure—
RIVETT-YARDE:	We've always wanted to have a double agent – particularly one with scientific qualifications – actually behind the Curtain. We'll find means of getting in touch.
HICKLEY:	But—
RIVETT-YARDE:	(Coldly) I suppose you want to do your best.
HICKLEY:	Oh, yes.
RIVETT-YARDE:	Splendid! Splendid! Show Mr Hickley out, would you, Train. Get him past the bulldogs!
TRAIN:	Right, sir. This way, Mr Hickley.

(FADE UP)

BOHUN:	I gather that you didn't entirely trust Rivett-Yarde. What was your idea?
HICKLEY:	I don't know. He seemed altogether too pleased with himself. I thought that all he really wanted was to get rid of me.
BOHUN:	Could be! What next?
HICKLEY:	I seemed to be in such a mess that I thought it would be simplest if I did just what I was told. For some time nothing happened at all. Then yesterday I got a message. It just told me to come to this flat and ask for

Mr Tangee. I was to bring no luggage and tell nobody. I did just that.

NOTE: (At this point, Bohun, as is his custom when asking an important decision, begins to pace up and down the room, pausing to 'throw' remarks at Hickley, who remains seated)

(THE ROOM HAS A PARQUET-BLOCK FLOOR WITH RUGS AND BOHUN'S FOOTSTEPS, THOUGH THEY DO NOT OBTRUDE, CAN BE HEARD)

BOHUN: Will anyone have missed you yet at Pond End? Or Chorminster?

HICKLEY: Not yet. I live in lodgings. And it was my day off. Miss Tappett might start enquiring. I had planned to have tea with her today.

BOHUN: And the laboratory?

HICKLEY: They'll miss me, of course, when I don't check in tomorrow morning. But they won't worry at once. They'll think I'm in bed with a cold.

BOHUN: That certainly gives us a breathing space. What I—

(RING AT DOOR BELL)

I wonder who that is.

HICKLEY: Don't open the door.

BOHUN: Easy. If it's our foreign friends I don't fancy they'd come back quite so openly. There's a chair in the hall. If I stand on it—

(BELL AGAIN)

I reckon I could get a squint through the fanlight.

HICKLEY: I don't trust them. Don't open the door.

(SOUND OF CHAIR BEING MOVED. KNOCKING ON DOOR)

BOHUN: (A little breathless) Looks all right. Only one man. As far as I can see he's wearing a dressing-gown. Let's see what he wants.

HICKLEY:	No – don't—

(<u>BOHUN OPENS DOOR</u>)

HORSNAIL:	Good evening. Are you the owner of this flat?
BOHUN:	Well – yes – I suppose I am, really.
HORSNAIL:	My name is Horsnail. I have the flat below you.
BOHUN:	Pleased to meet you, Mr Horsnail. Would you care to come in?
HORSNAIL:	I am here to lodge a complaint.
BOHUN:	Well, come inside. You can complain much more comfortably from there.

(<u>SHUTS DOOR</u>)

HORSNAIL:	I do not think I have ever met you before. (<u>To Hickley</u>). Or you.
HICKLEY:	No, I don't think you have.
BOHUN:	No. We have just – er – taken over from Mr Tangee.
HORSNAIL:	I am not a man who notices his neighbours much. I am a nature lover. That is why I came to Hampstead.
BOHUN:	I shouldn't have said there was an awful lot of nature left in Hampstead.
HORSNAIL:	Nature is everywhere.
BOHUN:	I suppose so.
HORSNAIL:	(<u>When he gets excited – as he is beginning to now – he starts each speech in a moderate tone but finishes it almost in a shout</u>) Also I came to Hampstead for Peace AND QUIET!
BOHUN:	I sympathise with you. I came to Hampstead for the first time this evening and I have already met two crooks and at least one madman.
HORSNAIL:	I am a long-suffering man. But that infernal din is more than I can stand. First it sounded like a fight.
BOHUN:	That was the crooks.
HORSNAIL:	I said nothing. Then the trampling of a herd of elephants.
BOHUN:	That would have been the police.
HORSNAIL:	I still say nothing. But when it comes to tramping backwards and forwards over my bedroom at midnight I lodge a mild complaint.
BOHUN:	I'm very sorry. The fact is we have been a bit disturbed

here tonight. It shan't happen again. Perhaps I could offer you a drink.

HORSNAIL: I drink only non-alcoholic apple wine.

BOHUN: I am sorry. We're out of that. Well, I hope we shan't disturb you again. (<u>At door</u>) Thank you for calling.

(<u>DOOR SHUTS</u>)

Odd character. Sounded as if he might go off pop at any moment. Now. You were telling me what happened when you got here.

HICKLEY: I got here about midday. Mr Tangee let me in. He seemed worried – and in a hurry to get away. Perhaps he was already feeling – you know – ill.

BOHUN: I shouldn't think it was that. He'd just had a letter ordering him to keep clear of his own flat! So he must have guessed that something was in the wind. What then?

HICKLEY: I sat about here for quite a long time. There was a little food in the larder. Mr Tangee said I could help myself. Then, about four o'clock, those two men arrived. They didn't say such – but I was frightened.

BOHUN: Konstant's enough to scare the pants off the Flying Squad. Why did they actually jump on you?

HICKLEY: When they told me about Mr Tangee being dead, I thought – I assumed—

BOHUN: You thought they'd killed him?

HICKLEY: I didn't know what to think. I lost my nerve. I said I wanted to go back. And I tried to run for it.

BOHUN: So man-mountain Konstant picked you up with one hand and tied you up with the other.

HICKLEY: That's about it. What are we going to do now?

BOHUN: It's quite a problem.

(<u>PAUSE. CLOCK STRIKES THREE-QUARTER HOUR</u>)

You've got to keep clear of the enemy. Find somewhere to lie up, and get in touch with Intelligence. Right? You can't go any further with your part of the game. Their treatment of you tonight shows quite clearly what they mean to do. Drop you out of an aeroplane over the North Sea, probably. No, you must get away for a bit.

HICKLEY:	But I can't do that. Commander Rivett-Yarde – you've never met him – he'll be very angry.

(FADE. FADE IN) (TELEPHONE)

RIVETT-YARDE:	Rivett-Yarde here.
TRAIN:	It's me, sir. Train. I'm terribly sorry. I've lost them.
RIVETT-YARDE:	(And he is angry) What do you mean, *lost* them?
TRAIN:	I'm afraid it was the rain, sir. It was so heavy. I went into the next door porch to shelter, and they must have come out then. It was just before the police car arrived.
RIVETT-YARDE:	At the Battle of Jutland I stood for thirty-six hours on the bridge of a destroyer. In the rain. I got wet. I didn't hide under a porch,
TRAIN:	I'm very sorry, sir.
RIVETT-YARDE:	I'm sure you are. Now listen. The police have gone, have they?
TRAIN:	Yes, sir. Some time ago.
RIVETT-YARDE:	But there's still a light on in the flat?
TRAIN:	Yes, sir.
RIVETT-YARDE:	Then stay where you are, and follow whoever comes out. If they both come out, follow Hickley.
TRAIN:	Right, sir.
RIVETT-YARDE:	Grrrrrr!

(FADE OUT. FADE IN)

BOHUN:	Even if he is as fearsome as you say, speaking for myself I'd rather be frightened than dead. However, the main point is that you've got to get away and hide up. That'll give us time to think. I might be able to have a word with the authorities myself. After all, if no one knows where you are, no one can bother you.
HICKLEY:	But where?
BOHUN:	I've got an idea about that, too. I mentioned my uncle at Barrowby-on-the-Marsh. I expect you know it – on the edge of the South Essex saltings. It's a pretty lonely spot even in summer. It's a great place for bird-watchers. They're almost the only human beings who ever do venture out there. My uncle doesn't mind. He likes solitude. He's an inventor.
HICKLEY:	Surely he's not the kind to—

BOHUN: No, no. You're quite wrong. He's as sane as you or me. I could give you a note to him and you could lie up snug for weeks.

HICKLEY: How should I get there?

BOHUN: First things first. We've got to get out of here without being seen. And that's going to take a bit of doing. What I had in mind was this. After a night of very heavy rain you usually get a bit of mist in the early morning. Five o'clock's about the time we want. The first tube trains start about half past five. I haven't thought yet how we're going to get out of the building, but once we're out the mist will be a help. If anyone comes after us, we separate. Make across the Heath for the station. Dodge about a bit until you're sure no one's after you. Then take a train to Barrowby from Fenchurch Street – it's about an hour – walk out to my uncle's place. Don't take a taxi. You should be there by the time he's getting up for breakfast.

HICKLEY: It's very good of you.

BOHUN: And another thing. I think I should get some sleep now. I'll wake you when the time comes. Use the bed in there.

HICKLEY: What about you?

BOHUN: It's an odd thing about me. I don't.

HICKLEY: Don't what?

BOHUN: Don't sleep; at least, very little. Sometimes ninety minutes a night. Sometimes less.

HICKLEY: Doesn't it worry you?

BOHUN: I got over worrying about it twenty years ago. Now off you go. I've got a lot of work to do on these papers.

HICKLEY: I don't suppose I shall be able to sleep myself.

BOHUN: You'd be surprised. You're almost asleep now.

(SOUND OF DOOR)

Not a bad little man, really. Now perhaps I *can* get on with these papers—

BOHUN: (Continuing as narrator) This time, with the clue of what Hickley had told me, I was able to make more sense of them. Putting aside his personal papers I concentrated on the records of L-E-F-T and the organising body C-L-E-F-T. I remembered having heard a certain amount about them before. There had been a bit in the newspapers. And

I think a question had been asked in Parliament. Their nominal heads were a couple of disreputable public characters – Lord Welwyn, who has been mad for twenty years and certifiable for the last five, and the notorious Archdeacon Laxater. But I hadn't read very far before I realised, with something of a shock, that the real indisputable head of the whole outfit was their General Secretary, my old friend Rupert Tangee. And there was something more to it even than that. There was a suggestion – not in the minute books themselves, but in some of the other documents – of a connection between C-L-E-F-T and a different sort of organisation altogether. There were three documents in particular. One was a memorandum, typewritten, and not very competently typed at that – rather as if someone had done it for themselves when their secretary was away – dealing with recruitment. One of the paragraphs was revealing. It said 'So far most of our active members have been women. This is acceptable in the formation stage, but it must be remembered that women rarely occupy the posts we particularly wish to reach.' I put that one on one side. Next was a small file of letters. They were unsigned, undated and had no address or any indication of where they came from. They all seemed to relate to the making of rendezvous in different parts of London. Some were odd. Some even had an amusing ring about them. 'Walk down the steps and feed the pigeons under the North-West Lion in Trafalgar Square.' The third thing was a list of figures in columns. I couldn't make head or tail of them. They had been written down on the back of a brochure for a Guest House on the Norfolk coast. 'The Travellers' Rest' (Mrs McWhirter). It was the figures themselves that were interesting. They looked as if they *must* mean something, but I couldn't for the life of me make out what.

Quite unconsciously, I had become absorbed in my thoughts and must have started to pace up and down.
It's a bad habit of mine. I can't sit still if I really want to think. I've worn holes in three carpets since I've been in Lincoln's Inn. I was interrupted by a loud and angry knocking on the ceiling of the room below.

(SOUND EFFECT)

I'd forgotten all about Mr Horsnail. I sank into a chair.

The knocking ceased. I looked at my watch. Time had gone on. It was almost five o'clock. Time to think about moving. And I hadn't yet made up my mind how we were to get out of the flat. Or had I? Subconsciously perhaps, I had already solved the problem. It is wonderful how problems *will* sort themselves out if you leave them alone. Rapidly I shovelled a selection of the more important of Tangee's papers into an envelope and stuffed it into my pocket. Then I tiptoed across to rouse Hickley.

BOHUN: (<u>Speaking just above a whisper</u>) Come on. Time to move.

HICKLEY: Wassat? Oh – it's you.

BOHUN: I thought you said you'd never get to sleep! You've had about three hours. It's just after five, and there's a lovely mist. Get on your coat and shoes. Did you have any luggage?

HICKLEY: No. They said I should be travelling light.

BOHUN: That was one way of putting it.

HICKLEY: How are we to get out of here?

BOHUN: I've got an idea about that. You remember that character who came up and shouted at us?

HICKLEY: From the ground floor flat?

BOHUN: That's right. Well, he's still awake. I'm afraid I disturbed him by pacing backwards and forwards again. Well, we're going to go on doing it.

HICKLEY: We?

BOHUN: Two will make more noise than one. And roll the rugs back. I want it to sound good.

HICKLEY: Have you gone mad?

BOHUN: Far from it. What do you think Mr Horsnail will do when he hears us?

HICKLEY: Rush up and tear us to pieces I should think.

BOHUN: Quite so. And we'll have our front door open so that he can come right in. Only – we shan't be here when he arrives.

HICKLEY: Shan't—?

BOHUN: I noticed a door on the opposite side of the landing – it looks like a broom cupboard—

HICKLEY: I think it's the bathroom for this flat and the one next door.

BOHUN: Better still. As soon as we hear Horsnail leave *his* flat, we nip out into that bathroom. As soon as he comes in here

45

	we run downstairs, into his flat – if he's really roused he won't have shut the door – and out of one of his ground floor windows.
HICKLEY:	But suppose—
BOHUN:	We shan't get anywhere by supposing. Now, ready? Go!

(THEY TRAMP IN STEP ACROSS THE FLOOR. THE NOISE IS IMPRESSIVE. IT IS SOON INTERRUPTED BY THUMPS FROM THE ROOM BELOW)

HORSNAIL:	(A distant bellow)
BOHUN:	We're tickling him. Keep it up.

(TRAMP, TRAMP, TRAMP. SOUND OF DOOR OPENING BELOW)

Quick! Into the bathroom.

(THEY SCAMPER OUT. BATHROOM DOOR SHUTS. HEAVY FOOTSTEPS ON STONE STAIRS)

HORSNAIL:	(His voice is muffled by the door between them, but is still extremely audible) This is deliberate SABOTAGE. Have you taken leave of your SENSES? Look here, I'm not going to put up with this any longer. (Continues to boom, distant, as he seeks for his aggressors)
BOHUN:	Now! Down the stairs.

(THEY CLATTER DOWN THE STAIRS)

In with you. And shut the door.

(HORSNAIL'S FRONT DOOR SLAMS)

(Whispering) No, don't go in the front room. The light's on. Try the other room. Now the window. Push the catch up, and I'll ease it open. Splendid! Out with you – Hey! Who's that? Run for it!

(A THUD – FOLLOWED BY FOOTSTEPS RUNNING ON ASPHALT AND DYING AWAY INTO THE DISTANCE)

BOHUN: (<u>As narrator</u>) I don't know who it was. A young man. I think he was surprised as we were. I pushed him more than hit him and he slipped and went down. I took to my heels. Hickley had disappeared. The mist was like a blanket. I walked blindly until I hit a road which, luckily, I recognised. After that fifteen minutes' hard walking took me to Hampstead Heath Station.

Once or twice, as I went, I got the idea that I was being followed. There were other people, in the mist, moving. It was difficult to know if they were interested in me or not. Once, on a lonely stretch, I was certain I could hear footsteps about twenty yards behind me. I stopped quickly, and they stopped, too. Could have been an echo.

It was twenty to six when I got to the station and the booking office was open. I realised that I probably was not looking my best. I peeled off my soiled gloves and pushed them into my side pocket. Then I brushed my raincoat down as well as I could, gave my hair a quick comb, and, having concluded this sketchy toilet, bought a ticket for Camden Town from the sleepy clerk.

I kept my eyes open for any sign of a pursuer, but I seemed to be quite alone. As I went out on to the platform it was getting light and the mist was clearing, which was a mercy, as I didn't fancy hanging round for hours waiting for the train. At first I thought I was alone on the platform, but suddenly I spotted him. A thickset man in a raincoat and a trilby hat – standing quite still, in the shadow between two lamps.

I tried not to jump. I don't think I gave myself away. After a couple of minutes the man started strolling towards me. It was obvious that he was going to talk. And equally obvious that I couldn't run away – unless I wanted to make myself conspicuous. Normally I wouldn't have thought twice about it. I should just have assumed that it was pure cursed idle curiosity. As it was—

(<u>FADE. FADE UP</u>)

D/SGT. HIBBS: Good morning, sir. Up early.
BOHUN: Yes. That's right.
HIBBS : Not a very nice morning.

BOHUN:	I expect it'll clear later.
HIBBS :	Be a real hot day, I wouldn't wonder. Oh, I beg your pardon. When I first saw you, I thought you were Mr Engleheart.
BOHUN:	Sorry. No relation.
HIBBS :	Ah. Now you come closer I can see you aren't anything like him. I thought I knew all the regulars on my train. My train I call it! I'm often the only one on it until it gets to Kentish Town.
BOHUN:	I'm afraid I'm not a regular. I don't live out here.
HIBBS :	Ah, I thought perhaps you weren't. But then again, I thought, if he doesn't live out here – I hope you'll excuse my curiosity – if he's just been stopping the night, where's his luggage?
BOHUN:	Oh, I travel light. Just a toothbrush in my pocket.
HIBBS :	That's the modern way. I'm always deducing things – a regular Sherlock Holmes. I put you down right away as an accountant or a solicitor.
BOHUN:	You're not far out. I'm an actuary.
HIBBS :	Well, there now! That's a curious thing. Someone was asking me the other day and I couldn't tell them. Just what does an actuary do, Mr—?
BOHUN :	Leslie.
HIBBS :	(<u>Thoughtfully</u>) Mr Leslie.
BOHUN :	He makes actuarial calculations. Works out sums with one or more unknown quantities. Calculates when people are going to die.
HIBBS:	(<u>Startled</u>) Die? Oh, you mean, in the natural course.
BOHUN:	That's right. In the natural course. There goes the signal. That must be our train.
HIBBS:	Seven minutes late. Must be the mist held her up. It's been interesting meeting you. If we'd had a bit more time I'd have got you guessing *my* profession.

(<u>TRAIN APPROACHING</u>)

BOHUN:	I haven't your knack, I'm afraid, Mr—?
HIBBS:	Hibbs. Detective Sergeant Hibbs – New Scotland Yard.

(<u>TRAIN NOISE CRESCENDO AND HALT</u>)

BOHUN: (<u>Narrating</u>) I managed to get into a different carriage – I hope without appearing rude – I just waited until Hibbs was inside, slammed the door on him and said: 'I always take a non-smoker.' Then I jumped in, three or four doors further down, and the train started.

I realised with sudden, awful clarity, what a fool I had made of myself: and what an awkward corner I'd got myself into.

If I'd stopped to think for a minute I should have stayed in the flat. There was less than no sense in running away. They knew I had been there – knew all about me. Now I had done something even sillier. I had lied – to a plain clothes detective – about my identity. The fact that I had imagined he was a plain busybody was neither here nor there. What I needed was time to think. There's only one place for thinking at that hour on a misty morning. I got quietly out of the train at Camden Town, took a bus to Euston Square and made for my favourite all-night Turkish Bath. By the time I came out again, feeling a lot better, it was a quarter to nine and I had settled certain things with myself. The first was that I must stay clear of *everyone* until that evening. Obviously as soon as the police caught up with me – and if they hadn't caught up with me by that evening I would go to them voluntarily – I must tell them everything. Them and M.I.5. Equally, if I told them too soon, it wouldn't give Hickley a fair chance to get clear. The answer to that was plain. Just stay out of sight for the rest of the day. Second, I had to put those Tangee papers somewhere safe. Third, I wanted some breakfast. I was ravenous.

After breakfast I went into a stationer's and bought a small flat cardboard box – the sort you pack books in and shoved all the papers into it. Before I fastened it up I sat down and scribbled out a short account of what I had done so far and what I intended to do, and I put that in as well. My training as a solicitor urged me to get that much on record. I had a feeling it might turn out useful. Then I sealed up the packet and, after some thought, addressed it to myself, care of The Law Society, Chancery Lane. Then I set off to walk home.

I lived, at that time, in a top floor flat above an Italian

restaurant near Cursitor Street, kept by a dear old lady called Mrs Magoli. I approached my destination cautiously, and it was as well that I did. I saw the crowd outside the door before they saw me. More trouble! I slid back, and nipped into a second-hand junk shop. I happened to know the proprietor.

BOHUN:	Morning, Mr Moss.
MOSS:	Morning, Mr Bohun. What goes on up there?
BOHUN:	Just what I was going to ask you.
MOSS:	You oughter know. En't that where you live?
BOHUN:	I didn't go home last night. What's up?
MOSS:	You may well ask. Early s'morning, from what I hear, some men got in. Tied old Ma Magoli up with her own apron. Cor, you should've heard her squeak when they untied her this morning:
BOHUN:	What did they do to her?
MOSS:	I don't think they *did* anything. Seems it was *your* stuff they were after. Spent a couple of hours up there – I hear, turning things inside out. You'd better get back and see to things, hadn't you?
BOHUN:	I think I had. But there's one thing I've got to do first. You haven't got a telephone, have you?
MOSS:	Box on the corner.
BOHUN:	So there is. And look here – do you mind not saying you've seen me – if anyone should ask?
MOSS:	I can mind my own business ...

(FADES – SOUND OF DIALLING)

BOHUN:	Hello! Horniman, Birley & Craine? Is Mr Craine in?
CRAINE:	Craine speaking.
BOHUN:	Roley ... it's me.
CRAINE:	What on earth have you been up to? Where are you speaking from?
BOHUN:	A call-box.
CRAINE:	Well, you have landed yourself in something now, haven't you? For goodness' sake keep the firm out of it if you can. I've only just got rid of those men.
BOHUN:	What men? What are you talking about?
CRAINE:	Two police officers. At least I suppose they were police officers. They said they were. They went through all your papers.

BOHUN:	Oh! (Pause) I suppose they didn't by any chance mention what offence I was alleged to have committed?
CRAINE:	Of course they did. They told me you had been stopped this morning at London Airport trying to smuggle a parcel of diamonds out of the country. Wasn't it true?
BOHUN:	(Slowly) As far as I know, the only actual offence I have committed in the last few hours is assaulting the police.
CRAINE:	(It is a yelp) What?
BOHUN:	Never mind. I'll ring you back later.
CRAINE:	Don't ring off—

(TELEPHONE RUNG OFF. FADE. FADE UP ANOTHER RECEIVER LIFTED)

RIVETT-YARDE:	Yes. Commander Rivett-Yarde here.
MAN:	I think I've just spotted him, sir.
RIVETT-YARDE:	Where?
MAN:	In a phone booth at the corner of Cursitor Street. He must have been making for his flat. But the crowd scared him off.
RIVETT-YARDE:	Right. Now listen to me, Jackson. Come rain or shine, come hell or high water, don't lose him again! He's the only chance we've got.

(MUSIC – FADE)

EPISODE 3

'MISS TAPPETT AND HER TORTOISES'

Transmission: Light Programme
Thursday, 4th August 1955 8.00–8.30 pm

(MUSIC – HOLD UNDER ANNOUNCEMENT)

| OPENING ANNOUNCEMENT: | We present William Fox in 'The Man Who Could Not Sleep', a serial-thriller in six parts by Michael Gilbert. Episode 3 – 'Miss Tappett and Her Tortoises'. |

(<u>MUSIC</u>)

ANNOUNCER: Bohun, a solicitor, discovering that he is sole executor of an Oxford acquaintance, Rupert Tangee, goes up, late in the evening to Tangee's flat to take over his personal papers. To his surprise he discovers two foreigners already in occupation. There is a fracas which ends with Bohun in possession of the field. The contents of the flat include one Albert Hickley, whom he discovers, gagged and bound, in the bedroom.

Under pressure, Hickley tells Bohun his sad story. A scientific worker and a double traitor, his original bosses have now begun to suspect him and have decided to remove him behind the Iron Curtain. This suits the book of Commander Rivett-Yarde of British Intelligence who is most anxious to discover just how these disappearing tricks are done.

RIVETT-YARDE: Hullo, Rivett-Yarde here. Yes. Give me Major Bagshawe will you?

OPERATOR: Extension number please.

RIVETT-YARDE: How should I know what his extension is? He's somewhere in the building. Find him. These signallers. No initiative. No drive. Lucky for Nelson he didn't have to deal with civil service telephone operators. When he asked for Trafalgar they'd have given him Waterloo.

BAGSHAWE: Bagshawe here.

RIVETT-YARDE: Oh – Bagshawe. Look here. Can you come up and have a word about the Hickley Case. There has been a most unexpected development. Come as quick as you can.

TRAIN: (<u>Very slight stutter</u>) W-well, sir. After that unfortunate business, out in the rain – when I sheltered in the porch and missed seeing Taylor and Koniatolitz coming out—

RIVETT-YARDE: Yes.

TRAIN: I thought I w-wouldn't take any chances on the next one, so I went into the garden. I could watch both doors from there – or I could have done, if the m-mist hadn't been so thick. There was a light in Tangee's flat – and after a bit a light went on in the ground floor flat as well, and I heard someone sh-shouting.

RIVETT-YARDE: Shouting? Ah. Good man, Bagshawe. Come in. You know young Train, I think.

BAGSHAWE:	Hullo Train. Where on earth did you pick up that black eye? It's a real smacker isn't it?
TRAIN:	Lost two teeth as well, sir.
RIVETT-YARDE:	Never mind your teeth. Go on. You heard someone shouting. What next?
TRAIN:	Then the man in the ground floor flat – the one who'd been doing the shouting, ran upstairs. There was more noise – and suddenly the window right beside me – the ground floor window – swung quietly open and the man jumped out.
BAGSHAWE:	Who *is* this other man?
RIVETT-YARDE:	(<u>Grimly</u>) That's what I'd give a lot to know. I'm looking forward to meeting him. I spoke to Farmer of the Special Branch about him a few minutes ago and he promised to ring me back. Go on, Train—
TRAIN:	Well, I was so surprised – they jumped almost into my arms – that the first one was away before I could do a thing. I'm pretty sure it was Hickley—
BAGSHAWE:	Yes, but what did you *do*, Train?
TRAIN:	I didn't really *do* anything. I tried to grab the second one, slipped in the mud, and went flat on my back and hit my head against the rockery. I don't remember anything else until I came round, in a pool of blood – my blood – with a splitting headache.
RIVETT-YARDE:	Never mind your headache. It's *my* headache that I'm worried about. They propose to take him across the Curtain.
BAGSHAWE:	The devil they do.
RIVETT-YARDE:	It's a process we've always wanted to watch. We've never been certain how the blighters really do get them out of the country. Of course, we know the lines from Europe – but they don't always take them to the continent now. I believe there's a jumping off point actually in this country.
BAGSHAWE:	So we watch Hickley to see how it's done.
RIVETT-YARDE:	Yes.
BAGSHAWE:	And you've lost him?
RIVETT-YARDE:	For the moment, yes. But Jackson – lucky we've got some brains in this department – heard early this morning that there'd been a bust-up in a small place off Cursitor Street. Nothing much to it. Two men broke in, and terrorised the Italian family called Magoli, who keep the Rising Sun

Restaurant on the ground floor. Then they went up and searched the upstairs flat. The only thing was, that from the descriptions given, one of the men sounded like Konstant Koniatolitz.

BAGSHAWE: Not a very easy person to be mistaken about.

RIVETT-YARDE: No. No. So he hurried round there and kept his eyes open. He's a sensible chap. About an hour ago he saw a man pushing his way through the crowd, stop, turn back, and dive into a shop. So he asked a few questions. He soon found someone who recognised the man. It was the man who lodges over the Magolis.

BAGSHAWE: And I take it that's the second man. The one who was with Hickley last night and helped him get away.

TRAIN: And gave me a black eye.

BAGSHAWE: Sounds a sporting character. Who *is* he?

RIVETT-YARDE: That's the next thing I want to know. And if Jackson keeps his wits about him—

(TELEPHONE)

RIVETT-YARDE: This may be him. Hullo.

FARMER: Hullo. Farmer here.

RIVETT-YARDE: Oh, hullo, yes. (Aside) It's Superintendent Farmer. (Into telephone) Any news?

FARMER: I've got plenty of background. The man's name is Bohun. B.O.H.U.N. Bohun. He's a solicitor. I got this from the Mobile Branch. Apparently one of their cars answered a call last night from a flat in Hampstead.

RIVETT-YARDE: Tangee's flat?

FARMER: Yes. When they got there they found the place in a bit of a shambles – and Bohun in possession.

RIVETT-YARDE: (Sharply) Alone?

FARMER: So I gather.

RIVETT-YARDE: That about Hickley?

FARMER: Not in evidence. He might have been there, of course, but the Sergeant says that Bohun certainly thought he was alone. Or maybe he's a very good actor.

RIVETT-YARDE: I'll act him when I catch up with him. What next?

FARMER: Bohun seemed to be O.K. Produced his credentials, and so on. He's a partner in quite a big firm in Lincoln's Inn. Absolutely above board – the firm, I mean. I don't know about him personally. And he had been appointed

Tangee's executor – so he'd a perfect right to be where he was.

RIVETT-YARDE: Rather an odd time of night to go executing.

FARMER: Well, I thought that. But I had a word with his partner, Mr Craine. Apparently Bohun doesn't sleep very well. Never gets more than about an hour's sleep a night. So he does a lot of his work whilst you and I are in bed.

RIVETT-YARDE: Speak for yourself.

FARMER: Craine said that Bohun hasn't turned up to work this morning. Perhaps that was to be expected. But there's another funny thing. As soon as the office opened two Special Branch men put in an appearance with a warrant: and searched Bohun's room. Went through it with a fine tooth-comb – opened all the drawers of his desk.

RIVETT-YARDE: Why is that funny?

FARMER: Speaking as acting head of the Special Branch, I can assure you that they didn't come from *us*. I wondered if perhaps your man—

RIVETT-YARDE: No. I'm afraid not.

FARMER: I see. Doesn't look too good. Well, I'll keep in touch with you.

(<u>RINGS OFF</u>)

RIVETT-YARDE: (<u>Slowly</u>) Well, it's beginning to add up, isn't it?

BAGSHAWE: Not to me it isn't.

RIVETT-YARDE: Bohun's the key to it. Maybe he's an honest man – maybe he isn't. What he's done is sail in and help himself to something of Tangee's that the other side mind about. In fact, they mind like Hell, for they've made two attempts already to get it back. One by ransacking his home, the other his office. My guess would be that it's papers of some sort.

BAGSHAWE: Papers showing Tangee's connection with CLEFT – or CLEFT's connection with espionage?

RIVETT-YARDE: Might be. I wouldn't have thought that papers of that sort would have provoked quite such violent reactions – after all, we knew most of it before.

BAGSHAWE: Do you suppose he's got the papers on him?

RIVETT-YARDE: Not unless he's a bigger fool than I take him for.

BAGSHAWE: Do you think he'll bring them to us?

(SHORT PAUSE)

RIVETT-YARDE:	Yes. I think he will. In his own time.
BAGSHAWE:	Always supposing he's left alive long enough to do it.
TRAIN:	Can I make a suggestion, sir?
RIVETT-YARDE:	No harm in trying.
TRAIN:	I just wondered – it was quite dark in the garden. I was flat out – on the ground – a lot of blood. Might he be stopping out of sight because he wasn't sure whether he'd killed me?
RIVETT-YARDE:	Why should he suppose we'd mind that?

(TELEPHONE)

	May be Jackson. Hullo.
JACKSON:	Jackson here, sir. I lost Bohun ten minutes ago.

(CRASH OF RECEIVER)

RIVETT-YARDE:	That blithering fool, that incompetent, muddle headed, jumped-up drip. He's lost Bohun.

(FADE. FADE UP)

BOHUN:	(As Narrator) When I came out of the telephone box, after speaking to my partner Roley Craine, I made for the Law Society. You know it. It's a solid building, two thirds of the way down Chancery Lane on the right, in the Big Business-Palladian style of architecture. Strangers frequently mistake it for one of the better class Insurance Offices. It's a good place for a quiet think and is practically empty at that hour of the morning. I pushed through the double swing doors, crossed the tiled hall (ECHOING FOOTSTEPS) took a look at the ticker tape on the way (FOOTSTEPS HALT) (England all out 256. Australia 180 for 2) and went through the inner door into the reading room. I picked up a newspaper but I didn't read it. One thing seemed to stand out. I *must* find out where Hickley had got to. Then I should be in a position to go to M.I.5. and say to this Rivett-Yarde character 'Look here, Rivett-Yarde. I know where Hickley is – he's safe, and another thing, I know where

some very interesting papers are. They're quite safe, too. But before I tell you anything, you must promise to go easy on Hickley. He's quite a well-meaning little man—'

At that moment my thoughts were distracted by voices in the hall—

HEAD PORTER: (<u>A very stately character</u>) Are you a Member of the Society, sir?

MAN: Well, not actually a member—

HEAD PORTER: In that case, sir, I'm afraid you are not allowed to use the Society's Premises.

MAN: I thought – I mean, as a country solicitor—

HEAD PORTER: Perhaps you would care to speak to the Secretary?

MAN: Oh, well, it doesn't matter. No.

(<u>DOOR TO READING ROOM OPENING</u>)

BOHUN: Who was that.

HEAD PORTER: I'm afraid I do not know *who* it was, Mr Bohun. But it was *not* a member of the Law Society. I sometimes think that half the office-workers in Chancery Lane imagine they can use this as a free library.

BOHUN: Shocking. Shocking.

(<u>As Narrator</u>) All the same – I wondered. We don't often get gate crashers. Was it possible that I was being followed? Quite suddenly I found myself experiencing that uncomfortable prickly sensation that afflicts the hunted man and makes him do stupid things. Calm yourself, Bohun. The whole of London is in front of you. Surely you have wit enough to shake off any pursuers. Without further ado I got out of my chair. I had a plan. I left the Law Society openly, by the front, without looking round, turned right and strolled down Chancery Lane. A little way along is a cul-de-sac, with a Law Stationers shop at the end of it. Only – unless you know that part of London well – you would not realize that you can walk *through* the Stationers shop and come out in Ball Yard at the back. I turned in, spent a few moments, dithering about buying a box of small wafer seals, then strolled out the other side. I had under-rated them. There were two watchers. The other one was standing on the pavement. A large young man. Never mind. I had reduced my pursuers by half. I walked fast down Ball Yard, and jumped a bus going down the Strand. The large young man caught it, too. I took no notice of him. At Charing Cross I got off and went down into the Strand Underground. The Strand Underground was particularly well suited for the manoeuvre I had in mind. Luckily there were not a great number of people about. As I strolled towards the ticket machines I kept one eye on the lifts. You probably know them. There are two of them, both automatic. When the lift comes up, the far gate opens to let the people out. Then the near gate opens to let the new lot in. But what I had noticed is this. There are always just a few seconds when *both* gates are open. The left hand lift was coming up now. (SOUND OF LIFT) I fiddled round a bit more – didn't want to be too soon – then dropped the pennies in, got my ticket, and walked slowly towards the lift. The big man was a little way behind me but I thought he looked suspicious. I slowed my pace. Both doors open. Not too fast. Now.

(SOUND OF 'MECHANICAL VOICE' SAYING 'STAND CLEAR OF THE GATES', AND BOHUN'S STEPS, FIRST AT A WALK, THEN AT A RUN. THEN THE CLANG OF THE GATE CRASHING SHUT. THEN MORE STEPS RUNNING, ECHOING AND RECEDING DOWN AN EMPTY CORRIDOR)

BOHUN: (Breathless) I'd timed it to a hair. Right through the lift and out the other side! I went the wrong way down an empty one-way corridor, and dodged into the entrance to the Emergency Stairs. In a minute I heard my man coming, fast.

(FOOTSTEPS RUNNING)

BOHUN: He went past within a few feet of me, and he looked pretty angry. I nipped out and walked back the way I had come. A minute later I was out in the Strand. I took a short stroll in the streets behind the Station to make sure I'd thrown off the pursuit. Then I walked down to the Embankment and found a telephone booth.

(<u>DIALLING</u>)

	Barrowby-on-the-Marsh 21, please. Barrowby. Yes, it's in Essex. On-the-Marsh. That's right.
OPERATOR:	One moment, sir. It's ringing now.

(<u>SOUND OF TELEPHONE RINGING</u>)

THRESHER:	(<u>hoarse voice</u>) Yes.
BOHUN:	Might I speak to Clarence Thresher?
THRESHER:	Speaking.
BOHUN:	Oh, it's you Uncle Clarence. I didn't recognise you.
THRESHER:	I've got a damnable cold. Nice to hear from you. I suppose you want a bed.
BOHUN:	Well – I may – what I really wanted to know was, has anyone turned up today saying he's coming from me?
THRESHER:	Coming to tea?
BOHUN:	Coming-from-me. That I sent him.
THRESHER:	Not a soul. Haven't seen a stranger for weeks. Except a pair of Rose Backed Oyster-Catchers. They set up house on my pond last week.
BOHUN:	This is a man. Not a bird. Name of Hickley.
THRESHER:	All right. What do I do with him?
BOHUN:	I wondered if you could keep him until I got down. I can't talk about it on the telephone.
THRESHER:	All right. Anything else?
BOHUN:	No. That's all for the moment. Goodbye.
THRESHER:	Goodbye.
BOHUN:	(<u>As Narrator</u>) My uncle Clarence is almost the only really reliable relative I possess. He is always ready to help and never asks questions. When I tell people that he is an inventor, I'm sure they picture someone with long hair and a lost look. Actually, he's not at all like that. He invents weapons. And, as far as I know, is living now on the reward he got from the Government for his Tank Busters. Although in his view he was badly underpaid for it. By this time I was getting a bit worried about Hickley. He had plenty of time to get to Barrowby-on-the-Marsh. I sat on a seat on the Embankment, and thought about it. For I had to find him. I had no doubt in my mind about that. I was pretty well in the soup already, but if I went along and said, 'I helped Hickley to escape and now I've

59

lost him', I could imagine the sort of reception I should get. But, curiously enough – for I'm as selfish as most people – it wasn't only myself I was worrying about. No. As I sat there that fine summer morning (<u>SEAGULLS</u>) listening to old Father Thames (<u>RIVER TRAFFIC</u>) all my worries centred on Hickley. I can't explain this, but I felt certain that I *must* find him and that he was going to *need* my help. But where – in the length and breadth of England – and at that moment a name came, unasked, into my mind.

VOICE OF HICKLEY:	'In fact one of them – a Miss Tappett – I even got quite friendly with'
BOHUN:	and again—
VOICE OF HICKLEY:	'Miss Tappett might start enquiring. I'd planned to have tea with her today.'
BOHUN:	Chorminster! If I was going down to my uncle's place, Chorminster was on the way. And Tappett wasn't a common name. There had been a sort of warmth in his voice when he had spoken about her. She was apparently one of the local supporters of D.E.F.T., that visionary left-wing debating society that Rupert Tangee had fathered for his own ends. It seemed to tie up. Anyway, it was the only lead left. I telephoned my uncle once more, after lunch, but no luck. After that I delayed no longer. I caught the bus to Fenchurch Street and the train to the depressing dormitory suburb of Chorminster. Outside the station, it was a bit difficult to know just where to start. I stopped the first intelligent-looking man I saw—
BOHUN:	I wonder if you happen to know a Miss Tappett?
MAN'S VOICE:	Tappett. Used to be a vicar here of that name, I believe.
BOHUN:	Would his family still be here?
MAN'S VOICE:	He died – oh – about 1902, I'd say. Before my time. Never heard he had any family.
BOHUN:	Thank you very much.

(<u>FADE</u>)
(<u>CHEERFUL WHISTLING</u>)

BOHUN:	I say. You don't happen to know where Miss Tappett lives?

BOY:	Whassat?
BOHUN:	I was looking for a Miss Tappett.
BOY:	I haven't got her.

(MORE WHISTLING. FADE)
(DOOR BELL. SHOP DOOR CLOSING)

BOHUN:	I was looking for a lady called Miss Tappett.
OLD WOMAN'S VOICE:	Sorry, I'm sold right out.
BOHUN:	Tappett.
OLD WOMAN'S VOICE:	That's right. Everything's scarce nowadays. Goodbye.
BOHUN:	Goodbye.

(FADE)

BOHUN:	(As Narrator) I went through a good deal of this. I tried the local telephone directory – no luck – and a street directory – but this was really only tradespeople – and I was seriously thinking of calling it a day when I saw the Family Stores. It stood by itself, rather on the South, on the open side of the town and looked a good old hotbed of gossip. I went in and was soon talking to an intelligent looking young lady behind the tinned food counter.
YOUNG LADY:	Well, as a matter of fact I do know the name. It's not a common name is it?
BOHUN:	Far from it.
YOUNG LADY:	She's not a customer here – I mean. But when I served in Holmes Drapery she used to come in. Sort of oldish.
BOHUN:	It would depend what you meant by old.
YOUNG LADY:	Oh. She must have been over forty.
BOHUN:	I see. Yes. That sounds possible. Do you happen to remember her address?
YOUNG LADY:	Well, I wouldn't have remembered it, of course, only she gave me a card. Well, not really a card. A sort of tract. I've got it somewhere.

(SNAPPING OF HANDBAG)

Here you are. (Reading) 'Are you interested in Democracy. Do you value Free Speech? Do you want

61

another War. L.E.F.T. stands for all of these. Local organiser Miss Tappett' – and there's the address – Paddock Cottage – you can keep it if you like. I only hung onto it for a joke.

BOHUN: I take it, then, that you don't subscribe to the – er – ideals so persuasively set out in this leaflet?

YOUNG LADY: Well, my boy friend's in the Marines—

(FADE)

BOHUN: (As Narrator) I found Paddock Cottage, a small, old fashioned, red brick building on the Southern outskirts of Chorminster, standing somewhat isolated, among trees, at the end of a lane. Big grounds for a mere cottage – and at the far end of them, backing onto another road, I glimpsed a building of the Village Institute type – which I fancied might be the meeting place of the Chorminster Chapter of L.E.F.T. Miss Tappett, who opened the door to me, was a comfortable lady, with a bright eye. I could well imagine, on seeing her, how poor Hickley had glimpsed in her a refuge and a haven from the stormy seas that were threatening to overwhelm him. It was obvious at a glance that nothing more exciting had ever happened to Miss Tappett than the breaking of a best tea cup or the death of a favourite cat.

(FADE)

MISS TAPPETT: And what can I do for you, sir?

BOHUN: I wonder if I might step inside – it's rather private.

MISS TAPPETT: You don't look like a smash and grab raider – nor yet a seller of vacuum cleaners – come in.

BOHUN: No, it's not vacuum cleaners

MISS TAPPETT: Please sit down.

BOHUN: Oh – thank you very much. (Sits) It's about a man – what the – Oh dear, I do hope I haven't hurt him.

MISS TAPPETT: Don't think twice of it. If you'd just get up for a minute and put him down on the floor. You can't hurt a mature tortoise by sitting on it.

BOHUN: You are fond of tortoises?

MISS TAPPETT: (Briskly) Devoted to them. And they are devoted to me. That is Gable. Such a handsome, dashing fellow! You were saying?

BOHUN:	(<u>Resettling himself</u>) I believe you are interested in the League for the Encouragement of Free Thought – L.E.F.T.—
MISS TAPPETT:	Indeed I am. I might perhaps say, without boasting, that I am personally responsible for the remarkable growth of Free Thought in Chorminster. When my father died he left me in comfortable circumstances. I might have spent the money on anything I wished – Religion, Politics, or even drink.
BOHUN:	Oh – I'm sure—
MISS TAPPETT:	A lot of rich old women do drink themselves to death, you know. You'd be surprised how many. It's usually Tawny Port. However, I decided to concentrate on Peace. I founded this Branch of the League, endowed it, and presented it with a meeting place.
BOHUN:	That building at the bottom of your garden?
MISS TAPPETT:	That is our Moot Hall. We have a meeting this evening. However. You mentioned a man.
BOHUN:	Yes. I was wondering if you remembered a worker in your Chapter – dear me – this is very embarrassing.
MISS TAPPETT:	Why?
BOHUN:	I'm quite sure there's another – ouch – yes.
MISS TAPPETT:	Oh dear. That will be Lamour. Rather a savage little girl. She hibernates behind the chair cushion. Perhaps you'd better change chairs.
BOHUN:	I think I had (<u>sits down carefully</u>). That's better. The man's name was Hickley.
MISS TAPPETT:	Oh. (<u>Pause</u>) Yes. I remember him. A very zealous member.
BOHUN:	(<u>Noting the change of manner</u>) When did you see him last?
MISS TAPPETT:	Well. I can't quite remember—
BOHUN:	Would it help you if I told you that my name is Bohun.
MISS TAPPETT:	Oh. *You're* Mr Bohun. I couldn't be sure. I was sure there was nothing seriously wrong with you, or Gable would never have walked off and ignored you. I had a dishonest insurance agent here once, and Gable savaged him at sight. Yes. Mr Hickley told me all about you. How kind you'd been.
BOHUN:	Where is he?
MISS TAPPETT:	Well – he's in the spare bedroom. He's been asleep since lunch. Such a trying time.
BOHUN:	I must have a word with him.

MISS TAPPETT: Then, if you'll excuse me, I'll knock on his door.

(<u>FADE</u>)

BOHUN: (<u>As Narrator</u>) I'd never realized before what sinister crea-
tures tortoises are. Particularly full-grown ones. Gable
had come quietly back and was nibbling the heel of my
shoes. Whilst a third one, which I had subconsciously
assumed to be some sort of book-end or ornament,
suddenly winked at me. I was quite relieved when
Hickley came in, doing up his tie.

(<u>FADE</u>)

BOHUN: Well, Mr Hickley. How are you feeling now?
HICKLEY: (<u>Still sleepy</u>) Much better. Funny what a difference it
makes – the place you're in, I mean – up in that spooky
flat, I was nervous as a kitten. But sitting down here, with
the kettle on the hob, and those blessed tortoises – ouch—
BOHUN: Don't be frightened. It's Gable. Just his love-talk.
HICKLEY: If you say so. It felt like a bite to me.
BOHUN: Whilst you've been snoozing here, things have been
hotting up. Someone got onto me. They ransacked my
flat and my office, and I was followed—
HICKLEY: (<u>Alarm creeping in again</u>) Followed?
BOHUN: But I threw them off.
HICKLEY: Are you certain?
BOHUN: Absolutely certain. It's not a thing you can easily be
mistaken about. What about you?
HICKLEY: Oh, I was all right. I got clear in the mist.
BOHUN: Look here. She'll be back in a minute, and I don't want to
say too much in front of her. Can you lie low here for a
day or two?
HICKLEY: I should think so. She won't mind.
BOHUN: The tortoises will chaperone you. All right, then. As soon
as it's dark I'll get up to town and open negotiations with
Rivett-Yarde. Here she is.

(<u>DOOR</u>)

MISS TAPPETT: I'll bring the tray in here. I've cut some cress sandwiches.
Can you eat cress sandwiches?

BOHUN:	Just try me! But aren't you going to join us?
MISS T:	No, I really haven't time. It's this special meeting this evening and I have my notes to get ready. It's a debate really. I expect you saw the posters. 'Should Science be International'. The Archdeacon was to propose and I had a sheet-metal worker, a Mr Cussack – such a superior man – to second. But he has tonsilitis. It really looked like the hand of Providence when you—
HICKLEY:	Me?
MISS T:	With your scientific knowledge.
HICKLEY:	Really – I hardly think. I have never addressed a public gathering before.
MISS T:	(Gaily) No time like the present. You persuade him, Mr Bohun.
BOHUN:	No, really, Miss Tappett. In this case, I must support Hickley. It would be most injudicious. You have very kindly refrained from asking what he is doing or why he has sought shelter here. But I can tell you this. It is of the highest importance that no-one should know he *is* here.
MISS T:	You can count on my discretion, of course. I am *not* the gossiping sort. Apart from the assistant secretary – or, I suppose, with the sad departure of Mr Tangee, he is now the Secretary—
BOHUN:	Do I gather you told this gentleman about Mr Hickley?
MISS T:	Oh, I mentioned no names. I just said that this old associate of our Branch – I may have mentioned that he was a scientific worker—
BOHUN:	Oh dear!
MISS T:	—Had arrived unexpectedly at my house after breakfast today, and might – I only said might – feel disposed to assist us in our discussions this evening.
BOHUN:	And this man you spoke to – he is one of the officials on the Central Body—
MISS T:	A most helpful and reliable man. A Mr Taylor.
BOHUN & HINCKLEY:	(Simultaneously) WHAT?
MISS T:	You know him? How splendid. He's joining us here for a cup of tea before the meeting. He'll be here any moment.
HICKLEY:	(to Bohun) What do we do?
BOHUN:	Keep your head. (To Miss Tappett) You say he's coming here?

MISS T:	Wasn't that the front gate?
HICKLEY:	(to Bohun) There must be a back way out.
MISS T:	I thought it was. (BELL) I'll let him in.
BOHUN:	Now keep your head. He can't do anything with a crowd of women about. It's no good panicking. (At window) I say. There are two more men out in the street. You wouldn't get a yard. Look, slip out the back way. There must be a way through the hall and out onto the road.
HICKLEY:	All right.

(DOOR SLAMMING AS HICKLEY RUNS OUT, AND THEN MISS TAPPETT RETURNS)

MISS T:	In here, Mr Taylor. I believe you know Mr Bohun.
TAYLOR:	We have met – once.
MISS T:	Splendid. And where has Mr Hickley disappeared to?
BOHUN:	Oh – well – he's just—
TAYLOR:	Perhaps he has gone ahead of us – across to the Hall. I can assure you he will find everything – in order. I went down myself with two of my men before I came up here. They are stationed on the doors and they will no doubt be able to give Mr Hickley any assistance he needs.
BOHUN:	Very thoughtful of you.
TAYLOR:	We try to leave no stone unturned. I make it a few minutes before six. I think we ought to be moving.
MISS T:	You're sure you wouldn't like to join us in a cup of tea? It's laid for you.
TAYLOR:	There appeared to be quite a large crowd in the hall. I should hate to keep them waiting.
BOHUN:	You anticipate a lively meeting?
TAYLOR:	It should, I think, be a very *interesting* meeting. (More sharply) I wonder if you could restrain your tortoise. It appears to be eating my trouser leg.
BOHUN:	That's Gable. An excellent judge of character.
MISS T:	Oh, naughty. I'll put him in the log-basket. There! Then perhaps we ought to be off.
BOHUN:	(To Taylor) After you.
TAYLOR:	On the contrary.

(FADE)
(IN THE BACKGROUND, THE SOUNDS CONNECTED WITH A LARGE AND OBSTREPEROUS AUDIENCE. IN

THE FOREGROUND THE 'PLATFORM PARTY' ARE ARRANGING THEMSELVES)

MISS T: You on my right, Archdeacon.
ARCHDEACON: Too kind, dear lady.
MISS T: And Mr Taylor on your right.
TAYLOR: Thank you, Miss Tappett.
MISS T: Then Miss Snooks, our honorary secretary.
MISS SNOOKS: Here.
MISS T: Mrs Philpot-Massingbred on *my* left.
MRS P-M: Thank you, my dear.
MISS T: Mr Hickley. That leaves an extra chair.
BOHUN: Perhaps if you'd allow me, I might afford Mr Hickley some necessary moral support.
MISS T: Excellent. Perhaps you will feel moved to speak.
BOHUN: (Grimly) I might even do that.

(FADE)

BOHUN: (As Narrator) I can't answer for Hickley, but I was feeling none too comfortable. There were at least three of Taylor's thugs in the hall – more than enough to stop us making a run for the only public exit. And possibly more in the road outside. Only one idea presented itself. It was hardly a plan – just a hope. If we could start a real schemozzle inside the hall – enough to draw in the outside watchers – then I had my eye on a small door leading from the platform, which, I felt pretty certain, gave onto an emergency exit. Also, beside it, a couple of fuse boxes and something which looked suspiciously like the main light switch. The Archdeacon, who had a really fruity delivery, was well into his stride. The audience was lapping it up.

(FADE IN)

ARCHDEACON: In the United States of America, a country which is, in many ways – I speak it more in sorrow than in anger – one of the most misguided ever to attain to a semblance of world power (CRIES OF 'HEAR, HEAR') in the United States, as I was saying, there is a salutary measure known as the Anti-Trust Law – a legislative measure designed to combat Monopolies. If the United States – in its wisdom (<u>LAUGHTER AND DERISIVE CHEERS</u>) has seen fit to legislate against the undue centralisation of economic power, why should we, or any other country, support a system of monopoly of scientific knowledge—

(<u>FADE OUT</u>)

BOHUN: (<u>As Narrator</u>) For some time I'd noticed Hickley getting more and more anxious. I thought it was just general anxiety about our position, but apparently there was something else on his mind.

HICKLEY: (<u>In a loud whisper</u>) I can't do it.

BOHUN: (<u>In a loud whisper</u>) Can't do *what*?

HICKLEY: Get on my feet and talk. I'd die sooner.

BOHUN: All right. Don't worry. I've got an idea. Kill two birds with one stone. Scribble a note and pass it to our Lady President. Ask her if she'd mind calling on me to speak.

HICKLEY: Would you really?

BOHUN: Yes. Hurry up. The old gas-bag's nearly finished.

(<u>FADE IN</u>)

ARCHDEACON: Only way to lasting peace and that the cause of our League is the cause of Enlightened Thought throughout the world.

(<u>SUSTAINED APPLAUSE</u>)

MISS T: Ladies and gentlemen. It had been our intention, as you know, to call on brother Cussack to second the motion. In his unavoidable absence, I have asked – (<u>Aside</u>) That's his name – oh yes – I have asked our dear friend Mr Bohun (<u>She pronounces it Bo-hun</u>) to say a few words. Mr Bohun.

(<u>MODERATE APPLAUSE</u>)

BOHUN: Madam Chairman, Archdeacon, ladies and gentlemen. I am, by profession, a lawyer, and spend much of my life in the courts of this country, listening to a variety of views put forward by a variety of different people. I think, however, that I can state with some confidence that never, in the course either of my public, or, for that matter, my private life have I ever listened to such a supreme example of unalloyed, fifteen-carat, blithering balderdash before.

(THE AUDIENCE, SOMNOLENT AT THE BEGINNING, NOW WAKES UP, AND BOHUN CONTINUES HIS SPEECH AGAINST GROWING INTERRUPTIONS AND COUNTER CALLS. AT THE END HE HAS TO SHOUT TO MAKE HIMSELF HEARD)

The Venerable Archdeacon, who would be far better employed looking after his archidiaconal affairs, assured you, as if it were a profound truth, that because economic secrets were shared *inside* America, scientific secrets should be shared *outside* it. This is one of the most child-like non-sequitur's that I have ever listened to. The world today is ruled by science. The country that is ten years – even five years – ahead of its neighbours in science is in a position to dominate them. That is the quite simple reason why no-one in their senses – and I suppose that *some* of you here tonight *are* in your senses – will support a one-sided traffic in scientific secrets with Soviet Russia.

(STORM OF PROTEST – ISOLATED APPLAUSE)

Ah – I see that has let an undesirable cat out of the bag. We don't say Russia – do we? We say 'our neighbours' and 'other countries'. Well, who do you think stands to gain? Who do you think is pressing for technical exchanges? Come to that – who is behind this silly society you belong to.

(THE FORMER PROTEST IS DWARFED TO INSIGNIFI-CANCE BY THE SHOUT THIS PRODUCES. IT IS QUITE OBVIOUS THAT THE PLATFORM IS ABOUT TO BE STORMED)

And another thing. Take a look around you. Who do you think these so-called stewards are – two more have just come in I see. (Aside to Hickley) Ready to jump when I do. They're not stewards at all. They're hired bullies! Hired by your precious Mr Taylor, who's trying to stop me speaking, and who's now going to get a poke on the snoot—

(THIS IS THE LAST WORD AUDIBLE. A CRISP CRACK DENOTES THAT MR TAYLOR HAS GONE DOWN. THE REST DISAPPEARS IN ROARING BEDLAM. A DOOR SLAMS – DIMINISHING THE NOISE SLIGHTLY)

BOHUN: Out with the lights. That door won't hold long.

(NOISE OF BATTERING – FOLLOWED BY THE STEPS OF BOHUN AND HICKLEY, RUNNING, FIRST ON GRASS, THEN ON MACADAM)

Here's a car, not locked. Tumble in.

HICKLEY: (Also out of breath) Whose is it?
BOHUN: No idea. Borrow it for five minutes. Then dump it and walk.

(CAR STARTING, BACKING, SLAMMING AWAY)
(FADE)

TAYLOR: (on telephone) Hello. Hello. Watch out at all points. As arranged. We think he has a car. Big blue saloon. Don't stop it. Follow it. No violence – yet. (RINGS OFF) I – don't – think – they – will – get – very – far.

(MUSIC – FADE)

EPISODE 4
'TROUBLE AT THE LAW SOCIETY'

Transmission: Light Programme
Thursday, 11th August 1955 8.00–8.30 pm

(MUSIC – HOLD UNDER ANNOUNCEMENT)

OPENING
ANNOUNCEMENT: We present William Fox in 'The Man Who Could Not Sleep', a serial-thriller in six parts by Michael Gilbert. Episode 4 – 'Trouble at the Law Society'.

(MUSIC)

ANNOUNCER: Henry Bohun, a respectable Lincolns Inn solicitor (who tells the story), has taken under his wing one Albert Hickley, who is a renegade scientist but a not unlikable little man. The two of them are on the run, pursued not only by the sinister Mr Taylor of CLEFT, the foreign espionage organisation, but also by Commander Rivett-Yarde of British Intelligence. CLEFT are in the lead. They want Hickley, but they want Bohun even more, for he has certain papers of theirs which they cannot afford to lose. Bohun is driving a stolen car and they are making for his uncle's farm on the lonely South Essex marshes.

BOHUN: (As Narrator) Thank heavens it was a car I could cope with. One of the good old-fashioned sort with a gear lever in the floor, not a modern thing with knobs on the steering wheel. After getting away from the Moot Hall, I slowed down. I had no wish to call unnecessary attention to our progress. We went through the main street at Chorminster, and on and out into the country. As we crossed the railway bridge, a man, who seemed to be leaning against the parapet watching the trains, gave us a careful look over. And a mile later on, I again got the feeling that our progress was being checked. It was getting dusk now, and ahead of me I could see the scattered lights of Barrowby. The problem had resolved itself into getting rid of the car without attracting attention; and then reaching my uncle's farm, which was some distance out on the Marsh. The limiting factor was Hickley. He was in very poor shape. What with the stresses and strains of the last twenty-four hours and the recent excitement, he was almost all in. I could hear his teeth chattering as he sat beside me in the car. Really, he wasn't the right calibre for a secret agent. We were running through the outskirts of Barrowby – if so small a place can be described as having outskirts – when I made up my mind. The station – Barrowby Junction – lies clear of the town, on the south side, towards the Marshes and the river. I drove straight up to the station, turned into the little car park in the yard, and switched off.

(FADE. HANDBRAKE. CAR DOOR SLAMMING)

BOHUN: (In undertone) Pull yourself together, Hickley. Ten minutes more and we'll be under cover.

HICKLEY: Where are we going?

BOHUN: You'll see. Do just as I say. And could you kindly stop your teeth chattering? Keep your mouth shut or something.

HICKLEY: All right.

(THEY WALK INTO THE STATION WAITING-ROOM. THEIR STEPS ECHO HOLLOWLY IN THE EMPTY ROOM)

BOHUN: Two third-class singles to (Very slight pause) Tilbury, please.

CLERK: Third returns?

BOHUN: No. Singles.

(TICKETS ISSUED AND PAID FOR)

CLERK: Over the bridge. Down train'll be here in five minutes. If we don't get no more lovely mist.

HICKLEY: What are we going to Tilbury for?

BOHUN: Quiet.

(THEY WALK ALONG THE PLATFORM)

We're going to go right along to the end of the platform, and then into the coal yard. Don't hurry. Stroll. Is the old boy in the signal box looking this way?

HICKLEY: I don't think so. But another car has just come into the yard.

BOHUN: Yes. I don't like that much. May just be a fluke. However, we don't want any other passengers rubbernecking. Quick as you can now. Over the fence. That's right. Up and over.

(PANTING AND SLIGHT TEARING)

Look out for your coat. Hold on, I'll unhook you.

HICKLEY:	Thanks (<u>MORE PANTING</u>)
BOHUN:	That's better.
HICKLEY:	What is it?
BOHUN:	As a matter of interest – it's a coal yard. And pretty full of coal. Now we climb out on to the road. Not so much need for hurry. We're out of sight. Let me give you a leg up. More barbed wire. Watch out.

(<u>PANTING AND HALVING</u>)

That's the boy. Along the road now for about four hundred yards ...

(<u>FEET ON ASPHALT</u>)

... then we cut down on to the Marshes—

(<u>FADE. FADE UP</u>)

HICKLEY:	I can't go much further. Could we stop for a minute?
BOHUN:	No sense in stopping. We're almost there. That's the light ahead. And I think this must be the front gate.

(<u>FEET ON GRAVEL</u>)

	The front door open too. He must have seen us.
THRESHER:	(<u>Booming</u>) Come along in, Henry. And bring your friend with you.
BOHUN:	That sounds like Uncle Clarence. The human foghorn.
THRESHER:	Come straight in. Shut the door behind you. First door on the right.
BOHUN:	Good evening, Uncle Clarence.
THRESHER:	Good evening, my boy. Introduce your friend.
BOHUN:	This is Mr Hickley. Mr Thresher.
HICKLEY:	Pleased to meet you.
THRESHER:	You look as if you could do with a drink. Sit down, sit down. That's right. I'll put a match to the fire. Gets a bit chilly out here after dark, even in summer. More mist tonight, I shouldn't wonder. There now. And grab hold of that. Rum and ginger wine.
HICKLEY:	It's very good of you. (<u>Splutters a bit as he drinks</u>)
BOHUN:	There's just one other thing. Would you very much mind if I drew the curtains?

THRESHER:	Of course. Why not? The police after you?
BOHUN:	They were this morning. But I think – on the whole – it's probably *not* the police who are after us at the moment.
THRESHER:	That's all right. Whoever it is, we shall get plenty of warning. You see that box there? That's my new approach recorder. It's hitched up to an electronic beam. If anyone breaks the circuit the bell inside there gives a 'ping'. Like that. One for each person. That's how I knew you'd arrived – and knew that you'd brought someone with you. Amuses the tradesmen. The butcher used to try and crawl underneath it. Of course, he couldn't. It's a fan beam.
BOHUN:	I see. Look here, I really think that if we're going to impose on your kindness, we ought to tell you what it's all about. Do you agree?
HICKLEY:	(<u>Unhappily</u>) Yes. I suppose we ought.
THRESHER:	Don't worry about me. I'm not curious at all. Come and go as you like.
BOHUN:	(<u>Slower</u>) It isn't entirely a question of satisfying, or not satisfying your curiosity. I have a feeling that it might be as well to have at least one other reliable person in on this story.
THRESHER:	Very kind of you to say so.
BOHUN:	Mr Hickley here is in trouble. He's a scentific worker. Works in the Government Station at Pond End. No sense in mincing matters. He's been a fool. First he was manoeuvred into giving away secrets to the Russians. Then British Intelligence spotted him, and – er – induced him to work for them.
THRESHER:	Double agent.
BOHUN:	Even more involved than that. Because after a bit the Russians spotted that he *was* a double agent and offered to take him back into their camp again. Actually take him back, I mean, behind the Iron Curtain. The first stage in his journey was Rupert Tangee's flat—
THRESHER:	Rupert Tangee. I seem to know the name.
BOHUN:	Yes. You've probably heard him on the wireless. And he lectures a bit. Anyway, the main point about Tangee is that he suddenly took and died.
THRESHER:	I see. Or rather, I don't see anything, yet – How did you come into it, Henry?
BOHUN:	I'm Tangee's Executor.
THRESHER:	And all this is part of your – ha – professional duties? Very conscientious chaps, you family solicitors!

BOHUN:	Well – not exactly. No. But I did start by taking over Tangee's flat.
THRESHER:	And Mr Hickley with it?
BOHUN:	In a way. I found him tied up in the bedroom – right, Hickley? Good Lord, he's asleep. Poor little chap. (<u>Softly</u>) I'm afraid he was never cut out for a spy.
THRESHER:	(<u>More softly too</u>) We haven't all got your peculiar constitution, my boy. Go on.
BOHUN:	That's about all there is to it. He came back to Chorminster where he lodges. Didn't go to his own digs, of course. Got a Miss Tappett to put him up. She keeps tortoises.
THRESHER:	Straws in the hair, eh?
BOHUN:	Oh, Lord, no. Quite charming, in an out-of-this-world sort of way – I think he's rather fond of her. Unfortunately, the other side got on to us – and we had to move rather quickly. So I stole a car—
THRESHER:	Yes. And left it opposite my front gate, I suppose?
BOHUN:	No. I parked it outside the Junction Station. We took tickets to Tilbury, but didn't wait for the train. We climbed out through the coal yard—
THRESHER:	Splendid. Do you suppose you succeeded in throwing them off?
BOHUN:	I really think we may have done – for the moment.

(<u>FADE. FADE UP</u>)

IMPERSONAL VOICE:	(<u>On telephone</u>) It is quite definite that nobody boarded the Tilbury train at Barrowby Junction.
TAYLOR:	(<u>Speaks good, careful English</u>) (<u>On telephone</u>) You are certain?
IMPERSONAL VOICE:	I was on the platform myself by the time it drew up.
TAYLOR:	What about their car?
IMPERSONAL VOICE:	It is still in the station yard where they abandoned it.
TAYLOR:	How far to the next station – on foot?
IMPERSONAL VOICE:	Copestake. About four miles.
TAYLOR:	All right. No need to hang about. Come in now.

(<u>RINGS OFF</u>)

	(<u>Speaking now – not on the telephone</u>) What do you think, Davis?
DAVIS:	(<u>He, like Taylor, speaks good, careful English, in his case, with a slight American twang. Almost too good and careful for a home-grown Englishman or American</u>) I do not believe that they can have intended to walk four miles to the next station and pick up a train. Bohun perhaps. Hickley no. He is not the open-air type.
TAYLOR:	What do you suggest?
DAVIS:	You have the map? Now – back from the station, on that side, are the Marshes – Saltings they call them locally. In the whole area there are not more than four – five – buildings. Farmsteads.
TAYLOR:	Six.
DAVIS:	Six at the most. You are bringing the other men here?
TAYLOR:	Yes. Konstant is fetching in the outlying posts now. I telephoned Hopper.
DAVIS:	Then I suggest we do a little domiciliary visiting. We can always pretend – let me see – to have lost our way in the mist.
TAYLOR:	It is possible that we may even do that.

(<u>FADE. FADE UP</u>)

BOHUN:	Hickley's safely in bed now.
THRESHER:	What about a night cap?
BOHUN:	Good idea.

(<u>CLICK OF GLASSES</u>)

	It's an odd thing, you know. I've only known Albert Hickley for twenty-four hours, but I seem to have spent most of that time either tucking him into bed or getting him up. I'm really beginning to feel quite warmly towards him.
THRESHER:	The paternal instinct.
BOHUN:	He seems such an impossibly ill-equipped little creature to be a spy. He's such a second-class person – and, I should guess, a pretty second-class scientist, as well. Now someone like you, Uncle Clarence—
THRESHER:	Don't be impertinent. My poor talents, such as they are, are at the service of my country. Not that they deserve them. An ungrateful set of baskets.

BOHUN:	How are you getting on with the Commission?
THRESHER:	The Commission has, very slowly and reluctantly, paid me about a quarter of what was due to me for my Tank Buster. In a month or two, or three, when they've all finished their summer recesses, they may get round to considering my aeroplane stopper.
BOHUN:	I hadn't heard about that one.
THRESHER:	It's quite a simple little thing really. I say 'aeroplane' but you could easily fit it on to any sort of vehicle. It transmits impulses, on a certain beat, which will be picked up by any other engine following and overtaking you. It's a matter of frequencies. All you have to do is transmit a frequency which is either the square or the square root of the frequency of the engine following you.
BOHUN:	No doubt – but what actually hapens?
THRESHER:	Oh, the other engine seizes up solid. Must do. It will practically put an end to aerial combat, as it used to be understood. Say you send up a flight of six aeroplanes. They'd all carry my box, and they'd be differentiated so as not to interfere with each other. No aeroplane coming to attack them could get within four hundred yards – that's about the present range. I shall probably improve on that in the course of time.
BOHUN:	The trouble with you people is you're spoil sports. A hundred years ago war used to be a perfectly gentlemanly pursuit – hullo—
THRESHER:	What is it?
BOHUN:	I thought I saw headlights swinging round at the end of the lane.
THRESHER:	If it was a car we shall see them again – the road goes on past the end of the field.
BOHUN:	Unless they're coming here.
THRESHER:	If they're coming this way, little Algy over there will tell us all about them.
BOHUN:	If they *have* turned their lights off and are coming down on foot it looks like trouble—

(A BELL – LIKE A MUFFLED BICYCLE HELL – RINGS
THREE TIMES – THEN TWICE MORE – THEN TWICE
MORE – THEN, AFTER A PAUSE, ONCE. AS IT DOES
SO THRESHER SPEAKS)

THRESHER:	Three. Five. Seven. That's the lot – no, one more. Eight. It's an invasion.
BOHUN:	I'd better get under cover in the bedroom. They're probably searching all the houses, this side of the line.

(DOOR SHUTS ON HIM. SHORT PAUSE. THEN KNOCK ON THE FRONT DOOR)

THRESHER:	(Shouting) It isn't locked. Come in, whoever you are.

(STEPS AND VOICES INDICATE THAT THREE MEN HAVE COME IN)

	Hullo. I don't think I've had the pleasure. Car broken down or something?
TAYLOR:	We were somewhat uncertain of our route. We left the road at Chorminster intending to make for Grays.
THRESHER:	Grays! Well, you've certainly come a long way round. Stranger here, no doubt.
TAYLOR:	Completely so. Seeing your light, we wondered if you – or your friend—
THRESHER:	Actually, I'm alone in the house.
DAVIS:	He is lying.
THRESHER:	(Turning on him) What the devil are you talking about?
DAVIS:	We saw a second shadow on the curtain. Someone left the room just before we entered. I *think* this is the place.
THRESHER:	You're talking balderdash. And may I say that I'm not used to being called a liar.
TAYLOR:	Then you won't mind if we search—
THRESHER:	Of course I mind. And now good evening to you. Ah – I see, a gun—
TAYLOR:	You are quite right. It is a gun.
THRESHER:	With a silencer. That's the old-fashioned sort, with baffle plates. It's terribly ineffective – and can be dangerous …
TAYLOR:	I think we shall find it good enough for the job. After all, you have no near neighbours.
THRESHER:	True.
TAYLOR:	Konstant. Search the ground floor rooms first—

(DOOR OPENING)

	Ah. Mr Bohun. So you were not alone, after all.
BOHUN:	(To Thresher) There didn't seem much point in hiding –

	or getting out of a window when there are five more thugs squatting round the house.
TAYLOR:	Your information is remarkably accurate.
BOHUN:	I must explain about Algy some day. Now, whatever you want – get on with it.
TAYLOR:	The first thing, I fancy, is to continue our search. There was one *more* person we most particularly wished to see.
BOHUN:	Hickley's asleep.
TAYLOR:	Then I very much fear we shall have to awaken him – perhaps somewhat roughly.

(FADE. FADE UP)

RIVETT-YARDE:	It's a good deal more than extraordinary, Bagshawe. I really don't know what to make of it. Unless he's mad.
BAGSHAWE;	Bohun? No, Rivett-Yarde, I don't think he's mad.
RIVETT-YARDE:	He seems to have provoked – quite deliberately provoked – a riot.
BAGSHAWE:	Riot all right. Police were swamped. They had to get the fire brigade out to stop 'em fighting. Women, mostly.
RIVETT-YARDE:	Incredible
BAGSHAWE:	More so when you consider that one of the big points in their programme is Peace. Bit ironical, really. Did you get any line on it?
RIVETT-YARDE:	I sent Train straight down. I told him to—

(TELEPHONE)

	Probably him now. Hullo. Yes. Yes, of course it's me.
TRAIN:	(Very indistinct)
RIVETT-YARDE:	Can't hear a word – it's this perishing line – these confounded bone-idle telephone people who won't do their maintenance properly.
TRAIN:	(More indistinct talk)
RIVETT-YARDE:	They got away in a car. And you went to see the lady – what lady? Oh, the Organiser.
TRAIN:	(More mumbling)
RIVETT-YARDE:	Look here, either get on to a better line or come in yourself and report.

(RINGS OFF)

Young idiot.

BAGSHAWE:	What's happened now?
RIVETT-YARDE:	As far as I can make out Train went to see the lady who organised the meeting that Bohun broke up.
BAGSHAWE:	Then what?
RIVETT-YARDE:	It sounded as if he said he got bitten by a tortoise.
BAGSHAWE:	What very odd things happen to that young man.

(FADE. FADE UP)

THRESHER:	It doesn't seem to me to be a proposition.
DAVIS:	What does not seem a proposition?
THRESHER:	Keeping the three of us here, under duress. One reads about it happening – but I don't believe it will work.
DAVIS:	Why not?
THRESHER:	Well, this is the English countryside. It's crowning characteristic is curiosity. Know thy neighbour as thyself. For instance, when the milkman arrives tomorrow morning, he won't just dump a couple of bottles on my doorstep and collect the empties you know, and depart whistling. He'll want to stop a few minutes and talk about his lumbago. He always talks about his lumbago. If I don't open the door when he rings, he'll assume that I'm ill.
DAVIS:	He will think that you have gone away – for a holiday.
THRESHER:	Don't be silly. He knows very well I had my holiday in June. I told him all about it at the time. And he won't just stop at wondering. He's a sympathetic type. He'll go round and climb in the kitchen window to see if anything's wrong with me.
DAVIS:	Then perhaps you *will* open the door. And talk to him about his lumbago.
THRESHER:	What, with you and your other thugs in the passage pointing guns at me? Well, it will be a rather stilted conversation. It might work. But what about the greengrocer?
DAVIS:	What about the greengrocer?
THRESHER:	He's our fast bowler. And I'm secretary of the Barrowby and Copestake Cricket Club. And tomorrow's the day we pick our team. He'll probably bring the Vicar with him. I can't see us having a selection committee meeting with guns pointing at us from every corner.
DAVIS:	Probably it will not arise. By that time I expect we shall be gone.
THRESHER:	I certainly hope so. Where are the others?

DAVIS:	I do not know. My orders are to stay here with you. I believe Mr Taylor is – reasoning – with your friend right now.

(FADE OUT INTO NEXT CONVERSATION)

TAYLOR:	Really, it seems to me quite logical, Mr Bohun. Unless you abstracted something from Tangee's papers you would not subsequently have behaved as you did. Whatever it was, I assume that you hid it somewhere early this morning. For that is the only time you have been out of our sight. Simple.
BOHUN:	Simple. Next question.
TAYLOR:	The next question is, what did you take and where did you hide it?
BOHUN:	That's two questions.
TAYLOR:	Then let us concentrate on the second one. Where did you put those papers? Konstant tells me they are not on you.
BOHUN:	He ought to know. He practically undressed me and picked my clothes to pieces stitch by stitch.
TAYLOR:	I am afraid Konstant enjoys demonstrating his strength.
BOHUN:	What's he doing now? Twisting Hickley's arm off or bullying Uncle Clarence. I don't think he'll get much change out of Clarence.
TAYLOR:	It is quite surprising what people can be made to say by suitable treatment. It is merely a question of selecting a treatment suitable to the particular individual.
BOHUN:	(Wearily) No doubt. But I can't think why you should imagine that I took anything at all.
TAYLOR:	Let's not go over all that again. Quite sufficient to say that at least one document of importance, which I had already put on one side for further consideration when you interrupted us yesterday evening – you see I am being quite frank with you – was no longer there when we went back this morning.
BOHUN:	You went back this morning?
TAYLOR:	Certainly. Shortly after you and Hickley left the flat yourselves. Incidentally, kindly disposing of the official watcher on the way.
BOHUN:	Oh, the chap in the garden? I hope I didn't hurt him.
TAYLOR:	A black eye and two teeth missing.
BOHUN:	You set my mind at rest. Even allowing for what you tell me – aren't there gaps in your reasoning? For instance,

	M.I.5 may have got there before you, and removed this – whatever it is you're worrying about – document.
TAYLOR:	(<u>Harder note</u>) No-one got there before us. And even if they had, I should still know that you were the guilty party.
BOHUN:	How?
TAYLOR:	Because you have been behaving in a guilty manner ever since.
BOHUN:	I deny it. What have I done that is suspicious? I did not go to the office this morning. Many solicitors take an occasional day off. I come to spend the night with my uncle – calling in for a cup of tea with my aunt, Miss Tappett, on the way.
TAYLOR:	(<u>Incredulous</u>) Your aunt?
BOHUN:	Not really *my* aunt. My mother's aunt's husband's sister. But I call her Aunt Clarrie.
TAYLOR:	I see. And after leaving her you stole a motor car—
BOHUN:	Borrowed.
TAYLOR:	Without the owner's permission.
BOHUN:	If you press the point – yes.
TAYLOR:	I do press it. Was that part of a normal day's activity?
BOHUN:	Well—
TAYLOR:	I think we will stop telling lies. And tell the truth. (<u>Very sharp</u>) Where did you put that paper?
BOHUN:	I deny that I have any paper of yours.
TAYLOR:	(<u>Amiable again</u>) You force me to say it – but this is an isolated house. I have seven men here with me. It should not be difficult to make you speak.
BOHUN:	Do you carry your instruments of torture about with you?
TAYLOR:	An ingenious man, Mr Bohun, has no need for racks and thumbscrews. Almost any simple kitchen implement will suffice. There is no real need even for violence. I only use violence when I am in a hurry. For instance, we could quite simply deprive you of sleep—
BOHUN:	Now that should be fascinating.
TAYLOR:	Why do you say that?
BOHUN:	I think I'll leave you to find that one out.
TAYLOR:	On the other hand, there are even more effective methods. Psychological methods—
BOHUN:	Such as—
VOICE:	(<u>A horrible scream of anguish rings through the house</u>)
BOHUN:	What's that?
TAYLOR:	I expect Konstant has become impatient.

BOHUN:	Let me – all right, you've got a gun.
TAYLOR:	Unless you want a bullet in your stomach, I suggest you sit still. Since, in a sense, he is suffering for you, would it not be simple to tell me what I want to know?
VOICE:	(Second, absolutely blood-curdling scream)
BOHUN:	This is your psychology, is it?
TAYLOR:	A sample.
BOHUN:	I think you're bluffing.

(DOOR OPENS)

TAYLOR:	Yes, Davis, what is it?
DAVIS:	(Whispers to him)
TAYLOR:	I see. Splendid. Fortunately, Mr Bohun, Hickley is made of less obstinate stuff than you. He has told us what we want to know.
BOHUN:	What have you done to him?
TAYLOR:	Absolutely nothing. Just psychology.
BOHUN:	I don't believe it.
TAYLOR:	Here he is. Why not ask him.
BOHUN:	What—
HICKLEY:	Bohun – what have they been doing to you? I couldn't stand it. Your screams. I thought it better—
BOHUN:	I'm afraid you've been tricked, Hickley—
THRESHER:	(Rushing in) What have those devils been playing at?
BOHUN:	Calm yourself, Uncle. No-one has done anything to anyone. Pure psychology. (To Hickley) How, Hickley, what did you tell them?
HICKLEY:	Everything that you told me.
BOHUN:	What about – the—?
TAYLOR:	Set your mind at rest, Mr Bohun. We know now that you placed the papers in a cloakroom, and posted the ticket to yourself at the Law Society. Davis – I think you have the most professional look – you could pay a visit to the Law Society at – let me see – lunch time tomorrow. It will be crowded then, I imagine. I suggest a black hat and rolled umbrella.
DAVIS:	And a brief-case.
TAYLOR:	Yes, of course. A brief-case.
DAVIS & TAYLOR:	(Laugh)

(FADE. FADE UP)

RIVETT-YARDE:	Tell me, Train, did *anything* happen to you at Chorminster – except getting bitten by a tortoise?
TRAIN:	W-well, sir – it depends what you mean – happen.
RIVETT-YARDE:	For God's sake – don't turn this into a quiz. We haven't got time. Let's have it. Navy-fashion.
TRAIN:	After I'd got away from Miss Tappett – and I really don't think she could have anything to do with any of this, sir. She looks exactly like my aunt—
RIVETT-YARDE:	Train!
TRAIN:	All right, sir … well, I called on the local police. They were still pretty sore about the meeting. Well, after a bit of talk about that, and how the Home Secretary ought to put a stop to it, and so on, I heard about the car—
RIVETT-YARDE:	Car?
BAGSHAWE:	What car?
TRAIN:	A 1938 blue saloon Marchbank-straight-six. Belonged to a Mrs Philpot-Massingbred. Bit of a local big-wig. J.P., and so on. Drives herself. She was at that meeting – actually on the platform. Someone threw a flowerpot and she caught it – on the chin. Broke a perfectly good set of bottoms and tops. The only really comfortable set she'd had since the war. Was she mad!
RIVETT-YARDE:	I trust this is leading us somewhere.
TRAIN:	Oh, yes, sir. You see, when she got out, she was madder still. Someone had stolen her car.
RIVETT-YARDE:	I see.
TRAIN:	But that turned out all right because the local police had found it. Parked outside Barrowby Junction. That's about four miles away. A half-pint station on the Chorminster-Tilbury branch line. I nipped out and had a word with the ticket clerk. No luck.
BAGSHAWE:	He didn't remember the car being left there?
TRAIN:	No. It was the wrong clerk. He wasn't on duty last night. So I hung round a bit more until the right one came back.
RIVETT-YARDE:	Tchah.
TRAIN:	I beg your pardon, sir.
RIVETT-YARDE:	Just a passing thought. Go on.
TRAIN:	*This* one was quite helpful. He remembered the two men who had left the car. And they certainly could have been Hickley and the other fellow – Bohun. Also he said that about three minutes later *another* car – sounded like a big one – he didn't actually see it, came tearing into the yard,

and a man got out. He asked for a ticket. The ticket collector said – 'Where to?' 'Where does the next train go to?' asks the man. The collector tells him 'Tilbury', so he buys a ticket for Tilbury, and walks out on to the platform. A few minutes later the Tilbury train arrives – and departs. And to the collector's surprise the man was still there.

BAGSHAWE: The second man?

TRAIN: Yes. The first two had gone by that time.

RIVETT-YARDE: By train?

TRAIN: Well – I suppose so—

RIVETT-YARDE: What do you mean?

TRAIN: The second man was obviously after them. If they caught the train, why didn't he? He was there in plenty of time to see whether they got it or not.

RIVETT-YARDE: (Grudgingly) There might be something in that. What did the second man do then? Just drove off, I suppose?

TRAIN: Yes. But not at once. He went into the public telephone booth first and put through a longish call.

BAGSHAWE: (Excited) Reporting back that he'd missed them. It's as plain as – as plain as my face. If Bohun and Hickley didn't even wait for the train they must have climbed out at the back end of the station and legged it.

RIVETT-YARDE: It still leaves a pretty wide field. They could have walked to the next station and caught a train anywhere.

BAGSHAWE: I suppose so – all the same—

RIVETT-YARDE: All the same. I agree it's time we took these two seriously. We'll put out a 'general'.

BAGSHAWE: Public?

RIVETT-YARDE: No. Not yet. Just an official general alert. I'll get Farmer to pass the details on to the police and you tip off the – well – all the Special Forces.

BAGSHAWE: Right.

RIVETT-YARDE: Let's have another look at the map. Barking – Tilbury and back to the Romford East Horndon road as an area of special search. Anything which comes up is to be reported to me here. I'll have a line manned night and day—

(FADE)

BOHUN: (As narrator) Of course, I only heard long afterwards exactly what did happen on that memorable mid-day. So far as I was concerned, I was a helpless prisoner, with my Uncle Clarence and Hickley, at the farm on the Marshes. With Davis gone there were only seven of them, but seven men who know their job, can keep three prisoners pretty safe. The postman had come and gone and the milkman had put in his appearance. Taylor dealt with him. He simply answered the bell himself and said that Mr Thresher had been called away for a few days and had left him in charge. The milkman had retired disappointed and not, I think, entirely satisfied. But not, on the other hand, dis-satisfied enough to take any useful action. At eleven o'clock, as I said, Davis departed. Perhaps a trifle too well dressed for an absolutely typical solicitor, nevertheless he looked quite impressive – pin-stripe trousers and black coat. Anthony Eden, rolled umbrella and brief-case. Thinking the matter over in retrospect, it was the purest bad luck for him that he should have had to deal with such a conservative body as the Law Society. The Law Society is the Body Politic of Solicitordom and lawyers, as a class, are apt to place great store by obser-vance of formalities. Particularly if it's a matter of handing over anything to anybody – and if you don't believe me, try getting money out of Court!

However – from what I have been told since, I can picture Mr Davis striding blithely down Chancery Lane, and up the steps of the Society's building—

(SWING DOORS)

VOICES: (Background murmur)

(CONSTANT PASSAGE OF FOOTSTEPS INDICATES THAT THE FRONT HALL IS A GOOD DEAL BUSIER THAN IT WAS WHEN BOHUN WAS HERE LAST)

CLOAKROOM
ATTENDANT: (Near foreground) Hat *and* umbrella. Hat only. You and your guest together, sir?

(THERE IS ONE MOVING GROUP GOING TO THE LUNCH ROOM AND ANOTHER, IN THE OPPOSITE DIRECTION, TO THE BUFFET)

VOICES:	(<u>A good deal of chatter</u>)
	How are you keeping these days?
	Overworking as usual.
	I wish *I* was a barrister and could rush off to the South of France immediately the courts shut. (*Etc.*)
	(<u>THERE IS ALSO A GROUP (STATIONARY) IN FRONT OF THE TICKER-TAPE</u>)
	(<u>Reading the latest results from Australia</u>) Scandalous. Of course, they doctor their pitches every night after dark. What do they put on them?
	Depends whether they are going to bat or bowl next morning. (*Etc.*)
	(<u>NONE OF THIS OBSCURES THE FOREGROUND CONVERSATION, BUT THERE IS AN IMPRESSION OF BUSY BACKGROUND LIFE GOING ON THE WHOLE TIME</u>)
DAVIS:	I say – er—
ROBERTS: (Second Porter)	Can I help you, sir?
DAVIS:	Thank you. I came to pick up a small package. I believe it was left here for me.
ROBERTS:	What name, sir?
DAVIS:	Boon. The spelling is B-o-h-u-n.
ROBERTS:	Oh, yes, Mr Bohun – one minute – I'll fetch the receipt book—
FIRST SOLICITOR:	We shall never win a Test Match in Australia until we take our own umpires with us.
SECOND SOLICITOR:	Come now, Bernard. That's rather sweeping. What makes you think that ours are any better than other people's?
FIRST SOLICITOR:	My dear fellow, British Justice is renowned for its impartiality—
SECOND SOLICITOR:	If you'd heard old Borman in Court this morning you wouldn't say that—
	(<u>FADE BACK SLIGHTLY</u>)
CLITHEROE: (Head porter)	Can I help you? I understand there is some question of a package.

DAVIS:	That's right. There. I think I can see it, in that glass case, under those gloves. You can see the name.
CLITHEROE:	(Puzzled) Excuse me, sir. I was given to understand that Mr Bohun had called for it in person.
DAVIS:	I—
ROBERTS:	'E *said* his name was Bohun, Mr Clitheroe.
DAVIS:	Well – as a matter of fact—
CLITHEROE:	Did you tell my assistant that you were Mr Bohun?
DAVIS:	(Scenting danger) No. Not at all. I was misunderstood. I came *from* Mr Bohun. As I was passing – you see – he asked me to pick up this package.
CLITHEROE:	Not indisposed, I trust?
DAVIS:	(Too quickly) Yes. Poor fellow. He's in bed. Influenza.
CLITHEROE:	Well, now, think of that. And I spoke to him in the reading room, only yesterday morning. He looked quite well then.
DAVIS:	Very sudden. He was taken queer – at my house, as a matter of fact – last night. And he's worrying about this letter.
CLITHEROE:	Then we must let you have it at once.
DAVIS:	Good.
CLITHEROE:	I expect you have Mr Bohun's written authority with you—
DAVIS:	(Blankly) Written authority?
CLITHEROE:	Oh, certainly, sir. We couldn't possibly hand over a member's property without written authority—
DAVIS:	(Beginning to get angry) But look here – that's absurd.
CLITHEROE:	Of course, if he were dead, a Grant of Probate—
DAVIS:	Nonsensical red tape. I can't waste my time—
CLITHEROE:	Possibly a written application to the Secretary – here – stop – stop at once

(CRASH AS DAVIS SPLINTERS THE FRONT OF THE GLASS CASE WITH HIS UMBRELLA HANDLE)

Hold him, Roberts! Police!

(SOUND OF FEET STAMPING AND STRUGGLING)

VOICES:	(Rapidly growing background hubbub)
ROBERTS:	(A sound like 'Ouch' as Davis drives his fist into his stomach) 'E 'it me. You saw him, Mr Clitheroe.

FIRST SOLICITOR:	Someone's gone mad!
CLITHEROE:	(It is noticeable that even his aitches go overboard in the excitement) 'Old 'is arms.
SECOND SOLICITOR:	Charles! Someone's gone mad and is assaulting Clitheroe.
FIRST SOLICITOR:	Hit someone your own size, sir. Ouch! I didn't mean me.
THIRD SOLICITOR:	Bernard's down.
FOURTH SOLICITOR:	Grab him round the knees.
SECOND SOLICITOR:	Bernard's gone for six.
FOURTH SOLICITOR:	Go for his ankles.
FIFTH SOLICITOR:	(Evidently a rugby enthusiast) Feet – feet.

(THE HUBBUB IS TERMINATED BY A MOST
ALMIGHTY CRASH AS ABOUT SIX PEOPLE GO TO
THE GROUND SIMULTANEOUSLY, CARRYING AWAY
THE TAPE MACHINE WITH THEM. THIS IS
SUCCEEDED BY A MOMENT OF COMPARATIVE
SILENCE, BROKEN ONLY BY:)

ALL:	(Strenuous panting)
CLITHEROE:	I think he's quieter now, Mr Foulkes. If you would perhaps remove yourself from his stomach. The police 'ave been summoned. Thank you very much, Mr Walker. I think 'e is quite safe now.
SEVERAL ELDERLY SOLICITORS:	(Together) Really. Scandalous. Disgraceful. I never heard of such a thing. Drunk at lunch time. *What* is the Society coming to? One expects that sort of thing on the Stock Exchange—
CLITHEROE:	Ah. Constable. This man. Charge of assault.
CONSTABLE:	Stand back there, please.
CLITHEROE:	Aggravated assault on the Society's premises.
CONSTABLE:	I think you'd better come along with me, sir. What – hullo—
VOICES:	(The hubbub dies right down)
CONSTABLE:	He's dead.

(MUSIC – FADE)

EPISODE 5

'CLOSING THE GAP'

<u>Transmission: Light Programme</u>
<u>Thursday, 18th August 1955 8.00–8.30 pm</u>

(<u>MUSIC – HOLD UNDER ANNOUNCEMENT</u>)

ANNOUNCER: We present William Fox in 'The Man Who Could Not Sleep', a serial-thriller in six parts by Michael Gilbert. Episode 5 – 'Closing the Gap'.

(<u>MUSIC</u>)

The Foreign Espionage Organisation, CLEFT, lead by the sinister Mr Taylor and his assistant, the giant, but moronic, Konstant, are holding three prisoners on Clarence Thresher's lonely south Essex farm. One is Thresher himself, a war weapons inventor. The second is Thresher's nephew, the London solicitor who tells the story, by name Bohun. The third, Hickley, a renegade scientist with whose affairs Bohun and his uncle have become involved.

CLEFT's first object was to recover certain papers which Bohun had removed. A Mr Davis, who was making the attempt, failed – and took his own life rather than face capture. The second object of the organisation is to remove Hickley (and possibly the other two as well) from England. Meanwhile British Intelligence, under Commander Rivett-Yarde, though a lap or two behind, is closing the gap.

MESSENGER: Superintendent Farmer for Commander Rivett-Yarde.

FARMER: Good morning. I thought I'd come round myself – we don't want too much telephone chatter about this.

RIVETT-YARDE: An astounding development. Have you found out anything more?

FARMER: Quite a bit. This chap Davis – or Davids, to be more accurate – is one of their assistant trade officials. That's

	what they call them. All of them are linguists and most of them are bad hats. Davids spoke good French and almost perfect English, with a slight American accent.
RIVETT-YARDE:	Yes. Yes. I can imagine his background. But what the devil was he doing in the Law Society? And why did he take poison? There's no doubt about *that*, I suppose?
FARMER:	None at all. Cyanide. He was wearing one of those heavy signet rings. A sliding top, and a container inside it. That's where he kept the stuff. *And* a reserve supply in his top waistcoat pocket.
RIVETT-YARDE:	Yes – but why did he take it?
FARMER:	Why? Because he'd failed. Not only failed, but failed badly – and over something they minded about.
RIVETT-YARDE:	He actually told the porter at the Law Society that he came *from* Bohun and said he was to pick up the package.
FARMER:	That's right. Then he overplayed his hand. When they wouldn't hand it over quietly he tried to snatch it – actually broke the glass and got his hand inside, but was sat on by half a dozen solicitors.
RIVETT-YARDE:	Hm. A very flattening experience, I should think.
FARMER:	It certainly flattened him.
RIVETT-YARDE:	I see. And realizing that he'd done exactly the opposite of what he set out to do – called attention both to himself and the packet, in fact – he took his own life.
FARMER:	That's right.
RIVETT-YARDE:	Where is it now, by the way?
FARMER:	The packet? Still there. We tried to get hold of it – material evidence – and so on, but they were very stuffy, very stuffy indeed. More or less told us to get a Judge's order or leave it alone. I expect we *shall* be able to get hold of it, but it's going to take a bit of time.
RIVETT-YARDE:	We may be able to short-circuit that.
FARMER:	You've got someone on the job?
RIVETT-YARDE:	I sent young Train round to see what he could do. He's a complete fool, but this happens to be the sort of thing he's good at.
FARMER:	If he gets any change out of their Secretary he's a better man than I am.
RIVETT-YARDE:	Oh, I don't imagine he'll trouble the Secretary. That's not his line at all. I'll let you know what transpires.

(FADE. FADE UP)

TRAIN:	W-well, sir. I've got it – for better or worse—
RIVETT-YARDE:	Splendid, Train. Housebreaking? Bribery? Impersonation? Or perhaps you'd rather not say?
TRAIN:	Oh, no. It was nothing like that. I just went round and had a w-word with the under-porter. A man called Roberts. Awfully nice chap. He and I were in the same Regiment. In fact, he was my b-batman once.
RIVETT-YARDE:	I see. Simple.
TRAIN:	Of course, he couldn't hand over the p-package. But he let me b-borrow it. I trundled it round to the nearest Law Stationers and had it photostated. Paid seven shillings out of my own pocket, sir.
RIVETT-YARDE:	I expect the funds will run to that. Got it there? Good. Now—

(CRACKLING AS THICK PHOTOSTAT SHEETS ARE UNFOLDED)

	This looks like a list of rendezvous. Trafalgar Square. British Museum. I sometimes think they're the only two places in London they've ever heard of. We could watch 'em, I suppose – not much sense in it now. What's this one? Memorandum on recruiting. That's one for the files, I think. Then what on earth's this—?
TRAIN:	I only photographed the back of that one, sir. It was an old brochure for a hotel, or something like that, but it was the figures on the back that looked interesting.
RIVETT-YARDE:	Yes. What do you make of 'em?
TRAIN:	Nothing much, I'm afraid, sir. 26. 1. 20. 39. 2. 2. 83. 3. 30. 83. 4. 0. 132. 5. 10.
RIVETT-YARDE:	Odd sort of sequence. Some of the numbers are in rising series, some in descending.
TRAIN:	It sort of looked familiar for a moment, sir – 26. 1. 20. 39. 2. 2. – it rang a sort of bell. But I couldn't quite put my f-finger on it.
RIVETT-YARDE:	All right. Get it across to the cipher department and let them have a go at it. They'll have it out in no time. Wonderful chaps. Use slide-rules. What's that last one?
TRAIN:	That's the p-pick of the bunch, sir. This chap Bohun seems a methodical sort of type – must have sat down

and written it all out yesterday morning. It's a sort of account of what he's done. He found out he was Tangee's executor. Went up to take over. Found Taylor and Konstant in possession. Dialled 999. Taylor & Co. got away. The police arrive. Then he finds Hickley tied up in the next room – that bit's new – and the two of them decide to wait for early morning and run for it. Then there's the bit about knocking me out – we know about that – it finishes – 'The few papers herewith looked the most interesting so I removed them. My present intention is to get Hickley away to some safe quarter – probably one of my family – and then have a word with Commander Rivett-Yarde, who sounds a tough character—'

RIVETT-YARDE: (<u>Complacently</u>) Hm. Remarkable. Remarkable. What are those words at the end?

TRAIN: '—but is probably not as tough as he thinks he is.'

RIVETT-YARDE: (<u>Pause</u>) I cannot say how keenly I am looking forward to meeting this young man.

(<u>TELEPHONE</u>)

Yes. Hullo.

FARMER: Farmer, here. We've finished the autopsy on Davids – no doubt about cause of death. Cyanide concentrate. Enough to kill a platoon. There's one other thing. He had the return half of a ticket on him. Chorminster. Could have been a blind, of course – but no reason it should be. He didn't know he was going to run into trouble.

RIVETT-YARDE: Chorminster. It looks as if we were right. They *haven't* moved very far out of the area. What are you doing about it?

FARMER: Quietly drafting in a few reinforcements. I'm going down to Romford now. You'll be able to get me at the police station, if you want me. Anything at your end?

RIVETT-YARDE: (<u>Slowly</u>) We've got one lead. Apparently Bohun *intended* Hickley to stay with some member of his family. We're looking into that one now. Also we've got something that may be a cipher.

FARMER: I don't want to hurry you in any way but I've got a sort of feeling that if we're going to break this we ought to break it fairly quickly.

RIVETT-YARDE:	(<u>Even more slowly</u>) Curiously enough – I have the same feeling myself – I'll keep in touch.

(FADE. FADE UP DISTANT SOUND OF COCK CROWING)

BOHUN:	I'm beginning to get a bit tired of this, Uncle.
THRESHER:	(<u>Yawning</u>) I've almost lost count of time. Two evenings ago, it must have been when you turned up like a bad halfpenny – and a pack of trouble with you.
BOHUN:	I'm sorry to let you in for all this.
THRESHER:	Don't apologise. It has its interesting side. It's always fun to meet the people your weapons are intended to destroy.
BOHUN:	I suppose you haven't got anything—
THRESHER:	A secret weapon! I'm afraid not. Most of my stuff isn't intended for use at close quarters. And I don't want to call attention to it. Some of it's rather valuable. That thing that looks like a knife box is a prototype sound wave unit. It projects sound waves and vibrations. Unpleasant ones. You know how some people can't stand hearing a finger rubbed on glass. Sets them all on edge. Well this is about twenty times as bad.
BOHUN:	Sounds horrible.

(OPENING DOOR)

	Well, we haven't heard anything from our friends this morning, you know.
THRESHER:	Where's Hickley?
BOHUN:	In the next bedroom. He's still asleep.
THRESHER:	Hullo.

(STEPS COMING UPSTAIRS)

	That sounds like our old pal, Taylor. And King Kong Konstant.
TAYLOR:	(<u>His voice is somehow less suave – colder and more abrupt</u>) Good morning.
BOHUN:	Good morning.
TAYLOR:	I come to warn you that food that may be a little short today. It will be evenly divided and there is plenty of water.

BOHUN:	You wouldn't like to give the whole thing up and let us go home?
TAYLOR:	I regret not. But you will not have to wait a great deal longer.
BOHUN:	I really don't know what you're worrying about. I take it your man Davis duly recovered the papers. As far as I'm concerned that's all there is to it.
TAYLOR:	Davis, unfortunately, did not succeed in recovering the papers.
BOHUN:	What—
TAYLOR:	All that Davis succeeded in doing was calling attention to them. I had always suspected that he was not as competent as he imagined he was.
BOHUN:	Was—? Is he—?
TAYLOR:	Of course. He is dead. What do you suppose. Having failed he realised that his life was forfeit. He anticipated matters by destroying himself.
BOHUN:	So your whole crazy scheme has gone up in smoke.
TAYLOR:	(Sharply) Certainly not. Because a set-back occurs, that does not mean failure.
BOHUN:	Who are you trying to convince? Us or yourself? This isn't something you can talk away, you know. You've *failed*.
TAYLOR:	I find you insolent.
BOHUN:	I couldn't care less.
TAYLOR:	Konstant.
BOHUN:	That's right. If you lose the argument resort to – ouch – brute force – ugh.

(SOUND OF TWO BLOWS)

THRESHER:	Leave him alone, you swine—
BOHUN:	(From floor) It's all right.
TAYLOR:	I will wish you both good day.
BOHUN:	(Winded) You see – a perfect example – the People's Democracy in action. If your opponent is getting the better of the argument – hit him.
THRESHER:	Are you hurt – the damned swine.
BOHUN:	Just winded. That was a couple of love taps. If Konstant really decided to hit you he'd tee you up like a golf ball, take one sharp swipe, and your head would land ten yards away from your body.

THRESHER:	Damned oaf. I wish I had a gun.
BOHUN:	No good. He's bullet proof.
THRESHER:	Not against the sort of bullets I'd use.
BOHUN:	Ouch – kick that chair across would you – that's better.

(CREAKS AS HE SETTLES INTO BEDROOM CHAIR)

	You know the thing that really worries me is this. When a crowd of this sort starts to show its teeth it means that they can see the winning post. I've got an idea that we're all three of us booked for a one way journey – first stop Moscow – if we get as far.
THRESHER:	How do you think we go?
BOHUN:	That's their big secret.
THRESHER:	And when do we start?
BOHUN:	Your guess is as good as mine. But I don't fancy we shall be stopping here a great deal longer.

(FADE)
(FADE UP FOOTSTEPS. DOOR OPENING AND THEN SHUTTING)

BAGSHAWE:	Mr Craine? Good of you to spare me a minute. My name is Bagshawe. Major Bagshawe. I'm attached to the Foreign Office – on Security Duties.
CRAINE:	(A very precise lawyer-like voice) Please sit down. I surmise that it is about my junior partner – Mr Bohun.
BAGSHAWE:	That's right.
CRAINE:	If you can tell me anything about him, I shall be more than grateful.
BAGSHAWE:	Then you've no news of him.
CRAINE:	I haven't set eyes on him for three days. He left the office on Monday in the ordinary way. He seemed perfectly normal. His secretary informs me that he was on his way to take over some property of which he had been appointed executor.
BAGSHAWE:	Rupert Tangee.
CRAINE:	That was, I think, the name. He did not arrive at the office at the usual hour on Tuesday – however, there was nothing in that. Young men nowadays are seldom punctual. Then, a little later, two policemen – or purported policemen – arrived and searched his room. They said

that he had been arrested for attempted diamond-smuggling—

BAGSHAWE: Yes. We know about those purported policemen.

CRAINE: About half an hour later Bohun telephoned. I told him about the charge of diamond smuggling – which he did not seem to take at all seriously. His actual words, so far as I can recollect them, were – 'The only offence I'm aware of committing this morning is assaulting the police.'

BAGSHAWE: Assaulting – Oh – yes, of course. That could have been when he sloshed young Train in the rockery.

CRAINE: Train in the rockery?

BAGSHAWE: (Hastily) Never mind. We'll explain it all to you some day. The important thing at the moment is, we've got to find out the names of his family.

CRAINE: Family?

BAGSHAWE: That's right.

CRAINE: But, so far as I am aware, he is not yet married.

BAGSHAWE: Oh, I expect he used the word in a more general sense.

CRAINE: Collaterals and ascendants?

BAGSHAWE: That's the sort of thing. How many – how many of those has he got?

CRAINE: I think—

(DIALS ON OFFICE TELEPHONE)

—would you ask Miss Prince if she'd come in – thank you very much. His secretary. A most intelligent girl. She's been with him a long time.

(KNOCK ON DOOR)

Come in.

(DOOR OPENS)

Oh, Miss Prince. It's about Mr Bohun.

MISS PRINCE: (Breathlessly) You've found him?

CRAINE: Well, no.

MISS PRINCE: (On a rising note) He's dead—

CRAINE: Calm yourself, Miss Prince. Mr Bohun is not dead. So far as we know – he is in perfectly good health – Is that not so, Major Bagshawe?

BAGSHAWE:	(<u>Drily</u>) We have no information to the contrary. Now, Miss Prince, I wonder if you could tell me – has Mr Bohun any family living? Father, mother, brothers, and so on.
MISS PRINCE:	He's got no brothers and sisters, that I do know.
CRAINE:	No collaterals.
BAGSHAWE:	No collaterals.
MISS PRINCE:	His mother was a widow – and she died quite recently. I remember Mr Bohun going to the funeral. It was snowing.
CRAINE:	No father. No mother. Grandfather and grandmother?
MISS PRINCE:	Oh, I shouldn't think so.
CRAINE:	Unlikely. Well, that leaves uncles and aunts and their issue.
BAGSHAWE:	What about it, Miss Prince?
MISS PRINCE:	I was trying to remember who he sent Christmas cards to. There was an aunt. She lived in Scotland and sent him a large box of Edinburgh rock each birthday. He never touched sweets himself. He used to give it to me. (<u>The reminiscence is too much for Miss Prince. She nearly dissolves into tears</u>)
CRAINE:	Calm yourself, Miss Prince. Was there anyone else?
MISS PRINCE:	The only other one was an uncle in Essex.
BAGSHAWE:	(<u>Sharply</u>) Essex. Whereabouts?
MISS PRINCE:	It may be in my address book. That's chiefly business addresses though – I could have a search.
BAGSHAWE:	I'd be obliged if you would – it's becoming rather urgent—

(<u>FADING</u>)

RIVETT-YARDE:	(<u>Telephoning</u>) Rivett-Yarde here. How are you getting on with that job?
CIPHER EXPERT:	Very interesting, Commander. I've rarely seen a sequence like it. I have a preliminary report here.
RIVETT-YARDE:	Splendid.
C. EXPERT:	The message consists, we think, of three different sequences. One of them is a regular rising sequence. One an irregular rising sequence and the other an arbitrary sequence.
RIVETT-YARDE:	Yes – but—
C. EXPERT:	The second sequence – second, fifth, eighth, eleventh, etc.

is simple, a unit sequence 1, 2, 3, 4. The first one, on the other hand, is very interesting. It runs 26, 39, 83, 83, 132. Rising, you see, but quite irregularly.

RIVETT-YARDE: Can you make out—

C. EXPERT: The third sequence – occupying the third places – is rather baffling. 20 – 2 – 30 – 0 – 10. It suggests a wheel cipher but the 2 is out of place.

RIVETT-YARDE: But what does the message mean?

C. EXPERT: Oh, I'm afraid we haven't reached any definitive conclusion in *that* point yet.

RIVETT-YARDE: Tchah.

(FADE, FADE UP)
(FARMYARD NOISES APPROPRIATE TO MID-AFTER-
NOON. HEN LAYING, COW MOO-ING IN THE
DISTANCE)

BOHUN: Uncle.

THRESHER: (Drowsily) Yes, m'boy.

(DURING THE FOLLOWING THE NOISE OF A
TRADESMAN'S VAN BUMPING UP THE DRIVE, THEN
THE RING OF A BELL)

BOHUN: I think I heard a van turn down your lane.

THRESHER: What time is it? Four o'clock. That'll be the greengrocer. He usually turns up just before tea.

BOHUN: Does he stop at the gate?

THRESHER: No. Drives his van right up to the door.

BOHUN: I wonder if we could wave to him as he gets out. No. Hold your horses. They've thought of that. Here come the bulldogs. Good afternoon, Konstant.

KONSTANT: Huh.

BOHUN: I gather you want us to keep away from the window. All right. All right. No need to throw your weight about. We're being as good as gold.

VOICES: (Distant murmuring)

THRESHER: I think he's brought the vicar with him.

BOHUN: Whatever for?

THRESHER: This is the day we pick the cricket team for Saturday. Poor old boy. He'll be frightfully upset at my going away without telling him.

KONSTANT: No talking.

VOICES: (For a moment)

(FRONT DOOR SLAMS. THE VAN STARTS UP)

KONSTANT: Very well.

(FOOTSTEPS AS HE AND OTHER MAN MAKE FOR DOOR. VAN CHANGING GEAR IN DISTANCE. ROOM DOOR SHUTS)

BOHUN: That's that. Don't take many chances, do they? I say. Did you manage to pick up anything from where you were?

THRESHER: I couldn't hear what our side were saying – except in a general way – I think I caught the vicar's ecclesiastical boom. I did get hold of one remark by Taylor. And I'm not sure that I liked it.

BOHUN: What was that?

THRESHER: He said, 'He'll be back by tomorrow morning. You could call round then.'

BOHUN: Back by tomorrow morning, eh?

THRESHER: It looks as if your guess was right. We're going out tonight. If we're going to pull anything off, we'd better think fast. It'll be getting dark by half-past eight. Just over four hours.

(FADE. FADE UP)

POLICE SERGEANT: 'E said what Constable?

CONSTABLE: 'E said that one of 'is regular customers 'ad absquatulated.

SERGEANT: There's no such thing.

CONSTABLE: 'Swat he said, Sergeant.

SERGEANT: You'd better ask him to step in here, and then perhaps we *shall* know what he wants.

(DOOR)

Absquatulated!

(DOOR AGAIN)

CONSTABLE: Mr Higgins.

SERGEANT:	Sit down, Mr Higgins. From Barrowby, I believe.
HIGGINS:	'S'right. Milk and Dairy Produce. Barrowby and Chorminster. Established nineteen-owe-five.
SERGEANT:	I understand from the constable here that you have a complaint against one of your customers.
HIGGINS:	Not *against* one of my customers. Good heavens and all, no. A very good customer. Major Thresher. He's got the farm down on the marsh.
CONSTABLE:	Swiggs Farm.
HIGGINS:	'S'right. Very nice gentleman indeed. Not just, 'leave two pints, my man, and send your bill weekly' – but friendly, see. Always have a word about his chickens or my lumbago. Well, he's been absquatulated.
CONSTABLE:	(Coughs)
SERGEANT:	Ab—?
HIGGINS:	Scuppered – press-ganged – kidnapped—
SERGEANT:	That's a very serious charge, Mr Higgins.
HIGGINS:	If it wasn't a very serious charge I shouldn't be wasting my time here. I know Major Thresher, see. He wouldn't go away without telling me. And who's that foreign smart Sam who opened the door. Tell me that?
SERGEANT:	Foreign? You mean he couldn't speak English?
HIGGINS:	Oh, he spoke English all right – but not like you and me, Sergeant. Too much flannel round the edge, if you follow me.
SERGEANT:	And you think that this foreign gentleman has ab – has kidnapped Major Thresher.
HIGGINS:	'S'right. Important government work, he's on. Hush-hush, see.
SERGEANT:	Well, thank you very much, Mr Higgins. We'll look into this.
HIGGINS:	(Suspiciously) Right away?
SERGEANT:	Certainly.
HIGGINS:	Then I can get back to my round with my mind at rest.

(SHUTS DOOR)

SERGEANT:	Well, what do you think of that?
CONSTABLE:	Barmy.
SERGEANT:	That's what I think. One born every minute. Spy mania. Why shouldn't Major Thresher take a holiday without telling his milkman.

CONSTABLE:	If it'd been a holiday, he'd have stopped the milk.
SERGEANT:	All right, Smarty. He's called away sudden. You don't always remember to stop the milk if you're called away sudden, do you?
CONSTABLE:	I don't drink milk.
SERGEANT:	Anyhow, better report it. Then we're clear.
CONSTABLE:	There's a Special out for this area.
SERGEANT:	So there is. Where's the signal? All reports to Romford. If they can make anything special out of *this* one they're welcome to it.

(STARTS DIALLING AND FADE)
(FADE UP)

BAGSHAWE:	(<u>Patiently</u>) You'd have thought it was simple enough to find an address. I'd always imagined that lawyers were well-organised over things like that – files and address books and so on.
RIVETT-YARDE:	Tell her she must keep trying, Bagshawe.
BAGSHAWE:	She's trying all right. She was nearly knee-deep in paper when I saw her last.
RIVETT-YARDE:	Can't she remember his name?
BAGSHAWE:	She thinks it is something like Medley.
RIVETT-YARDE:	Medley?
BAGSHAWE:	And then, again, she thinks it might be Trubshawe.
RIVETT-YARDE:	Pah. What about the aunt?
BAGSHAWE:	Oh – we found her address. The Wee Hoose, Strathpeffer – that's in Inverness-shire.
RIVETT-YARDE:	Doesn't sound very probable. Tell the girl she's *got* to unearth that uncle – and quick.
BAGSHAWE:	(<u>Doubtfully</u>) I'll tell her.

(<u>FADE. FADE UP</u>)

RIVETT-YARDE:	Yes, alright, Train, what else have they reported?
TRAIN:	(<u>On telephone – it is evidently the end of a long list</u>) A Mrs Prendergast at Grays reports that three sailors stopped her and spoke to her. One of them was black.
RIVETT-YARDE:	Highly suspicious.
TRAIN:	A Mr Philpot at Romford has heard very odd sounds from his old air-raid shelter three nights running.
RIVETT-YARDE:	Why doesn't he look inside?

TRAIN:	He doesn't feel it to be his business. And the last one is a milkman from Chorminster who reports that one of his customers, a Major Thresher, has been kidnapped.
RIVETT-YARDE:	Is that all?
TRAIN:	That's all for the moment, sir.
RIVETT-YARDE:	Where are you speaking from?
TRAIN:	I'm down at Romford, sir – with Superintendent Farmer.
RIVETT-YARDE:	All right. Keep at it.

(TELEPHONE AGAIN)

RIVETT-YARDE:	Hullo, Rivett-Yarde here.
OPERATOR:	There's a Mr Craine on the line, sir.
RIVETT-YARDE:	Who? Mr Craine? Never heard of him.
OPERATOR:	He wanted to speak to Major Bagshawe, sir.
RIVETT-YARDE:	All right. Put him through to me.
CRAINE:	Is that Major Bagshawe?
RIVETT-YARDE:	It's Commander Rivett-Yarde here. Major Bagshawe works with me.
CRAINE:	My name is Craine. Senior partner in the firm of Horniman Birley & Craine—
RIVETT-YARDE:	Oh yes. The firm where Bohun works.
CRAINE:	(Very precise) Mr Bohun is a partner in this firm. Yes. And I understand that Major Bagshawe is anxious for reasons best known to himself to discover the name and address of Mr Bohun's surviving uncle, who is thought to be resident in Essex.
RIVETT-YARDE:	Yes. Have you got it?
CRAINE:	No. But a thought occurred to me which might shorten your enquiries. Since Mr Bohun's secretary was unable to recollect the name of this uncle it was clear that it was *not* a paternal uncle – or the name would have been Bohun. I therefore obtained a sight of Mr Bohun's birth certificate.
RIVETT-YARDE:	Of course! Why on earth didn't we think of it? Well played, Mr Brain.
CRAINE:	Craine. I have it in front of me. Mr Bohun's mother was Alice Patricia Bohun, formerly Thresher.
RIVETT-YARDE:	What!
CRAINE:	Thresher. T-h-r-e-s-h-e-r—
RIVETT-YARDE:	Dammit. The milkman.

CRAINE:	What did you say—

(CLICK. RIVETT-YARDE HAS RUNG OFF)

RIVETT-YARDE:	(To the operator) Romford Police Station and make it fast. (To himself) A break at last. I only hope that we're not too late. Half-past seven. If they were there this morning, they'll hardly move before dusk.

(BELL)

	Hullo. Yes. Superintendent Farmer?
FARMER:	Speaking.
RIVETT-YARDE:	Look here. A break at last. Chorminster put in some routine reports this afternoon. One of them was from a milkman who said that his customer, a Major Thresher, had been kidnapped.
FARMER:	Yes. I think I remember that one.
RIVETT-YARDE:	Well, Bohun's uncle is called Thresher.
FARMER:	Is he now? That looks very possible, doesn't it. I think the report had the address. Anyway, I can get it from Chorminster. Yes. We'll look into that at once.
RIVETT-YARDE:	It's up to you, of course. But I think I should get the house surrounded now, and 'walk it up' after dark. They're an unpleasant crowd. Don't want another Sidney Street.
FARMER:	You may be right.
RIVETT-YARDE:	And I'm coming down myself.

(FADE. FADE UP)
(FARM NOISES AS BEFORE)

THRESHER:	(Yawns) What's the time, m'boy?
BOHUN:	Nearly seven.
THRESHER:	Can you see anything out of that window?
BOHUN:	I can't see much of the landscape. But I can see one of the enemy – he's the one with only one ear. He's sitting in the ditch watching the window and if I so much as twitched the blind he'd blow his little whistle.
THRESHER:	Wonder where he lost his ear.
BOHUN:	I expect he annoyed Konstant.
THRESHER:	I've been thinking.

BOHUN: Anything come of it?

THRESHER: In a sort of way, yes. Our guess is that they're going to move us this evening.

BOHUN: I should think so.

THRESHER: Then we'll go by car – or cars. They've got three of them.

BOHUN: I guess so.

THRESHER: And we'll have to take a certain amount of luggage – say a suitcase each.

BOHUN: (After a pause) If my guess is right, we mayn't have a lot of need for suitcases.

THRESHER: You mean they'll finish us tonight?

BOHUN: I think of it this way. They've got an exit somewhere. It's either on the coast – or maybe it's a little air-strip or something like that. But wherever it is, it won't be more than a night's drive away from here.

THRESHER: And when we get there?

BOHUN: (Another pause) They may hang on to Hickley for what he's worth to them. But we're supercargo. They'll dump us overboard as soon as they clear the coast.

THRESHER: You're a confoundedly cheerful person to talk to.

BOHUN: No point in not facing facts.

THRESHER: I agree. But I still think they'll allow us to take some luggage – if we play it right. They don't *want* trouble. It suits their books better if we behave ourselves.

BOHUN: Lambs to the slaughter.

THRESHER: They'd rather have two nice little well-behaved lambs than a couple of rampaging bulls. And if when we say 'What about luggage' they say, 'Oh, you won't need luggage – we're dropping you in the sea tonight—', then we *must* put up a fight.

BOHUN: Something in that.

THRESHER: We wouldn't get away with it – but they might have to shoot us – and we might do them some damage – you never know what's going to happen when a scrimmage starts.

BOHUN: I agree. But supposing they do let us pack—

THRESHER: All right. I'll offer to lend you a suitcase – this blue one – and some kit. Which you'll pack. I'll take this red one – which I'll pack.

BOHUN: They'll watch us like lynxes whilst we do it.

THRESHER: Of course they will. They're not fools. When the cases are packed we'll stand them down behind the door. Yours –

and this is most important – on the outside. Mine on the inside – so that it's bang up against this curtain.

BOHUN: Understood.

THRESHER: When the moment comes for departing – I want you to make some kind of diversion – kick Konstant on the shins or something – don't go too far – I don't want you to get killed.

BOHUN: Much obliged. And whilst I am diverting them—?

THRESHER: I shall simply push the red suitcase behind the curtain and pick up another identical suitcase which I shall have placed ready—

(<u>SUITCASE PUSHED</u>)

So.

BOHUN: I say – that's neat. But what's in that second suitcase?

THRESHER: The second one is a *very* special suitcase.

(<u>FADE. FADE UP</u>)

TRAIN: (<u>On telephone</u>) Is that cipher section?

CIPHER CLERK: Speaking.

TRAIN: Train here. Are you working on that figure cipher that our section submitted?

C. CLERK: That's right.

TRAIN: Made anything of it yet?

C. CLERK: Well—

TRAIN: You haven't. Have you got it there? I haven't got a copy with me, and I've just had an idea about it.

C. CLERK: Got a pencil? I'll read it in threes. That seems to be the way it's meant to go. 26. 1. 20; 39. 2. 2; 83. 3. 30; 83. 4. 0—

TRAIN: Of course! I thought I recognised it. That's it. What mugs we have been. The old Rivett is going to be mad.

C. CLERK: I say, if you know the key you might just as well pass it on.

TRAIN: Sorry. No time—

(<u>FADE. FADE UP</u>)

TAYLOR: (<u>Sharply</u>) Now. If you've finished packing, the cars are ready.

BOHUN:	Just one small point, Mr Taylor.
TAYLOR:	Yes, Mr Bohun.
BOHUN:	Where are you taking us?
TAYLOR:	I'm afraid I cannot tell you.
BOHUN:	Then I'm afraid I must refuse to go with you.
TAYLOR:	You have no option.
BOHUN:	No? Catch this one.

(THUD)

| TAYLOR: | (Gasp) Konstant! Konstant! Konstant! |

(THERE IS A THUDDING OF FEET AS TWO MORE
MEN ARRIVE. SOUNDS OF STRUGGLE)

BOHUN:	All right. All right. I see your point – ouch—
TAYLOR:	That's enough.
BOHUN:	(Winded) A good deal – more – than enough.
TAYLOR:	You should never appeal to brute force unless the balance of force is on your side.
BOHUN:	Napoleon said the same thing – only more neatly.
TAYLOR:	We won't waste any more time then. (To one of the men) Is Hickley ready?
DRIVER:	He is in the front car.
TAYLOR:	Good. Mr Bohun. Out with you. Major Thresher. You have your luggage.
THRESHER:	Thank you very much. I have my luggage.

(SOUND OF CAR, TRAVELLING AT A MODERATE
RATE)

TAYLOR:	Turn right at the end of the drive. No need for lights yet.
DRIVER:	Right, sir. All the others with us?
TAYLOR:	Yes, they are behind us. Not too fast, we don't want to lose them.
DRIVER:	(Sharply) What's that?
TAYLOR:	Where?
DRIVER:	Straight ahead. A police barrier. And a policeman.
TAYLOR:	Straight at it.
DRIVER:	But I can't—
TAYLOR:	(Shouting) Go on. Faster. It's only a pole. Smash it.

(<u>CAR ACCELERATING</u>)

DRIVER:	But the man is standing—
TAYLOR:	(<u>Screaming</u>) Go on.

(<u>THERE IS A RESOUNDING CRASH</u>)

MAN:	(<u>Cry, as if mortally hurt</u>)
DRIVER:	We've killed him.
TAYLOR:	Drive on, drive on—

(<u>THE NOISE OF THE CARS DYING AWAY INTO THE DISTANCE</u>)
(<u>FADE. FADE UP</u>)

FARMER:	Anything from the hospital, Sergeant?
SERGEANT:	He isn't gone yet, sir. But they don't sound hopeful.
FARMER:	Drove straight at him and over him.
SERGEANT:	Yes, sir. And one of the other cars went over him when he was on the ground.
FARMER:	I'll get those swine, if it's the last thing I do – evening, Commander.
RIVETT-YARDE:	(<u>Abruptly</u>) So they got away.
FARMER:	For the moment.
RIVETT-YARDE:	What happened?
FARMER:	Our people were round the house. They'd just got there. The barricades weren't finished when they made a break. Three cars, without lights.
RIVETT-YARDE:	So you haven't got much description.
FARMER:	The other man at the barricade – the one who wasn't hurt – says the first car was a big saloon, dark colour, old-fashioned lines. The others were smaller and newer. That's all.
RIVETT-YARDE:	Not a lot to go on.
FARMER:	They can't get across the Thames – except at Tilbury. I don't think they'll risk that – anyway, we've warned the car ferry. The likely ways are east, to the coast. Or perhaps north.
RIVETT-YARDE:	How much start?
FARMER:	I'm afraid it was half an hour before we got any effective control out.
RIVETT-YARDE:	It's quite a lot.

FARMER:	Hullo. Something for me.
SERGEANT:	(<u>Apologetic</u>) Well, Sir. You asked to see *anything* that came in from that area.
FARMER:	Where's this from?
SERGEANT:	Billericay, sir. Just came in over the telephone. A Mr Pardoe.
FARMER:	What's happened to Mr Pardoe?
SERGEANT:	His car's seized up. Solid.
FARMER:	He ought to try using oil.
SERGEANT:	That's what I thought, sir.
RIVETT-YARDE:	Where do you think they'll be making for?
FARMER:	Well – it's a matter of guesswork either way. If they've got some secret bolt-hole, the Norfolk or Suffolk coast's the obvious place – gives them the shortest run across the North Sea.
RIVETT-YARDE:	Or Lincolnshire.
FARMER:	Yes. Might be Lincolnshire.
RIVETT-YARDE:	And that's about two hundred miles of coast.
FARMER:	It's not easy. What we want is – yes?
SERGEANT:	Two more, sir.
FARMER:	Two more *what*?
SERGEANT:	Cars seized up, sir. One, three miles out of Maldon, on the Chelmsford Road. One at Tiptree.
FARMER:	Sounds like an epidemic. Where's the sense in it?
SERGEANT:	Dunno, sir. It's just happening.

(<u>TELEPHONE</u>)

	Yes. Oh. Yes, he's here. For you, Commander.
RIVETT-YARDE:	Rivett-Yarde here.
TRAIN:	(<u>His voice squeaky with excitement</u>) I've done it, sir.
RIVETT-YARDE:	Done what, Train? And don't squeak. We're in no mood here for picking daisies.
TRAIN:	I've solved the cipher.
RIVETT-YARDE:	What? *You've* solved the cipher. But you don't know the first thing about ciphers.
TRAIN:	That's j-just it, sir. That's why I solved it. It isn't a cipher at all. It's something someone has been scribbling on the back of that brochure.
RIVETT-YARDE:	How do you know?
TRAIN:	Because I recognised it. It's the score in the Test Match. Australia's first innings. 26 for 1, last man 20. 39 for 2,

	last man 2. 83 for 3, last man 30. Then 83 for 4, last man nought. That's the bit I recognised. I'd remembered two wickets falling at 83—
RIVETT-YARDE:	Oh, all right. I hand it to you. Just another dead end.
TRAIN:	I wondered, sir.
RIVETT-YARDE:	Don't tell me now that you think the Australian team are involved in this—
TRAIN:	No, sir. But it did occur to me. As the opposition were so keen to get hold of these papers – and the other papers really didn't seem terribly important – I just wondered about this one. Not the figures on it, they don't mean a thing, but the paper itself. It was a sort of advertisement – a brochure—
RIVETT-YARDE:	Good Lord – so it was. What was it for—
TRAIN:	I can't remember the details, but it was a Guest House, called the 'Traveller's Rest', on the coast.
RIVETT-YARDE:	Which coast?
TRAIN:	A place called Battlesham. It's south of Dunwich in Suffolk.
RIVETT-YARDE:	Knock me down with a ship's biscuit! Train, you're a genius. Get here as fast as you can, and you may be in at the kill.

(<u>RINGS OFF</u>)

	Superintendent, we've broken in at last. Slide the map over. All those places the cars have been seizing up, Billericay, Tiptree, Maldon. Lay your ruler across 'em and go on till you hit the coast; where does it bring you out?
FARMER:	Why – what have the cars got to do with it?
RIVETT-YARDE:	I've no idea. No idea in the world. Just draw the line. Where does it come out on the coast?
FARMER:	Just below Dunwich, but—
RIVETT-YARDE:	Come on, then. Get aboard.
FARMER:	Where are we going to?
RIVETT-YARDE:	First stop – and last stop – the 'Traveller's Rest'!

(<u>MUSIC – FADE</u>)

EPISODE 6

'THE TRAVELLER'S REST'

Transmission: Light Programme
Thursday, 25th August 1955 8.00–8.30 pm

(MUSIC – HOLD UNDER ANNOUNCEMENT)

OPENING
ANNOUNCEMENT: We present William Fox in 'The Man Who Could Not Sleep', a serial-thriller in six parts by Michael Gilbert. Episode 6 – 'The Traveller's Rest'.

(MUSIC)

ANNOUNCER: Two sets of people are making for the 'Traveller's Rest' a guest house on the coast of Norfolk (Proprietor, Mrs McWhirter) The first group, in three cars, is the espionage organisation known as CLEFT; it is headed by a Mr Taylor. They have with them, as unwilling passengers, Hickley, a renegade scientist, Bohun, a solicitor (who tells the story) and Bohun's uncle, Major Thresher, an inventor. What CLEFT do *not* know is that Major Thresher has brought with him in the last car a new frequency expresser which causes any car coming up behind them to seize up. Following this trail of broken down cars and infuriated motorists comes a rescue party headed by Superintendent Farmer of the Special Branch and Commander Rivett-Yarde.

BOHUN: (As narrator) The drive was a nightmare. I, Bohun, was in the second car, with Hopper – I think he hailed from Germany – at the wheel and two more sitting beside me. One of them had a gun in his pocket, and I don't think he took his hand off it during the whole drive. If there had been half a quarter of a chance of jumping him I'd have tried it. After we ran over that policeman, I had no illusions left. We were for it. I wondered why they didn't knock us off there and then and leave us in a ditch. I could only suppose that they were acting under orders and had the whole thing planned for later on, so that our bodies would never turn up to embarrass then.

Thresher was in the car behind me – that was the last of the three. Which was the only piece of good luck we had had. If that infernal machine of his was working, and supposing he could get it turned on without his guards noticing, then the engine of any car that came up from behind us was going to seize up solid; and surely *someone* must sit up and take notice, if we left a chain of immobilised cars behind us. Whether they could or would do anything effective, or in time, was a matter I tried not to think too much about.

After ninety minutes running I could sense that we were getting near the sea. Presumably, therefore, near our destination. We had been going along fast, without much check, and I calculated that we might have covered fifty miles. During the last half hour we had passed no traffic and I had not seen the lights of any coming up behind us. Presently we turned off the main road on to a minor one, and then on to a worse one still, almost a cart track. This was a short cut, presumably to avoid a village, because we came out eventually on to the coast road, went along it for about a mile, and turned into a driveway. I saw a notice board. It was some sort of hotel or guest house, but we were past it before I could read the name. The driveway was concrete. I heard the noise of the tyres purring on it – then we drew up in front of a building. The young moon was coming up and by it I saw the 'Traveller's Rest' for the first time—

(A CAR DOOR OPENS AND SLAMS)

TAYLOR: Everyone stay where they are. Hopper, run your car back, so that we can have some light. Don't go off the ramp. I want no wheel marks.

(CAR REVERSING)

That's enough. Now we can see what we're about. Please dismount. Milo, ring the bell.

(BELL)

MILO:	She will be down in a minute. I see a light.
THRESHER:	The 'Traveller's Rest', my boy – delightfully appropriate.
TAYLOR:	Do not talk. And stand apart—

(CHAINS BEING MOVED. HEAVY DOOR CREAKS
OPEN)

MRS McWHIRTER:	(Scots) Good evening to you.
TAYLOR:	Mrs McWhirter?
MRS McWHIRTER:	Aye.
TAYLOR:	I telephoned you that we were coming. Is everything ready?
MRS McWHIRTER:	Aye. Everything's ready. My lambs are all of them in bed long since. It's the sea air, ye ken. It gives them braw appetites and sends them to their beds as tired as bairns.
TAYLOR:	Good. Then we'll go in. You three first. Then put the cars away. You know where to put them – not in the garages.
THRESHER:	What about our suitcases?
TAYLOR:	(Coldly) I do not think you will need a suitcase, Major Thresher.
THRESHER:	Oh?
MRS McWHIRTER:	Come away in. You'll find we have every home comfort at the 'Traveller's Rest'.
TAYLOR:	Straight ahead.

(SOUND OF FRONT DOOR CLOSING BEHIND THEM)

Down to the end of the passage.

(THEIR FOOTSTEPS, WHICH HAVE BEEN MUFFLED
BY WOOL, SUDDENLY RING OUT ON ROCK)

Down the steps, one at a time.

(THERE IS THE THUD OF A VERY HEAVY DOOR
CLOSING BEHIND THEM; FURTHER FOOTSTEPS ON
ROCK OR CONCRETE)

Now. I'll leave you to your devices. Make yourselves comfortable. We have some little time to wait.

(HIS FOOTSTEPS PASS UP THE RAMP AND DIE AWAY)

BOHUN: (Softly) Comfortable! Is there room for me beside you on that packing case, Uncle? Come on, Hickley, you can squeeze up beside me.

HICKLEY: Right.

THRESHER: This is a queer set-up and no mistake. What happened? One moment we were in the hall of that horrible guest house. Then, before you could say Jack Robinson – we were here. What on earth is it?

BOHUN: As far as I could make out, we went straight along the hall, then, when we got right up to the end – where you'd expct the outside wall – there was an opening – and some steep steps down – and this.

THRESHER: Yes. But what is it?

BOHUN: Listen!

(IN THE SILENCE THEY ALL HEAR THE LIPPING AND SUCKING OF WATER)

THRESHER: Did you hear that?

BOHUN: It's open to the sea, down at the far end. That's the tide going out.

THRESHER: If it wasn't for the fact that it's so obviously hand made, I should have said it was some sort of pirates' or smugglers' cave. But the walls and floor are concrete.

And – I can't see very clearly in this light – but isn't that some sort of launching ramp down at the far end?

BOHUN: It could be.

HICKLEY: (Breaking in suddenly. Speaking louder than the other two) What are they going to do with us?

BOHUN: Well.

HICKLEY: You might as well tell me. I've been through so much lately. It'll be almost a relief to know.

BOHUN: All right, Hickley. It's only a guess, of course. But I think they've got some arrangement for a boat to come in here at low tide. A motor boat of some sort. And I think they plan to take us out to something rather bigger – which would presumably be lying out in the North Sea, waiting for us—

HICKLEY: And then?

BOHUN:	Then – (Pause) I think they plan a burial at sea.
HICKLEY:	Is there *any* chance—?
BOHUN:	A mighty thin one. We've left the best trail behind us we could manage. If our friends can follow it they may get here. The question is whether they'll be in time to do any good—

(FADE. FADE UP)

TAYLOR:	(Jovial) You got the messages, Mrs McWhirter?
MRS McWHIRTER:	Aye. I got the messages.
TAYLOR:	What time is the boat due?
MRS McWHIRTER:	Between two and three in the morning. They couldna be more pree-cise.
TAYLOR:	And the trawler?
MRS McWHIRTER:	Och, it's been off and on for days now. You could see it with a glass from the old look-out.
TAYLOR:	(Sharp) I trust you did no such thing.
MRS McWHIRTER:	Sairtinly not. I mind my business.
TAYLOR:	(To Hopper) We'll take all three of them with us, Hopper.
HOPPER:	All the way?
TAYLOR:	I don't know. There will be instructions when we reach the trawler. I should imagine not.
HOPPER:	(A sneer) What about the famous scientific worker?
TAYLOR:	I rather think that even Hickley has outlived his usefullness. Mrs McWhirter, how are things going with you here?
MRS McWHIRTER:	Fine. Fine. I've just the four regulars, you understand. I look after them myself. The old leddies are no trouble. No trouble at all. They like a little walk to the beach in the afternoon and a clack in the evenings. The Colonel whiles more difficult.
TAYLOR:	I have no doubt you can manage him, Mrs McWhirter.
MRS McWHIRTER:	Mostly he's quiet as a lamb, but he has moments when he rants and rages.
TAYLOR:	Is there any chance that they heard our arrival?
MRS McWHIRTER:	None in the world. In bed by eleven. It's the rule of the house. And they sleep at the back.
TAYLOR:	(Breaking in) What is that?
HOPPER:	Did you hear it too, sir? It sounded like a car.
TAYLOR:	Keep away from the window, you fool.
HOPPER:	There. It's coming nearer.

TAYLOR: Yes. And more than one car. They passed the gate – then stopped, I think. Get everyone below stairs.

(HOPPER CLATTERS OUT FAST)

You know what to do, Mrs McWhirter?

MRS McWHIRTER: To do? I've naething to do. I'm just a householder. I'll go to my room, I think. Don't forget Mr Hopper's gloves.

VOICES: (A whistle, in the corridor)

TAYLOR: Everything set. We'll get below.

(THE TWO OF THEM STEP INTO THE PASSAGE. TAYLOR'S FOOTSTEPS ON THE CONCRETE RAMP; FOLLOWED BY THE THUD OF A HEAVY DOOR SLIDING TO)

(FADE. FADE UP)

FARMER: This is the place, Commander. Shine your torch on the road, Bennett. (Pause) No sign of tyre marks. Not that you could expect it, with this damned concrete drive.

RIVETT-YARDE: Concrete drive? Bit unusual – for a private establishment—

FARMER: Very unusual – and unhelpful. We'll leave the cars here, I think. We don't want to give any unnecessary warning. Cole, you take three men, on foot, round to the back – that's the seaward side. Bennett, wait with the cars. The rest of you come with me. Lucky there's a bit of moon. Less chance of a slip up.

(NOISE OF STEPS ON CONCRETE. THEN A PAUSE. OWL IN BACKGROUND)

We'll give Cole a little longer to get into position.

RIVETT-YARDE: (Whispering) Big garages for a place of this size. Large enough for half a dozen cars.

FARMER: (Whispering) It's an odd set-up altogether. Reminds me of something. I can't quite place it. All right. Here goes.

(PEAL OF OLD-FASHIONED BELL. SILENCE. THEN YOWL FROM CAT)

Woken pussy, anyway. Try again.

(REPEATED PEALS. ANOTHER PAUSE. FARMER
KNOCKS REPEATEDLY)

MRS MCWHIRTER: (Her voice seems to have become not only shriller but
somehow even more Scottish. Her speech is not repro-
duced phonetically) Who is it?
FARMER: Would you mind opening the door?
MRS MCWHIRTER: Go away and come back at a Christian hour.
FARMER: Open up.
MRS MCWHIRTER: Who are you?
FARMER: Police.

(A RATTLE AS THE DOOR OPENS, BUT ON THE
CHAIN)

MRS MCWHIRTER: I'll no take the chain off until you show me your warrant.
FARMER: Inspector. Have you got your warrant card with you?
INSPECTOR: Yes, sir.
FARMER: Push it through the door.
INSPECTOR: Right sir.
MRS MCWHIRTER: Hmp.
FARMER: Now will you very kindly get the door open.

(RATTLING OF CHAINS)

We won't all go in. I want the front of the house watched,
and the garages. Put some sort of block across the drive
– heavy enough to stop a car this time. Inspector, bring a
sergeant and three men and come with me. Perhaps you'd
come along too, Commander.
RIVETT-YARDE: Try and stop me.
MRS MCWHIRTER: You'd better come in here. I'll blow the fire up. And keep
your voices down. We don't want to wake the guests.
FARMER: How many guests have you got?
MRS MCWHIRTER: Just the four.
FARMER: Their names?
MRS MCWHIRTER: What's that to you?
FARMER: (Politely) Then perhaps you'll show me your hotel
register.
MRS MCWHIRTER: (Uncomfortably) Well – I don't always keep it up – these
four are regulars, you see. More like boarders than
guests.

FARMER:	What are their names?
MRS McWHIRTER:	There's Mrs Mainprice. She's been with me longest. She's a wee bit deaf. And the Misses Trimble – they're sisters and very attached to each other. And then there's Colonel Potter.
FARMER:	I see. And besides yourself those are the only four people in this house?
MRS McWHIRTER:	Aye. I have a man and his wife round the house by day, but they sleep at home.
FARMER:	Have you had any visitors tonight?
MRS McWHIRTER:	Visitors?
FARMER:	By car.
MRS McWHIRTER:	The last car to stop at this door was the doctor. He came before tea. We don't get much in the way of the car trade.
FARMER:	Then why have you got four garages?
MRS McWHIRTER:	Tuts! I didna build them. They were there when I came. You're welcome to see into them if you so wish. They're all empty, barring one that has the coke in it.
FARMER:	Thanks you. I'd like to look at them, in due course. Meanwhile, the house—
MRS McWHIRTER:	The house? You're not going to disturb those puir creatures.
FARMER:	We'll disturb them as little as possible, I can assure you. Sergeant, takes Bates with you and start with the bedrooms.

(FADE)
(FADE UP)

POLICE SERGEANT:	Well, Bates? You done that one?

(DOOR SHUTS SOFTLY)

CONSTABLE:	Whew! Yes, Sarge. A piece of cake. She must be deaf as a doorpost. Never stirred.
SERGEANT:	Look everywhere?
CONSTABLE:	I'll say I looked everywhere.
SERGEANT:	Under the bed?
CONSTABLE:	Certainly.
SERGEANT:	And there wasn't nothing there?
CONSTABLE:	Yes. But not what we're looking for.
SERGEANT:	All right. All right. Now try this one. Go on. Better knock.

(TIMID KNOCK)

All right. She's asleep. In you go.

(DOOR OPENING AND SHUTTING)

FIRST LADY/
SECOND LADY: (Piercing shrieks)

(DOOR RE-OPENING RAPIDLY)

CONSTABLE: Hey, Sergeant.
FIRST LADY/
SECOND LADY: (Further shrieks)
CONSTABLE: They're awake.
SERGEANT: (Sourly) I can hear.
CONSTABLE: I can't go in there. They're sitting up in their beds, two of 'em, creating something horrible.

(THE SHRIEKS ARE PUNCTUATED, NOW, BY THE RINGING OF A HAND BELL)

SERGEANT: You've got your duty to do. In you go.

(DOOR)

CONSTABLE: It's all right, ladies. We're not going to harm you.

(VOICES, SHOUTS AND BELL ARE MUFFLED AS THE SERGEANT HASTILY CLOSES THE DOOR, BUT CAN STILL BE HEARD)

Just a routine search.
FIRST LADY: Help! Murder! Mrs McWhirter! Police!
CONSTABLE: I *am* the police.
SECOND LADY: Murdered in my bed! Oh dear! Mrs McWhirter! I'll leave this moment!

(MORE BELL. DOOR RE-OPENS AND NOISES BECOME CLEARER)

CONSTABLE: It's all right, I tell you. (To Sergeant) There's no-one in there, Sergeant.

SERGEANT: (<u>Remorseless</u>) Have you looked under the beds?
CONSTABLE: Under the beds? Cor stone a crow!
SERGEANT: Then look under 'em. Go on. They can't bite you.

(<u>THE DOOR OPENS – NOISES CORRESPONDINGLY
LOUDER – AND SHUTS AGAIN. DIMINUENDO. DOOR
RE-OPENS</u>)

CONSTABLE: You're wrong, Sarge. One of 'em did.

(<u>DOOR SHUTS</u>)

In the shoulder.
SERGEANT: That's all right. You can get a pension for that. Received in the course of dooty. Only one more.
CONSTABLE: Look, I can't do it. I'm demoralized.
SERGEANT: All right. All right. I'll tackle this one myself. Firmness. That's all you need. Firmness and tact.

(<u>DOOR OPENS. GUN GOES OFF FROM INSIDE AND
BULLET CRASHES INTO WALL. BOTH MEN FALL
FLAT</u>)

SERGEANT: Hey!
CONSTABLE: (<u>To himself</u>) Firmness.
COLONEL POTTER: (<u>In a clear, military voice</u>) If any man dares set foot in this room, I shoot. And I warn you, gentlemen, I *can* shoot.
SERGEANT: You can't do that to us. We're the police.
COLONEL: You have not found me unprepared. I have long known it was coming.
SERGEANT: Known *what* was coming, Colonel?
CONSTABLE: Tact, see.
COLONEL: The Fascist Revolution. Secret Police. Midnight arrests. You don't take me alive – I've eleven bullets left. The first ten are for the first ten men through that door before I kill myself.
SERGEANT: I think we'd better report this to the Inspector. You stop here and watch.
CONSTABLE: Supposing he comes out?
SERGEANT: Take him in charge.

(<u>FADE. FADE UP</u>)

RIVETT-YARDE:	You're absolutely certain?
FARMER:	I can only believe my own eyes, Commander. We've searched every square inch from ground floor to garret. Total result: one of my men with a bullet hole in his helmet – lucky it wasn't an inch lower; and one man bitten in the shoulder.
RIVETT-YARDE:	And there's no-one here?
FARMER:	It isn't as if we are looking for a boy and a dog. There must be six or seven of them, to say nothing of our three chaps. You can't hide ten grown men up your sleeve.
RIVETT-YARDE:	I wonder. Maybe we've been *too* quick – and got here before they did. Or are we wrong about the whole thing?
FARMER:	Here comes madame. And she looks damned pleased with herself.
MRS McWHIRTER:	A-weel, gentlemen. Are you satisfied with the trouble you have caused?
FARMER:	Most of the trouble, if I may say so, was made by your own guests. Did you *know* that Colonel Potter had a loaded revolver in his room?
MRS McWHIRTER:	Sairtinly. He's a grand shot – at the bottles on the beach.
FARMER:	I hope he has a licence for his gun, or there may be trouble about that.
MRS McWHIRTER:	I should predict that there will be trouble in any event, Superintendent. I have friends who will not stand by and see me put upon. Is it within your rights to search a leddy's bedroom? At night? And the leddy in her bed?
FARMER:	In an emergency, ma'am, we have to do as we think best. I will now wish you good evening.
MRS McWHIRTER:	(<u>Venomously</u>) And-a-verra-guid-evening-to-you.

> (<u>SLAMS FRONT DOOR AND OSTENTATIOUSLY RE-CHAINS IT</u>)
> (<u>FADE. FADE UP</u>)
> (<u>DOORS SLAMMING. CARS STARTING AND DRIVING OFF ONE AFTER ANOTHER. NOISE DYING AWAY INTO THE DISTANCE. FADE</u>)

TAYLOR:	Are you sure the police have all gone, Hopper?
HOPPER:	Yes. I think so.
TAYLOR:	I don't like it.
HOPPER:	As long as they *have* gone away—?
TAYLOR:	The real question is, how did they get here at all?

HOPPER:	What does that matter now?
TAYLOR:	You have not given it enough thought, Hopper. So far as I know the only lead to the 'Traveller's Rest' was the fact that Tangee happened to have in his possession one of its advertising brochures. How he got it I do not know. When I noticed it, I at once put it on one side for destruction. If I had not been disturbed, it would have been burnt – that night. You see?
HOPPER:	But—
TAYLOR:	The point is, why should that particular brochure catch the eye of anyone who did *not* know the truth. It was simply one among a thousand other papers.
HOPPER:	Then perhaps it was not the brochure that led them here.
TAYLOR:	You put the matter in a nutshell. But if the brochure did not lead them here, what did? If they have any other reason – any real reason – for suspecting this place, we can never use it again. They have gone away for the moment, but a little enquiry in the right quarters will show them the truth.
HOPPER:	As long as they do not find the truth before morning, *we* shall be safely away.
TAYLOR:	Leaving Mrs McWhirter to make what explanations she can.
HOPPER:	I have no doubt she will prove herself equal to the task.
TAYLOR:	No doubt.
BOTH:	(Laugh)

(FADE. FADE UP)

RIVETT-YARDE:	What next?
FARMER:	I've got a feeling, Commander, that the next thing we ought to do is put ourselves right by the local authorities. What's the nearest town?
RIVETT-YARDE:	Battlesham. Not really a town. Small seaside resort.
FARMER:	It'll have a policeman of some sort, I expect.
RIVETT-YARDE:	Are you going to leave anyone here?
FARMER:	Yes. But I think we'll practice a little deception. We've done enough bull-at-a-gate for one night. Sergeant, follow us in your car for about a quarter of a mile, then turn round, coast back down the hill, and get your men into position around the house. Not to interfere. Just to watch. And don't be seen or heard. If that old Scotch package catches you, she'll skelp you properly.

SERGEANT: Right, sir. I'll watch out for it.

(DOORS SLAMMING. CARS STARTING AND DRIVING OFF ONE AFTER ANOTHER. NOISE DYING AWAY INTO THE DISTANCE. FADE)
(FADE UP)

RIVETT-YARDE: Is this the place?

(CAR DOOR SHUTTING)

It doesn't look like any sort of police station.

FARMER: You're in the country now, Commander. Put the torch on that gate-post. Suffolk County Constabulary. That's it. Probably just the Sergeant – and his family.

(BELL)

RIVETT-YARDE: Yes, I don't think we'd better all burst in on him. He'll think it's an invasion. You come with me, Commander. Inspector, get the cars parked.

(FOOTSTEPS AND DOOR)

P/SGT MULLINS: (Who speaks in a pleasant, Norfolk accent) Well, gentlemen. What can I do for you?

FARMER: I'm Superintendent Farmer, from the Central Office. I wonder if I could come inside for a moment?

MULLINS: Why, of course. I'm Detective Sergeant Mullins by the way. You're a long way from London, Superintendent. May I ask who your friend is?

FARMER: This is Commander Rivett-Yarde. He's with the Foreign Office.

MULLINS: Oh, yes? (These introductions are made as they move along the passage) If you'll allow me, I'll light a lamp. We haven't the electricity yet. That's it. Now what can I do for you, gentlemen?

FARMER: It's security business. And it's a long story. But first of all, can you tell us anything about a Guest House – it lies two miles along the coast road—

MULLINS: The 'Traveller's Rest'.

FARMER: You know it?

MULLINS:	Yes. I know that. It's run by an old catamaran of the name of McWhirter.
FARMER:	Do you know anything against her?
MULLINS:	Nothing except her tongue. She has a Residential Hotel. Just the few regular guests. Patients, you could almost call them. She keeps herself to herself. As she can do, with those big grounds she has. The hotel has its bit of coast, and its own beach.
RIVETT-YARDE:	What does an establishment like that want with four garages?
MULLINS:	She would not have built them. I take it they would have been there when she bought the place – after the war, of course.
RIVETT-YARDE:	How does the war come into it?
MULLINS:	It was a Naval Establishment of some sort – you'd know more of that than me, Commander.
RIVETT-YARDE:	A Coastal Watch Headquarters?
MULLINS:	Something of that sort. But it was more than that. That was only the cover story, you see. It was really something different.
RIVETT-YARDE:	That sounds intriguing. What sort of thing?
MULLINS:	I wasn't here myself in the war. I was up to Cromer. But I heard of it. They used to send out parties in motor torpedo boats. Agents, and so on. Very secretive they were about it.
RIVETT-YARDE:	But of course. An MTB(X) Station. That would explain a lot.
FARMER:	What was that?
RIVETT-YARDE:	One of our hush-hush places. There were half a dozen of them. On the face of it a Rest House or a Commander's Residence or something of that sort. Actually the place from which they sent out top secret missions. There'd be a hidden way down to the sea, with water deep enough for a motor torpedo boat to come alongside. The people upstairs would know very little about the other side. One or two types would arrive, and stay there a day or two – then suddenly they'd disappear through some hole in the wall – and the next you'd hear of them – if you heard of them again – would be from Occupied France or Holland.
FARMER:	Then we know it's got some sort of secret exit. Something down by the water-line. But we still don't know the way down to it!
RIVETT-YARDE:	There's one way of finding out. We must get through to

the Admiralty – you've a telephone here? Would you see if you can get them? Ask for Naval Intelligence Division. Commander Vaisey.

MULLINS: Very good, Sir.

(<u>MULLINS GOES OUT</u>)

RIVETT-YARDE: (<u>To Farmer</u>) They may have had local men working on that station, who will know how the disappearing trick was staged. It's an outside chance.

FARMER: When you're speaking to the Admiralty, couldn't you ask them to try to stop the bolt-hole?

RIVETT-YARDE: Get a destroyer out, you mean? Easier said than done. Depends where the nearest one happens to be. And if they're prepared to do it, on my say-so.

(<u>MULLINS COMES BACK</u>)

MULLINS: The Admiralty on the telephone, Commander. It's in my front parlour.

RIVETT-YARDE: Thank you. That's quick work.

(<u>FADE OUT TO DISTANT LAPPING OF WATER</u>)

<u>Note</u>: (Bohun and Thresher whisper throughout following scene)

BOHUN: It's the only chance.

THRESHER: Fairly long odds, my boy.

BOHUN: I agree. But what's the alternative? It's nearly half-past two now. If a boat's coming it must be here soon. They can't be going to embark us in broad daylight. Hickley's gone to sleep again.

THRESHER: I'm damned nearly asleep myself. It's on occasions like this, my boy, that I envy you your peculiar constitution. Let's go through it again.

BOHUN: Right. You see that man by the passage way. The one nearest to us. He's damned near asleep. We could reach him in three quick steps. You grab him round the neck, Uncle. I'll get hold of his gun. It's in his coat pocket, I know. He travelled in the car with me, and he never took his hand off it.

THRESHER: All right. But what then? There are four more of them at the seaward end, and Taylor and Konstant aren't far off.

BOHUN: Yes. But you see those packing cases – no – don't look round now. Pretend to blow your nose or something. You see them?

THRESHER: Yes. Vaguely. At the back of the cave.

BOHUN: Right. As soon as we've got the gun we nip back behind them – and barricade ourselves in. That's the blind end of the cave, so they can't get round behind us. And those packing cases look thick enough to stop a bullet. They won't be so keen to come poking their heads over the top if we've got a gun.

THRESHER: They'll winkle us out in the end – we might hold them up for a bit, though.

BOHUN: Hold them up till it's light, and we get another chance. Anything can happen.

THRESHER: When do you plan to start?

BOHUN: Well, we'll wait as long as possible. The later we kick off the better. Now wake Hickley up quietly and tell him what we've worked out. All he's got to do is hop back behind those packing cases and lie down.

THRESHER: Sounds easy when you put it like that.

(FADE. FADE UP. A SMALL, CHEAP CLOCK SOUNDS THE HALF HOUR)

Note: (They are all feeling the tension imposed by waiting)

RIVETT-YARDE: Half-past two. They ought to have rung back before now.

FARMER: If they've had any luck.

RIVETT-YARDE: You're sure you gave them the right number?

MULLINS: Battlesham 123. It's an easy number.

FARMER: They oughtn't to make a mistake about—

(TELEPHONE BELL. THEY ALL MOVE AT ONCE)

RIVETT-YARDE: I'll take it. Hullo. Yes.

(TELEPHONE NOISES)

Good man. Where? Where's that? (To Mullins) Where's Brimber Bay?

MULLINS:	'Bout two mile down the coast.
RIVETT-YARDE:	(Into telephone) All right. Our local man knows where that is. Golf Club cottage. Give me the name again.

(TELEPHONE NOISE)

Shaughnessy. Yes, that's all right. I've got it. Good. Very good. Thank you.

(RINGS OFF)

	We've got to get out to Brimber Bay. Lieutenant Commander Shaughnessy is our man. It'll be quicker to go out and see him than try and explain on the telephone.
FARMER:	I hope he'll play.
RIVETT-YARDE:	(With sublime conviction. Following conversation takes place as they are moving out of the house and down the path) He's been in the Navy. He'll play. We want your fastest car.

(FRONT DOOR, STEPS ON GRAVEL. GATE)

FARMER:	All right. Inspector. (Pause) Good Lord, they've all gone to sleep.

(SOUNDS CAR HORN)

INSPECTOR:	(Hurriedly waking up) Yes, sir.
FARMER:	Wake up, everybody. The game's moving. Inspector, I want you to leave us one car – who's the best driver – Williams? – all right. Take everyone else back to the 'Traveller's Rest'. Contact Sergeant Betts and the crew we left there. Make a cordon round the landward side of the house. Do it quietly. I don't want any trouble till we get back.
INSPECTOR:	Right, sir. What about the beach?
RIVETT-YARDE:	We hope to be able to block the sea exit. A Hunt Class destroyer on patrol off Thames Mouth. Bit of luck. They were able to intercept her and send her up. This the car?

(A LOT OF OPENING AND SHUTTING OF DOORS AND BACKGROUND NOISES)

SERGEANTS: (<u>Running commentary, in background</u>)
Turn her round, Hibbs.
Back the way we came.
Look alive there.
Who told you to turn your lights on.

<u>Note</u>: (There is a sense of urgency as the whole machine jerks into motion again)

FARMER: That's right. Mullins is coming with us. Better sit beside the driver, Mullins, and tell him the way. We'll get in the back.

(<u>THE CAR IS MOVING NOW, QUITE FAST</u>)

MULLINS: Sharp right fifty yards ahead.

(<u>SQUEAK AS THE CAR BRAKES AND DOES A SKID TURN</u>)

Straight on now, for almost a mile.

(<u>CAR GATHERS SPEED</u>)
(<u>QUICK CUT. FADE UP</u>)

That's the place, sir.

(<u>CAR BRAKES</u>)

That little white one. Looks pretty in the moonlight, doesn't it?

(<u>CAR DOORS</u>)

He'll be fast asleep.
RIVETT-YARDE: Soon remedy that.

(<u>PROLONGED FRONT DOOR BELL. WINDOW OPENING</u>)

SHAUGHNESSY: (<u>Irish and proud of it</u>) What the devil—?
FARMER: Commander Shaughnessy? It's the police here. If you'll very kindly let us in we'll tell you what it's all about.

SHAUGHNESSY: Is it war that's declared?

FARMER: Not quite.

SHAUGHNESSY: All right. I'll be down.

(QUICK CUT)
(FADE IN)

The Traveller's Rest? Certainly I know it. There's a cellar under the building, and under the cellar there's a cave. Or it was a cave. We brought it up-to-date, you might say. We put in ventilation. The cave mouth's under water at most tides. That's what made it so safe, you see.

FARMER: But how did you get into the cellar? We saw no sign when we searched the house.

SHAUGHNESSY: (Enthusiastically) Nor you would. Not if you searched for a week. Oh, 'tis most ingenious. The whole of the wall at the end of the passage moves on a counter-weight. The machinery that does it is in the kitchen. When I handed the place back we dismantled it all—

RIVETT-YARDE: Well, someone's re-mantled it again, that's clear.

FARMER: The thing is, could you work it now?

SHAUGHNESSY: I think so. Whatever they have done to it, the principle would be the same. There's the counter weight to unlock, and a starting lever to pull—

FARMER: I wonder if you'd mind coming and showing us.

SHAUGHNESSY: (Slightly startled) In my pyjamas?

FARMER: I'm afraid there's terribly little time to spare.

RIVETT-YARDE: It's a matter affecting the security of this country – and, incidentally, the lives of three people.

SHAUGHNESSY: Why didn't you say so before. I'll grab a coat as I go through the hall.

(FADE. FADE UP)
(IN THE SILENCE OF THE CAVE THE WATER CAN BE HEARD SLAPPING AGAINST THE ROCKS AND THE LANDING PLATFORM AS THE TIDE EBBS. THEN, VERY FAINTLY, IN THE DISTANCE, THE SOUND OF A BIG MOTOR BOAT COMING IN)

BOHUN: (Whispering) Here's the boat with the rest of the gang. This is it, we've got to do it now or not at all.

THRESHER: You go for his gun. I get him round the neck. Right?

BOHUN: Right. Now grab him.

(MOTOR BOAT LOUDER. FOOTSTEPS)

VOICE: (Hails quietly, from end of cave)

(STAMPING OF FEET)

BORIS: (Shout, strangled at birth)

(NOISE OF STRIFE)

BOHUN: (Shouts) Take cover.

(A LONG SLITHERING BUMP AS BOHUN AND THRESHER GO TO EARTH)

TAYLOR: (Savage) What's happened? More light there. Boris! What is it? Where are they?

BORIS: (Still gasping) I wasn't asleep. I was watching.

TAYLOR: Who accused you of sleeping? WHERE ARE THOSE MEN?

BORIS: They jumped on me.

HOPPER: They cannot have gone far. The outer door is down. They could not have passed us at the cave opening. They must be up there. Among those packing cases.

TAYLOR: Konstant.

KONSTANT: Huh.

TAYLOR: Our friends are up there, playing hide and seek. We should like them out, and quickly.

(BOAT CRESCENDO, AND THEN MUTED, AS SHE CUTS HER ENGINES TO COME IN. IN COMPARATIVE SILENCE THE HEAVY STEPS OF KONSTANT CAN BE HEARD, AS HE CRUNCHES TOWARDS THE CAVE-HEAD)

BOHUN: (Clearly) I warn you. Stop where you are, or I'll shoot.

(THE FOOTSTEPS CONTINUE WITHOUT FALTERING. THE SLAMMING ROAR OF AN AUTOMATIC – TWO SHOTS – DEAFENINGLY LOUD IN THE CONFINED

SPACE. NO SOUND FOR A MOMENT. THEN A CRASH
AS KONSTANT GOES DOWN)

THRESHER:	(Whispering) Who said he was bullet proof?
HOPPER:	The boat's in.
TAYLOR:	I can hear. Keep back. We want no unnecessary casualties. (Raising his voice which echoes slightly in the cavern roof) Mr Bohun.
BOHUN:	Go on, Mr Taylor. I can hear you.
TAYLOR:	I'll give you a minute to come out from behind those packing cases. All three of you. With your hands up.
BOHUN:	You've got it all wrong. The idea is for you to come down here and fetch us out. Quite a few shots left in this gun. *And* a spare magazine.
TAYLOR:	(Patient) On the contrary. You will come out.
BOHUN:	I hate to contradict you.
TAYLOR:	If you do not come out, this grenade which I am holding in my hand will be thrown over your barricade of packing cases. The effect of a grenade exploding in the confined space in which you are lying should be quite remarkable.

(PAUSE)

BOHUN:	You're bluffing.
TAYLOR:	Half a minute.
BOHUN:	I suppose you want me to put my head up and look – so that you can take a pot shot at me.
TAYLOR:	You are at perfect liberty to look. No one will shoot you. This way will be far more effective. Twenty seconds.
BOHUN:	(Rather desperate) You'll kill Hickley as well. I thought you wanted him.
TAYLOR:	He will have to be sacrificed for the greater good. Ten. Nine. Eight. Seven.

(CROSS FADE)

THRESHER:	See if you can pick him off before he throws it.
BOHUN:	No. He's behind the buttress.
TAYLOR:	Six. Five. Four.
THRESHER:	Look out, Hickley. If you show yourself they'll shoot you.
TAYLOR:	Three.

HICKLEY: Out of the way, Bohun, let me go.

BOHUN: Stop him, Uncle! What's he doing? He's mad!

HICKLEY: Drop that grenade, drop that grenade.

(A RUSH OF FEET)

HICKLEY: (A desperate scream)

BOHUN: (Shouting) Good Lord. He's got him. Down for your life.

(A ROAR WHICH DWARFS ALL PREVIOUS SOUNDS AS THE GRENADE GOES OFF. THE SOUND REVERBER- ATES AND BOOMS AND FINALLY FADES AWAY INTO SILENCE, BROKEN ONLY BY THE RINGING OF A DOOR BELL)

FARMER: What was that?

RIVETT-YARDE: Sounds as if the whole place is blowing up.

MRS McWHIRTER: What is it?

FARMER: Open up, Mrs McWhirter.

MRS McWHIRTER: What is it this time?

FARMER: I'm not arguing. Open the door, or we'll break it down.

MRS McWHIRTER: Ye'll no do that in a hurry.

RIVETT-YARDE: There's a French window here. I think that's a better chance.

FARMER: Break it open.

(SOUND OF SPLINTERING OF WOOD AND GLASS)

All in.

RIVETT-YARDE: Right, Sergeant, watch that door.

(HALF A DOZEN MEN BURST INTO AND THROUGH THE ROOM)

MRS McWHIRTER: (Suddenly shrill) This is an outrage.

FARMER: We'll see about that. Watch her, Sergeant. If there's any trouble, handcuff her. Now, Commander Shaughnessy, let's see if you can do your stuff.

SHAUGHNESSY: As I remember it, the kitchen was on the right, at the end.

(DOOR)

Yes, that's it. The apparatus was worked from inside that cupboard. It looks like a pump handle. First the lock of the counterweight.

(SNAP)

Then the pulley-lever—

MRS McWHIRTER: Come out o' my kitchen.
SHAUGHNESSY: —which works the door.

(SOUND OF DOOR SLIDING UP AND A HEAVY THUD AS IT SETTLES INTO PLACE)

FARMER: All right. Spread out. Gag that woman if she tries to shout. I'll go first—

(THE CLATTER OF FOOTSTEPS AS THEY RACE DOWN INTO THE CAVE. THEN A MOMENT'S SILENCE)
(VERY FAINT CHUGGING OF MOTOR BOAT IN DISTANCE, AND RECEDING)

RIVETT-YARDE: Ahoy, there.
BOHUN: (From far end) Ahoy, there.
RIVETT-YARDE: Whoever you are, come out of there – and quick.
FARMER: And come out with your hands up.
BOHUN: It's all right. We're coming as quickly as we can. Some of the men got away in the boat after the grenade went off. Not the important ones, though.
FARMER: Who are you? And who's – this?
BOHUN: That is – was – I'm afraid – Albert Hickley. A scientist. A silly fool, and, ultimately, a brave man. Taylor – yes, that's him, in the corner – was just going to lob a hand grenade into our hiding place. Hickley went for him. The grenade went off and killed both of them. The rest of them scarpered – except Konstant – I'd shot him.
FARMER: Oh. You'd *shot* him.
BOHUN: That's right. He's in the other corner. As I was saying, the rest got away.
RIVETT-YARDE: They won't get far, I fancy. There's a destroyer between them and their rendezvous. They won't get round *that* so easily. Now. Who are *you*?

BOHUN: This is Major Thresher. And my name is Bohun. Spelt B-o-h-u-n.

RIVETT-YARDE: (<u>Grimly</u>) And mine is Rivett-Yarde. Spelt as it sounds. I can't say how I have been looking forward to meeting you—

(<u>MUSIC – FADE UNDER ANNOUNCEMENT</u>)

CLOSING
ANNOUNCEMENT: That was the final episode of 'The Man Who Could Not Sleep', a serial-thriller in six parts by Michael Gilbert.

MY AUNT SHE DIED A MONTH AGO

The Mitchison family was lower middle-class until grandfather James Mitchison made the best part of a million pounds out of buttons – in the days when ladies wore rather more buttons than they do now. When he retired he built, on a bend in the Thames between Windsor and Henley, a sort of 'week-end palace' of red brick and curly tiles, with a private river frontage, called 'Shalimar'.

Three of his children lived most of their lives in it with him; they will be dealt with in a moment. The eldest, and more independent, Samuel Mitchison, became a schoolmaster, eventually owning and running his own school. He died about ten years ago, leaving the one son, Howard Mitchison, the well known writer of light fiction. Howard makes quite enough money for a flat in Albany, a nice car, and a lot of foreign travel. Although all his novels have nickel-plated heroines, he himself knows absolutely nothing about women and is scared of them.

He has rather lost touch with the rest of the family.

Reverting now to the other three of old James Mitchison's children (Howard's uncle and aunts). The youngest was Aunt Minna. She had married an Italian, Carlo Paradolce, who had presented her with a daughter Pippa and then returned to Italy and was heard of no more. Minna herself died of an obscure liver complaint when Pippa was nine years old.

The next was Uncle Bernard, a bachelor. Five years ago he was drowned whilst out punting. The third was Aunt Rachel, also unmarried. A month ago (whilst Howard was in the wilds of Sardinia, picking up background for his new novel), Aunt Rachel was knocked down and killed by a hit-and-run motorist, whose identity has never been discovered. Howard was too late for the funeral. But on his return he received a summons from old Mr Rumbold of Wragg & Rumbold, solicitors, who explained to him the effect of her death.

Mr Rumbold explains to Howard that Aunt Rachel, the survivor of that generation, has been able to leave him the house and contents and the use of a large fund to keep it up. Apart from this, grandfather has tied the money so tightly that the first person who will be able to touch it will be the surviving grandchild. 'That's Pippa or me' says Howard. 'As she's only eighteen and I'm forty one the chances are on her'. 'Quite so' says Mr Rumbold, 'but if you accept your aunt's bequest you will be able to live meanwhile, free, and in some comfort. There is an excellent staff at Shalimar. Mrs Musker, though a somewhat formidable woman, is a most efficient housekeeper. Her husband, little Mr Musker, acts as steward or butler. I remember him as a young man, when he was a junior clerk in this office. There are two or three maids and also a garden staff. The funds, although you cannot touch the capital, will pay for all of that.'

Howard's first reaction is that he wants none of it. However, it is a golden summer that year; and the thought of a house by the river is attractive. He decides to spend a week there before making his mind up whether to dispose of the house and contents (as he can do, under the Will).

In fact, he enjoys himself enormously. The house is marvellously run, and although old fashioned, offers a sort of solid, well-organised comfort that went out fifty years ago. He postpones the decision, and decides to settle there for the rest of the summer and finish his current novel.

He is also highly intrigued by Pippa, a most unusual girl of eighteen; very uninhibited. A wearer of clothes that would perhaps have been more usual on a girl of fourteen; she has never been to school having been governess-taught and seems to delight in saying (and doing) the first things that come into her copper-coloured head.

The nearest neighbours are the Wrattens, who have the house next up the river. She is a retired (minor) opera star (Diva Deliciosa); he is a retired opera star's retired husband. Howard is invited to tea with them, and finds them a source of information about the family. Their hints that Bernard's death *may not have been entirely accidental* are the first disquieting element.

Then a second, much more disquieting thing happens. Mr Rumbold has said that his Aunt Rachel has left him a letter telling him her wishes about the house and staff. It was not part of her official will but was to be handed to him if he decided to take up residence. Howard asks Mrs Musker for it. After some delay and prevarication, she produces it. It seems quite harmless, naming a number of things Aunt Rachel wished him to keep up, subscriptions and so on. But what really startles him is that (a) the ink is quite fresh. He judges not more than two days old and (b) It is *not* in his Aunt's handwriting – which he happens to know well.

*

Another neighbour is Bill Millman. A huge, athletic, creature, who seems to have nothing to do but scull up and down the river looking magnificent or drive round in a biscuit-coloured De Magnus Coupé. A conversation, accidentally overheard at night in the garden, shows Howard that although Pippa may dress and talk like fourteen, she is quite capable of behaving like eighteen. Bill is clearly infatuated.

Mrs Musker becomes 'difficult'. Howard decides to have a showdown, and sack her. He finds he cannot. He can either sell the whole house and get rid of everyone (in which case the money will belong to the estate, not him) or else leave it as it is. Pippa promises him that Mrs Musker will behave in future. After further conversation with the Wrattens, Howard gets the idea that there may have been something funny about *all* the deaths. (Minna's liver, Bernard's punt, and Rachel's motor accident.) Alarmed, he spends the evening writing a long letter to Mr Rumbold.

Going out to post it, he hears a car coming behind him. Howard thinks nothing of it until he suddenly sees it has *no lights on*. He jumps through a hedge, just missing being knocked for six, and takes to his heels. In the moonlight he has noticed that the car is a light coloured coupé.

Howard's first reaction is to pack up and leave. He is somewhat re-assured when he reads in the paper next morning that a car, driven wildly and without lights and with a man and woman in it (both unknown to him), has been involved in a crash at a place about five miles off. Presumably, therefore, the harrowing incident of the previous evening was just an accident. Be goes back to look for the letter he was going to post, finds it in the ditch, and posts it.

He calls on the local doctor, who attended Aunt Minna. The doctor makes light of the idea that her death could have been anything other than natural.

His next call is to the police. The local Inspector proves friendly. Howard asks him a question. How did he *know* that Aunt Rachel died from a hit-and-run driver? The Inspector says that little Mr Musker heard a car's brakes squealing, then accelerating away again. It was he who went out and found her. He is also told that they recovered, from Aunt Rachel's clothing and hair, a number of splinters of thick, convex, glass which, when reassembled, formed about two thirds of what was obviously a headlight glass of standard pattern.

That afternoon, Howard has an urgent telephone call and goes up to see Mr Rumbold, the lawyer, who has got his letter. Howard tells him all that has happened – including the so-called 'letter of instructions' from Aunt Rachel that first aroused his suspicions. 'I know a good deal about handwriting,' says Howard. 'I had to study it for a book I was doing. That is a clever forgery of Rachel's writing'. With a pretty white face, Mr Rumbold takes out a folder of requests for money, and endorsed cheques for large amounts 'Then what are these?' he says. 'About half forgeries, half genuine,' says Howard, when he has studied them. 'Then someone had about five thousand pounds in the last year that they shouldn't have had,' says Mr Rumbold.

Though unwilling to go back to the house, at Rumbold's urgent request, Howard returns to Shalimar. 'You *must* find the truth,' says Rumbold. 'No matter *who* it involves. The person who has been embezzling this money,' he adds, 'is probably the murderer of one, or more of your family.' Howard has no plan except to keep his eyes wide open.

That evening he notices something. He is sitting, trying to write, in the summerhouse at the foot of the lawn, when Pippa goes past in a canoe with Bill Millman. Howard has field glasses with him, and quietly keeps them trained on the next bend of the river. The minutes pass but no canoe appears. Howard walks along the bank until he can see round the immediate bend. The canoe has disappeared.

Piqued, Howard leaves the house, crosses the river lower down by the bridge, and comes back on the other bank. Part of the mystery is explained. The elbow of the river at that point is formed by a small island, almost impenetrably covered with nettles and brambles. It does not look, however, as if any boat could have made its way down the backwater which separates this island from the bank on the other side. Part of the mystery therefore remains.

After tea that day, Howard decides to take Mr Musker, to a very limited extent, into his confidence. Mr Musker admits that he himself was not very happy about Uncle Bernard's death. Bernard wasn't a swimmer, but he was a capable, rather violent, puntsman. Musker suggests that Howard have a word with Mr Battle, the boat builder.

Mr Battle tells Howard about the so-called accident. Apparently, when Bernard went up to town for the day, Pippa, (then only a girl of 13) used to paddle the Shalimar punt down to a landing stage belonging to an inn on the other bank; and (sometimes) wait for Bernard or (more often) walk home over the bridge. Bernard would arrive on the evening train, walk up the road to this inn, have a drink or two, then punt himself home. On this occasion, apparently, the punt pole broke under one of Bernard's first violent pushes, Bernard went in, unnoticed in the dark, and was drowned.

Howard sees that Mr Battle is not entirely easy about this. He presses him. Had he ever known a punt pole break in that way? *Could* you break a punt pole by just leaning on it? In the end Mr Battle leads him into the back of his boat house and says 'I'll show you something I picked up two weeks later down at the weir.' It is half a punt pole. And, although partly broken, it is clear that it has also been three quarters sawed through.

'Why on earth didn't you show this to the police?' asks Howard.

'There's no way of proving that this is the punt pole he was using,' says Mr Battle, 'and anyway, Bernard was a drunken old wastrel, not much use to anyone – and I've known Miss Pippa since she was three.'

Howard has now to face the fact that Pippa may be an embezzler and, at least, a double murderer. If the doctor was right, Minna died naturally, and even the most fiendish child would hardly have poisoned her own mother. Nevertheless, so clever has she been that everything is surmise, nothing proof.

Howard has a further talk with Mr Musker. This time about Rachel's death. Musker says that, when he ran out and found her lying there, his first instinctive move, after summoning the doctor, was to get hold of Pippa. He ran up to her room, but it was empty. She was nowhere in the house. Thinking she might be next door with Bill Millman, he had telephoned but, although he had got the number twice, he had only heard the ringing of the telephone. So that house was empty too. Then he had got onto the police, and in the ensuing excitement had forgotten about Pippa. She had turned up much later, having (apparently) been out in Millman's car at a road house, dancing.

Howard asks Musker about the Island. Musker explains that it is Shalimar property, and, though now overgrown, was once a well-kept-up retreat. There is an old summer house tucked away in the middle of it. You get at it by running your boat in under the willows at the tip of the island. He adds that it has long been a favourite retreat of Pippa's.

That evening Howard manages to break into Millman's garage – it's not locked – and make a quick inspection of Millman's car. Although the headlights are pretty much alike, in fact, the offside one is slightly larger and slightly newer than the near-side one.

Howard can think of nothing better to do than watch Pippa unostentatiously. The following evening he sees her slipping out and making for the bottom of the garden. When he gets there the canoe is gone, but he takes the dinghy and follows. He finds the landing place – though no canoe – and picks his way through the almost tropical undergrowth, into the middle of the island, where, in a clearing in the moonlight, stands the derelict summer house. He searches round a bit and eventually climbs in. Under a loose board he finds the battered remnant of an off-side head light. Howard suddenly hears a noise, and realizes that someone is climbing in after him. He makes for the opposite window, but much too late. Someone jumps on him, and a pair of very powerful hands grasp him by the throat.

As the breath is going out of him, Howard realizes that it is Bill Millman. Bill is beserk, and is shouting, 'What have you done with her, you swine? What have you done with her?' Howard manages to bend one of his fingers back enough to gasp out, 'She isn't here, you fool.' Millman lets go of his throat enough for Howard to talk. Howard manages to convince him that Pippa is nowhere on the island. And asks him what the devil he is up to, trying to murder him.

Millman says that he has been told that Howard had got Pippa *drunk* at dinner that night, and taken her across to the island. His deductions as to Howard's intentions were fairly natural. 'If I had done anything of the sort,' agrees Howard warmly, 'I should deserve murdering. But it's absolutely untrue. And who told you?'

'Musker told me,' says Millman.

The two men sit together in the dark and try to work this out. 'If Musker said that,' says Howard, 'he said it in order to make you come after me and kill me. If that's right, it makes Musker the villain. It was he who cut through Bernard's punt pole, and staged it so as to throw blame on Pippa. It was he who hit Aunt Rachel – and staged it to throw blame on both of you.'

'How could he have hit her with *my* car, when I was miles away driving Pippa to a dance in it?'

'Easy,' says Howard, 'have you looked at your headlights lately?'

'No,' says Millman. 'What's wrong with them?'

Howard explains his theory. Some weeks before Aunt Rachel's death – presumably when Millman was away for the night and had left the car behind – Musker had gone into his garage, removed the offside head lamp complete, and substituted another one almost, but not quite like it. Then, when the time came – and he saw Pippa slip off in the car for a jaunt with Bill – he had waited in the hedge for Aunt Rachel to take her usual evening constitutional and had bashed her *with the head light* carefully leaving a lot of the broken glass round the body. The rest of the head light he had hidden in the hut to be used as damning evidence if it were necessary to swing the crime onto Bill.

'Why was he doing this?' asks Bill.

'For money,' explains Howard. 'As an ex-solicitor's clerk he was well placed to swindle the estate; and with everyone except Pippa disposed of, there would be almost no limit to what he could turn into his own pocket.'

At that moment, Millman says, 'Hush. Someone's coming. It must be him. He's coming to see what sort of mess I've made of you.'

Musker arrives. Howard and Millman go for him. He gives them the slip, runs back to the landing stage, and pushes off in the punt he has brought. Millman and Howard go after him in the dinghy. In his haste, Musker slips and goes overboard. They watch the surface, but he doesn't come up. 'There's a dangerous undertow here,' says Millman, 'right into the weeds under the lee of the island. We'll never get him now.'

'No-one helped Bernard either,' says Howard, callously.

The whole thing is hushed up. All the deaths, including Muskers, are on the record as accidents. The house has been sold. Mrs Musker turns out to have been acting very much under her husband's order. Pippa is going to marry Millman and some day either she or Howard will have a million pounds (less what the ingenious Musker has filched). Howard's readers all notice a change in his books. His heroines are now much more human.

THE GAME CALLED JUSTICE

On the surface, the position of Birnie Ancrum is enviably happy. For four years he has been one of the stars of the First Division football team, 'North London', and next year may captain it. He has naturally become a considerable newspaper personality. He has a sweet wife Cathie, a generous income, and a nice home at Edgware.

There are superficial worries of a type not uncommon to a man in his position. In spite of his income he never seems to have much money to spare – certainly none to save. One particular newspaper seems to be pointedly anti-Birnie and his team. The scribe in question is Frank Lorimer and the motives for his bitchiness are not obscure. He himself captained North London six years ago (when Birnie first joined the team), and on retirement from active play had hoped to be made manager. A personality difference with the Club Chairman, Colonel Lambert-Empson, J.P., T.D. prevented this. Frank never got a managerial job. He has taken to sporting journalism and alcohol.

A third worry is that he is being afflicted with anonymous notes, a campaign which is beginning to affect his play. He half suspects that the source may be Lawrence ('Larry') Marks, a brilliant winger, who would be a natural Number Two in the team hierarchy if he was not addicted to an expensive social life, to an extent which, in the opinion of the Team Manager Joe Philpot, jeopardises his training schedule. Joe is the no-nonsense Mancunian who got the job when Frank Lorimer was passed over.

The campaign of anonymous notes and pin-pricks would be much easier to bear if Birnie could discuss it with Cathie. Unfortunately it is a double-edged attack. It not only accuses him of selfishness, cowardice and lack of concentration on the field but it also contains sly references to an episode in his past of which he is not proud; which he has never discussed with Cathie, and to which he has no desire to draw her attention.

Claudia, his former mistress, is a rich woman, in her middle/late thirties now, with a weakness for young men, and the money to indulge it. She owns a mews cottage in Knightsbridge, converted regardless of expense. Her home is situated in a smallish cul-de-sac lined with what used to be coachmen's cottages and which are now fabulously expensive mews residences with painted front doors, fancy ironwork lamps, dolphin knockers and all the trimmings. Her household is a middle-aged French maid, Francine Cordeau, who lives in; and a German chauffeur, Hans Biederbach, who lodges a couple of streets away and looks after the two cars.

Four years ago, Claudia captured Birnie, then at the beginning of his serious football career. The standing arrangement between them was that she would send Hans, with the car, to a discreet after-match rendezvous. If a distant away match was involved, then they went off to a hotel. If a home match took place, then back to the London mews cottage. Discreet though the arrangement was, Frank Lorimer certainly knew about it and Larry Marks seems (from snide remarks he lets fall from time to time) to have found out about it. Birnie suspects that both men may from time to time also have enjoyed Claudia's favours; Frank as his predecessor, Larry as his successor.

This regular arrangement lasted for three years. It was then broken off amicably; but there was a sting in the tail. Claudia, though generous with her body and occasional expensive gifts (one of them a gold cigarette case which Cathie has always wondered about), was remarkably business-like and tight-fisted about money. She never *gave* money. If she did hand over cash – (as she did to Birnie from time to time – he was a great deal poorer then) – it was always as a loan and properly covered by I.O.U's. These, now that he has retired from her retinue, he is forced to redeem. He does so by drawing regular monthly cheques 'to cash', and sending bank notes, without any covering letter, to Claudia. Claudia, the complete business woman, sends him receipts, which he destroys, and she notes the transaction in her private cash journal, along with a number of other such transactions.

In spite of this, Birnie has remained coolly friendly to Claudia. He does not, for instance, suspect her of being behind the persecution he is being subjected to. But he is a bit shaken when an extremely intimate photograph of himself with Claudia on her bed arrives in his morning mail. He suspects that it was taken through the fanlight of the bedroom – but who by? And how did he get into the house? Or was it one of the substitute boyfriends who was hidden somewhere in the house at the time? He is on the point of telephoning Claudia when she rings him, at the pre-match hotel in the Midlands at which he, with the rest of the team, is staying on that Friday evening. The call gets put through to Larry, who passes it, with a grin, to Birnie.

Birnie's account of the telephone call – which is given by him in the *second* version to the police, is as follows. He says that Claudia sounded very upset. She said that something most unpleasant and difficult had come to light that morning. She didn't know which way to turn. Could he please help her. He could catch an early train, be in London by half past eight and at her cottage by nine. And home with his Cathie before midnight. Birnie says that he didn't want to go, but something she said suggested that this business might be connected with the anonymous letter campaign and help to clear it up. He tells Joe some taradiddle about Cathie not being well and is allowed to slip away quickly after the game.

He says that he got to the cottage about 9 p.m. and found it locked up and in darkness. Knowing that Claudia is vague about times, he assumed she had gone out and would be back later. He went to a nearby pub for a drink and a snack, returning to the house at ten o'clock. Still no sign of life. He hung around for a bit, and in the end gave up and went home, getting there just before midnight. He told Cathie that there has been a bit of a party to celebrate that afternoon's victory (3–0), about which Cathie, of course, knows, having watched Match of the Day on television.

Next morning at nine o'clock Francine, the maid, returning from her regular Saturday off, (which she spends at her sister's), finds Claudia strangled on her bed. She summons the police. The story is in all the papers on Monday morning. Birnie and Cathie read of it at breakfast. GLAMOROUS SOCIALITE FOUND STRANGLED – DEATH IN MEWS COTTAGE.

The police investigate. They assume from the first that it is a sex-killing. Francine will not mention any names. She clearly knows a lot, but does not wish to get involved. However, an address book with a great number of names and addresses in it is found and the police, with their customary ant-like persistence, investigate all the men in the list. This brings them to Birnie. It is a routine enquiry, which falls to Detective Sergeant Blount. Birnie says he was a friend of Claudia's, but has not seen her for more than a year.

The first real break for the police occurs when a youth, himself an ardent North London fan, reports that he saw, and recognised Birnie in the pub near the mews cottage. The police now concentrate their enquiries. They learn from Larry Marks about the Friday evening telephone call and about Birnie slipping away from the match from Joe Philpot. Cathie tells the police about his arriving home at midnight. This leads to a second, far from friendly, interview with Birnie, conducted by Detective Superintendent Farthing. Birnie changes his story. He has, by now, consulted local solicitors, Alfred Belling of Belling & Rapp. He tells his story of the telephone call and his response to it; but still maintains that Claudia was 'just a good friend'. The police continue their enquiries.

This version of Birnie's story is blown sky high by Frank Lorimer. He produces to the police a print of the famous photograph. He says that he thinks 'it is his duty to let them see it'. He explains that it was sent to him anonymously. He had meant to tear it up. Perhaps it was fortunate that he kept it. Detective Superintendent Farthing agrees that it was very fortunate.

This leads to a third interview, which takes place on Saturday afternoon immediately after one of North London's home games. Birnie is picked up as he actually leaves by the players' entrance. The police put it to him that he was – and still is – Claudia's lover. Birnie admits the liaison – he can hardly deny it, in the face of the photograph – but says it was broken off more than a year ago. 'Then why,' says Farthing (who has seen Claudia's careful cash record) *are you still paying her money every month?*' Birnie's explanation is disbelieved. He blusters and bluffs and contradicts himself, and is charged with Claudia's murder.

There were strong reactions at Birnie's home, in the press, in the modest offices of Belling & Rapp and in the far from modest Boardroom of 'North London'. In the Boardroom, three different views are expressed, with equal force. Colonel Lambert-Empson expresses the traditional view that if the police have charged the chap, he probably did it. The vice-chairman, a self-made business tycoon, Arthur Gould, says that the police are perfectly capable of framing an innocent party. He has had experience of them both in business and as a motorist. He doesn't trust them an inch. Joe Philpot simply points out that the team are lying seven from bottom in the League table and it will cost them at least £200,000 to buy a comparable centre-half – even if they can find one. And if they don't, they'll go down to the bottom like a stone.

Mr Gould says, 'One thing's quite clear, the boy must have the best solicitors, *my* solicitors, Lawtons of Norfolk Street, and we must put up the money. Better to put up £20,000 and give him a chance of getting off than to say goodbye to a £200,000 investment.' The Colonel is indignant. He says, 'You can't buy justice in this country. If the boy's innocent, he'll be acquitted.'

Sir Walter Lawton (President last year of the Law Society) accepts the assignment. He is not everyone's idea of a distinguished solicitor. Solicitors do very little of their work in public, and their personal appearance is not as important as, for instance, that of a barrister. He is a dumpy little man with a bristling moustache and (occasionally) a bristling manner. He has a large and competent staff. The man, deceptively youthful in appearance, to whom he assigns the principal part, is Noel Anthony Portarlier Rumbold, known to a wide circle of friends of both sexes as Nap.

By the time that Nap has extracted from Birnie *his* version of the events of the fatal Friday and Saturday, and has seen Cathie and learned about the previous events, he expresses a preliminary opinion to Sir Walter. He says, 'I'm not at all sure he didn't do it. He was fed up with Claudia, fed up with calls on his time, fed up with paying her money. She was a standing threat to his position, which was just beginning to be important in the world of sport. And I believe that his wife thinks the same.'

Sir Walter says, 'Never mind about whether he did it or not. The police have to *prove* that he did it. To a jury, we don't have to prove the contrary. What we have to do is to produce an equally credible alternative, based on sound evidence. That's your job. You can drop everything else and concentrate on it.'

Nap sees several possible lines of enquiry. The first is technical, and will be better handled by his firm. However, the two points about which pathological and forensic science evidence will be adduced – that is the precise time of death and the precise method of the killing – are for him to deal with. The marks indicate strangling by ligature, not by hand. But what ligature? Nap wonders. Is it a tie, a scarf, a piece of cord? And where is it?

Nap ponders a further point. A woman who is being strangled usually manages to scratch her attacker. This marks him – and leaves traces of blood, skin and tissue under her nails. Were her nails examined? If so, with what result? Was there any blood there? If so, of what blood group? If not, was there any other matter?

Sir Walter reassures him, 'We will have the best man obtainable at the commital proceedings. He will listen to their evidence, and will tell us what to do, and the line to take at the trial.' Meanwhile Nap investigates the domestic staff. Here he receives a set-back. Hans Biederbach has been allowed to return to Germany. The police, when challenged, say that he was not a witness of any importance. His evidence, if required by the defence, could be taken on affidavit in Germany. The prosecution did not intend to call him. 'Fine,' says Nap, 'but where is he?' The police seem unable or unwilling to say. Sir Walter, through a friend at the top of the

Home Office, is allowed to use the Interpol network, and an address is discovered.

The third line of enquiry is the journalist Frank Lorimer. Nap soon becomes convinced that he was behind the anonymous letter campaign and that he was doing it not (primarily) to be anti-Birnie, but to get his own back on the team manager Joe Philpot. He is too obviously delighted at the non-success of North London and openly prophesies that they will go down to Division Two at the end of the season and that Joe will be sacked. The compromising photograph, Lorimer says, came through the post. He suggests that it might have been taken by Francine the maid. Incidentally, Lorimer reveals that winger Larry Marks also came up to London that Friday evening. He must have been on the same train as Birnie. Why didn't he travel up with Birnie? Frank saw him at a night-spot, just before midnight. What was *he* up to? Much of this information comes out in an indiscreet conversation at El Vino. Nap has a harder head than Frank!

With Francine, Nap has more success than with the male witnesses. She clearly has a soft spot for him, and is not convinced that Birnie was the murderer. She produces one new, and possibly significant fact. The evening before her death, Claudia had told Francine that some of her most valuable jewellery was missing. When Nap asks her how this can be proved, Francine says, 'All her good pieces were insured. There is a list of them in the escritoire in her bedroom.' Nap knows that the police made an inventory of everything when they sealed up the house; and that Claudia's own solicitors have a copy and would oblige them on a solicitor-to-solicitor basis with a sight of it. A comparison of the lists will show which pieces were missing. He feels that this needs following up, although he is far from sure where it is going to lead.

Francine reveals that she has always had, and has retained a key to the mews cottage. She offers to accompany Nap there so that they can get hold of the insurance schedule. The visit to the cottage duly takes place. It produces the list (in the course of locating which they discover that one of the drawers, normally kept locked, has been forced). It also produces something much more exciting. Nap climbs on a chair to examine the fanlight between the passage and the bedroom to see whether it could have been used for photography, and sees, quite clearly in the light of his torch, a set of right-hand finger prints.

Quick action is called for. A photographer with flash-light apparatus is organised by Sir Walter and set up to photograph the print. As this is being done, Superintendent Farthing, alerted by neighbours, arrives. There is a blazing row, but Nap has his photograph. But whose prints are they?

There is a further, very small, incident in the flat. In the course of their original search, the door of one of the rooms is found jammed shut. Nap tries to open it and fails. Francine, one of those powerful French country-women, says, 'Let me' – and pulls it open with a quick jerk. She has obviously got very strong wrists and arms. Significant when one considers that she also possesses a key of the cottage.

Francine volunteers her own prints. They do not match the ones found. Frank Lorimer, when appealed to, does the same. Still no luck. When Nap at last manages to track down Larry Marks, to discuss with him the question of where he went on that Saturday night and why, he gets a complete brush-off. Marks refuses to co-operate and maintains that if the police want to question him, they can do so. However, Nap has got a nice set of right-hand prints on the card he handed Larry at the outset of the interview. Unfortunately, these prints do not correspond either.

The commital proceedings produce few surprises. The police witnesses, apart from normal map-drawers and photographers, comprise Larry Marks, Joe Philpot, Sergeant Blount (as to Birnie's first statement), Superintendent Farthing (as to his two subsequent ones), the boy who identified Birnie in the pub, Francine, Dr Ramsay (the well known Home Office Pathologist) as to the time of death, and Professor Penny of the Forensic Science Laboratory on the possibility that the liga-ture was a North London Club silk tie which has been found in one of the drawers in Claudia's bedroom. The evidence of the discovery of minute threads of coloured silk in the creases of the strangulation mark is technically interesting, and obviously impresses the magistrate. It does not impress Sir Walter's expert, who is sitting in Court making notes for the defence.

The only cross-examination is of these two technical witnesses and is on the subject of Claudia's *nails*. The pathologist agrees that he removed certain matter from behind them as a routine precaution. There was *no* identifiable human tissue; but there were certain small shreds of blue/grey wool.

The magistrate finds a prima facie case and commits for trial. North London are defeated 3–0 away by Leeds United. Nap flies to France, Sir Walter goes to see Mr Hargest Macrea Q.C. and Cathie visits Birnie in prison. Birnie is completely disheartened, disillusioned and inclined to whine. He says, 'When the machine is against you, you've had it.' The cumulative effect of the commital evidence has, in fact, been impressive.

Birnie has every reason to be depressed as the Crown traditionally sews up its cases very neatly. Furthermore, it is curious how a case which sounds water-tight when only one side of it is presented, sounds quite different when it is properly defended.

The real weakness of Birnie's position is that he has lied to the police. In fact he told them three different stories. He did so, he says, to keep his not very creditable early experiences as a gigolo from Cathie, particularly since he was still paying Claudia money, and had his public image to consider.

As to the general line of defence, Macrea advises that although he is now reasonably certain that Frank Lorimer was behind the anti-Birnie campaign – it will not get them anywhere if they try to prove it in Court. As far as the murder is concerned, it is an irrelevance. Moreover, if they can keep him friendly, he may be willing to co-operate in one small but important matter. Macrea asks, 'Do you happen to know what his christian name is?' Sir Walter says, 'No, why?' Macrea says, 'I was hoping it was Quentin.'

The evidence which must be attacked, according to Macrea, is the technical evidence. He feels that it can be shaken. Not only the laboratory evidence about the tie, which he has his own ideas about, but also the more important question of the time of death. Dr Ramsay, the Home Office Pathologist, saw the body at 10 a.m. on Sunday morning. It had been undisturbed (presumably) since death, and was in a closed room of fairly low temperature. He was therefore able to say, with fair certainty, by fall of body heat and onset of rigidity, that death had occurred between twelve and fifteen hours prior to his examination. This put the latest likely time of death at 10 p.m. Now the boy who identified Birnie says that he came into the pub at nine o'clock, seemed 'restless', kept an eye on his watch, and left again 'about an hour later'. This fits in much better with the view that Claudia was already dead by nine o'clock. If Birnie had himself killed her, *is it conceivable that he would have hung around for an hour afterwards?*

Nevertheless, they are not going to get home unless they can find a substitute murderer. They are not going to have to *prove* that it is Francine or Larry Marks or Frank Lorimer or the missing chauffeur; merely that it is just as likely that it is one of them as that it is Birnie. That photograph, was almost certainly taken by the next boy-friend, at the period when the affair with Birnie was cooling off, and No. 2 had the run of the house. He took it, possibly with Claudia's cognisance, as a form of insurance policy or blackmail lever. If they can find the owner of the right-hand prints they will be a long way on. The most satisfactory method would be to finger print all the men in Claudia's address book. *This is the sort of thing that*

*the police might be able to organise, but is right outside their capabilities
as private litigants.*

Meanwhile Nap is at the Headquarters of Interpol at 37(bis) Rue
Valery in the Parisian suburb of Lagny-Pomponne. He presents his credentials to the Deputy Director, M. Lachaise, and asks for an 'enquiry'. He is
told that a request for an official 'enquiry' can only be made through the
British correspondent at Scotland Yard. Nap says that the British Foreign
Office has requested co-operation. 'That may be so,' says M. Lachaise, 'But
regulations are regulations.' He is either being stupid, or deliberately
obstructive. Nap says, 'Very well, I will telex my enquiry to Scotland Yard
with a request to re-telex it to you. I will pay for the outward and inward
transmission.' With some reluctance, M. Lachaise agrees. Nap says, 'Since
I shall be on the move, might the result of my enquiry, *if positive*, be sent
to a firm of lawyers in London? I will pay for that, too.'

Following the ceremonial opening of the case of Regina v Ancrum at the
Old Bailey, Mr Adrian Goff, Senior Treasury Counsel, presents the bare
bones of the case against Birnie. He prepares to call the witnesses of fact –
Joe Philpot, Larry Marks and the two policemen. Macrea somewhat takes
the wind out of his sails by saying that insofar as this evidence concerns the
untrue stories told by his client, there will be no need to take up the time
of the Court. They are admitted. He would, nevertheless like to ask some
questions of the boy, Fred Smithers, who saw Birnie in the pub.

When Fred gives his evidence it is clear that the police now realise the
vital connection between it and the time of death. He says (in answer to
his own Counsel) that Birnie left 'Some time after he arrived. It might have
been an hour. It might have been three quarters of an hour or even less.'
'Maybe half an hour?' suggests Mr Goff. Macrea is on his feet in an
instant. He objects to words being put into the boy's mouth. He also reads
to him the unequivocal statement he made in the commital proceedings.
'Birnie Ancrum left around ten o'clock.' 'Who has persuaded you to
change your mind?' says Macrea. 'Have the police been coaching you?'
The Judge is down on the defence counsel so heavily for this that he
comments to Sir Walter as he sits down 'Judge hostile'.

Nap is now in Darmstadt. He has an address for Hans Biederbach's
family. He is met by an enormous, hostile, Prussian father who says that
of course he can't see Hans; he is caravanning on his honeymoon. When
Nap asks where this is, not only does he refuse to tell him, but he asks
what authority Nap has for such questions. Nap departs, with a flea in his
ear but not without hope. He has noticed a depot for caravan hire in the
next street.

Back at the Old Bailey the cross examination of Frank Lorimer is proceeding. Macrea says, 'I did catch your name correctly, did I not? Frank Quentin Lorimer?' He then asks him about a number of entries in Claudia's famous account book showing F.Q.L. as paying her certain sums of money from time to time. Lorimer admits that Claudia loaned him money on I.O.U. The entries are notes of repayment. Macrea says, 'I am not making any imputations about this. I put the questions only so that the jury might learn of the businesslike habits of the deceased, and attach rather more weight to the explanation by the accused of the payments *he* made.' The judge said, 'The jury must form their own conclusions on that point, Mr Macrea.'

A few tactful questions at the caravan centre in Darmstadt produced the information Nap was after. 'Hans and his Gretel have gone to Baden-Baden. They spoke of using the Nachtigal site, where Hans had been before. Very suitable for a honeymoon couple,' says the man in charge with a grin. 'Very remote. At this time of year they might be the only ones there.'

In the meantime Herr Bierderbach senior, Han's father, is telephoning the police.

Nap arrives at the Gausthaus Zum Nachtigal, and learns that the honeymoon couple are caravanning up in the woods. The lady of the Gasthaus thinks that Hans has driven down to the market town of Weitensfeldt for stores. Nap explains that he is a very old friend of Hans. He will go up and say 'Hallo' to Gretel.

After Macrea has cross-examined Dr Ramsey with considerable expertise, on the question of the time of death, he deals with Professor Penny of the Forensic Science Laboratory. He says, 'You admit that you are uncertain that this tie was used to strangle Miss Mountpenny?' The professor, an honest man, says, 'Yes'. 'Then,' says Macrea, 'let me put another question to you. *If* you had used a tie or scarf to strangle someone, would you have left it behind for the police to find?' The Professor is forced to say 'No'. Macrea sits down.

When Macrea continues the defence, he says, 'I have a number of witnesses to call. They will prove photographs taken of a right-hand set of finger prints. I shall also call the prisoner himself. I had intended to call technical evidence, but in view of the showing made by the technical witnesses for the Crown, I see no necessity to do so.' The judge says, very coldly, 'You must be the best judge of that, Mr Macrea.'

At the caravan site, Nap makes his mark with Gretel. He is dressed as a tourist, in leder-hosen, and looks absurdly young. He says he is on a walking tour. Gretel, who is a bit piqued at Hans leaving her behind, is not unwilling to chat. He claims to have known Hans well in England. This serves as an introduction. They get on well.

Nap persuades Gretel that it would be a nice idea if he took her photograph. He poses her suitably against a background of the caravan and photographs her with the surprisingly expensive camera which he is carrying. Since he seems to require a head and shoulders photograph, he takes it from quite close-up with a fine adjustment on the focus.

At the moment the camera clicks Hans returns to the Gasthaus. The innkeeper's wife says something to him in German. Hans looks extremely surprised and departs at the double. He arrives back at the caravan a minute too late. Nap has gone, and is now making his way back towards civilisation – and a post office. Hans returns to the Gasthaus and telephones the local police.

At the Old Bailey, the judge is addressing Macrea. He says, 'We have listened patiently during the whole of the latter part of this afternoon, Mr Macrea, to witnesses called by you who have proved that a photograph, showing the prisoner in a most improper attitude of intimacy with the deceased, *could* have been taken from the fanlight over the bedroom door. You have then produced an official certificate from the files of the Interpol organisation in Paris (which, with some hesitation, I have been prepared to accept without actually calling on an official of that body to give evidence). This demonstrates that the print of a right-hand found on the same fanlight was that of the deceased's German chauffeur, Hans Biederbach, now returned to that country, and that this indicates that he took the photograph and was himself intimate with the deceased. The Jury will have to form their own conclusions as to the validity of *that* argument. What I am not clear on is what bearing any of this has on the charge of murder. I imagine the Jury is puzzled too. Perhaps you will be able to explain that to us tomorrow. The Court is adjourned.'

In Macrea's chambers that evening after Court, Macrea says, 'With any other judge, I believe we might have done it. Arbuthnot is notorious for his ultra-puritan views. The mere thought of Birnie having extra-marital relationships with a woman was sufficient to make him believe him guilty of murder too. The Jury is on our side. I'm pretty certain, in fact, that the foreman is a North London supporter. Also the beefy character too, to his left. They would like to acquit. But they won't do it arbitrarily. We've got to convince them that Hans was a bad hat – and had a motive for murdering Claudia.' The telephone rings, the voice of the exchange asks if Sir Walter Lawton is there. He says he has a person-to-person call for him from Munich. Sir Walter says, 'That sounds like Nap.' He takes up the telephone, and says, 'Who? Oh – yes,' and similar non-committal things. Then rings off. Macrea, puzzled, says, 'If that wasn't your young partner, where is he?'

'In prison,' says Sir Walter. 'That was a German client of mine, Herr Rauss, the chemical millionaire. Nap got to his office one step ahead of the police and gave him a roll of film. Herr Rauss has had the one photograph in it developed and is sending it by telex, to his London branch. We can have it first thing tomorrow.'

Macrea says, 'Fine. I hope it helps us. But what about Nap? Why was he arrested? And what for?'

'The charge,' says Sir Walter with a smile, 'was voyeurism coupled with taking indecent photographs of a young wife innocently sunning herself in the nude in the Black Forest. His camera was impounded. Since, however, the roll of film now in it contains nothing but eight different views of the Munich Brau-haus I imagine he will have little difficulty in refuting the charge.'

During the fourth and last day of the trial, Macrea says to the judge, 'Before addressing the Court, I would ask permission to recall Mlle Francine Cordeau.' Permission is reluctantly granted. He asks her, first, about the broken open drawer in the desk. What did Claudia keep in it? 'All I know,' says Francine, 'is that she had my passport and work permit in it.' Also, she thought, Hans Biederbach's passport and permit were kept there. He then asks her about her mistress's jewellery. Could she identify it? She says she could probably identify the main pieces.

Macrea is on delicate procedural ground. He says, 'I would like to hand the witness a photograph. I have not been able to supply copies previously to the Court and the prosecution since it only came into my possession early this morning. I have, however, had sufficient prints made for my Lord, for my learned friend, and for the jury.' He hands these to an usher, who dishes them out. The judge says, 'I assume you will be proving this photograph in the normal way, Mr Macrea.' Macrea says, evasively, 'I will do my best.'

He says to Francine, 'You will see the curiously shaped diamond brooch with a larger stone in the middle. Can you identify it for us?'

'Why certainly,' says Francine. 'It belonged to my mistress. It is one of the pieces that was stolen.' Macrea then explains the provenance of the photograph. The judge says, 'I assume you are calling Mr Rumbold to prove the taking of this photograph?' Macrea says, 'Unfortunately owing to a misunderstanding, he is detained by the German police.' The judge says, 'This is most irregular. The photograph should not have been produced.' He then says to the jury, 'You will disregard it.' The foreman says, surprised, 'You mean we have to imagine we've never seen it?' The judge says, 'That is my ruling.' The foreman says, 'It's going to be rather difficult,' and a glance passes between him and the man two to his left who is the other North London supporter.

Macrea, who has observed this with an eagle eye, now addresses himself exclusively to these two men. He says, 'Nothing in this case is certain. All we can do is surmise. The case I put to you is this. Hans Biederbach had the run of his mistress's house. His finger prints show this, whether he took that photograph or not. I suggest he did. And I suggest that for some time she had been *his* mistress. He desired to break off the liaison and get married to his Gretel. He also felt entitled to some recompense. So he stole valuable pieces of jewellery which, as we have heard, are missing. Although we are supposed not to know where they are now! The deceased, who though lavish with her body was passionate over money, discovers the loss and charges Hans with theft. She also wants help and advice and sends for Birnie Ancrum. Hans Biederbach cannot get away, since she is holding his passport. Hans decides to recover his passport by force. He breaks open the escritoire drawer, but is caught in the act. He kills her. You will note that my version fits in with *all* the technical evidence – both as to time of death and the fact that whilst Birnie was wearing a macintosh over a linen suit, Hans Biederbach's chauffeurs jacket was undoubtedly made of blue-grey wool—'

A few weeks after the trial, North London are at home to Burnley. Birnie is playing the game of his life, cheered on by a huge crowd which happens to include the foreman and two members of the jury.

THE LAST CHAPTER

TRANSMISSION: Saturday, 10th January 1970   8.30–9.58 p.m.   Radio 4
Rec. Rpt. 12th January 1970   3.15–4.45 p.m.   Radio 4

CAST:

Laurie	Anna Cropper
Gordon Loftus	James Bolam
Naylor-Smith	Maurice Denham
Batson	Alan Barry
Jessica Wrayburn	Kathleen Helme
Leslie	Nigel Anthony
Randolph Applin	Allan Cuthbertson
Ben Bannister	John Pullen
Inspector Vigars	Peter Tuddenham
Policeman	Geoffrey Collins

Produced by Nesta Pain

BATSON: (<u>Fading up</u>) And I should bloody well think so too. Do you realize how long we've been waiting for this book. Two years. (<u>Pause</u>) That's what I said: '*TWO YEARS*'. If you don't believe me, look up your records. (<u>Pause</u>) I know. I know. He's a bloody awkward customer. He promises and doesn't do it. Sit down Loftus.

<u>(GORDON SITS DOWN DELICATELY)</u>

I'm most terribly sorry for you. Really I am. That splashing noise you can hear is my tears falling all over the desk. (<u>Pause</u>) Well, you're an agent. That's how you earn your ten percent isn't it?

<u>(GORDON HAS TAKEN OUT A CIGARETTE AND IS CLICKING HIS LIGHTER)</u>

If you light that cigarette, you'll have to smoke it in the passage I'm afraid.

(GORDON HASTILY PUTS THE CIGARETTE AND LIGHTER AWAY)

Yes, I'm listening. I've been listening for six months, BUT MY PAPER CAN'T PRINT EXCUSES. I want the bloody book. We've paid for it. What happens if I call the whole thing off. (Longish pause) Exactly. He can't pay back the advance because he's spent it. Do you know what a court of law would call that? They'd call it fraud. F-R-A-U-D. (Further longish pause) (In a slightly more moderate voice) All right, one month. Thirty days, until the end of August, but not a day more. Not an hour more! Not-a-single-bloody-minute-more.

(BANGS DOWN THE RECEIVER)

GORDON: Did I sound angry?
GORDON: You did.
BATSON: I am. That was Bannister's agent.
GORDON: Ben Bannister?
BATSON: None other. We've bought serial rights in his book of reminiscences.
GORDON: They should make good reading.
BATSON: They might be if he'd write 'em.
GORDON: Won't he?
BATSON: Months now they've been feeding us the same sort of crap. 'It's *nearly* finished'. 'It's all *but* finished.' 'It practically *is* finished'. 'Just the last chapter to come, then you can have it.'
GORDON: If it's just the last bit, couldn't we publish what he *has* written?
BATSON: In the ordinary way we might.

(THE TELEPHONE BUZZES. EDITOR PICKS IT UP, LISTENS FOR A MOMENT)

Tell her she can jump off Beachy Head.

(REPLACES RECEIVER)

But, in Ben's case no. Ben's an odd character. On the surface he's tough as old boots. But like a lot of these rugged characters, he's a lot softer inside. He doesn't like hurting people. I've got a feeling he doesn't want to write that chapter.

GORDON: But why's the last chapter so important?

BATSON: Why? Because it's that sort of book. If he was writing a detective story, it'd be the chapter that answered all the questions. The chapter that told you who the villain was. Only this is real life. And maybe the villain's still alive and Ben doesn't want to hurt his feelings.

GORDON: Then I suppose we've got to wait until all the villains are dead.

BATSON: Wait, nothing. We've paid money for this book. A hell of a lot of money. If we can't get the book we're going to get a story. *Why* won't Ben write the last chapter? *Who's* he protecting? *What's* it all about? Get the idea?

GORDON: Er – yes. I think so.

BATSON: Go down and talk to him. Find out what is holding him. (Half to himself) Of course his agent mayn't be telling the truth. They're terrible liars. He mayn't have written the book at all.

GORDON: Do you think he'll talk to me?

BATSON: If he won't, twist his arm.

GORDON: Judging from his reputation I don't suppose he'll be a very easy man to intimidate.

BATSON: If *he* intimidates *you*, that'll be a story too.

GORDON: (Unhappily) I suppose it will. I'll go down first thing tomorrow.

BATSON: Go this evening. Remember what Nelson said: Lose not an hour. He hangs out in an old game-keeper's cottage. The local squire lets him use it I believe. They were in some hush-hush outfit together during the war. I've got *his* name somewhere.

(RUMMAGES THROUGH PAPERS ON HIS DESK)

Naylor-Smith, J.P., D.C. M.C., Halsfield Manor, Halsfield, Kent. If Ben won't talk, maybe Squire Naylor-Smith will.

GORDON: Has he got a wife?

BATSON: Who are you talking about? Ben or Naylor-Smith?

GORDON: I meant Bannister.

BATSON: Well the answer's the same in either case. No. Naylor-

Smith's a bachelor. Ben's a widower. His wife died soon after the war. She was a French girl he met in the Resistance.

GORDON: Any children?

BATSON: Children?

(<u>TELEPHONE RINGS. PICKS UP RECEIVER</u>).

Listen darling. The answer's no. It always has been. It is now and it always will be. N-O. No.

(<u>RINGS OFF</u>)

Children? Yes. It comes to my mind that he has got a daughter, somewhere. She's a student. She was involved in one of their nonsenses. Come to think of it, if she's inherited Ben's temperament, the authorities had better watch out.

(<u>FADE OUT. FADE UP SOUND OF A CAR STOPPING, REVERSING. DOOR OPENING. FEET ON ROAD</u>)

POLICEMAN: (<u>A man of Kent</u>) What's all this.

GORDON: Oh, hullo officer. I didn't see you.

POLICEMAN: I saw you. You nearly went back into the ditch.

GORDON: Well, it isn't a very wide road, is it? I was backing to get my headlights on that signpost.

POLICEMAN: Ah.

GORDON: I wanted to see which of them pointed to Halsfield.

POLICEMAN: They both do.

GORDON: That's helpful.

POLICEMAN: That way, you go through Halsfield Village. That way, you go through Halsfield Street. Which were you wanting?

GORDON: I didn't want either of them, actually. I wanted Halsfield Manor.

POLICEMAN: Mr Naylor-Smith's place.

GORDON: That's right, only I don't want that either.

POLICEMAN: Ah.

GORDON: I want the game-keeper's cottage.

POLICEMAN: Mr Bannister.

GORDON: That's right. You know him?

POLICEMAN: Oh, we all know Mr Bannister. Yes, we all know *him*. He's what you might call a character.

GORDON: So I'd heard. Which of these roads—

POLICEMAN: You could take either of 'em.

GORDON: Oh.

POLICEMAN: The right-hand one goes through the Village, like I said. Then on a mile, and you find the lodge gates. Down the drive, past the house. You'll have to leave your car there. Walk the last hundred yards to the cottage. Right?

GORDON: Quite clear, thank you.

(STARTS UP CAR)

POLICEMAN: (Over the noise of engine) Or you *could* take the left fork. That'd bring you up to the back of the cottage – but it's not so easy to find. Not in the dark.

GORDON: No thanks. I'll take the high road. Goodnight officer.

POLICEMAN: Goodnight sir.

(FADE OUT. FADE UP CAR SLOWING DOWN. STOP-PING. IT IS RUNNING ON A GRAVELLED DRIVE)

(Gordon is humming to himself as he gets out)

(DOOR BANGS SHUT)

GORDON: Ah, this must be it.
'For I'll take the high road, and you'll take the low road, and I'll be at Halsfield afore ye.'
I hope he doesn't think I'm a burglar and take a pot at me. It's damned dark.
'For me and my true love will never meet again. By the bonny bonny banks of—'

(CRASH)

Damn. What is it? Someone left a tree stump lying about.

(FOOTSTEPS, STILL ON GRAVEL, FADING OUT AND IN AGAIN TO DENOTE AN INTERVAL BEFORE.)
(FEET ON FLAGSTONE. KNOCK ON DOOR. SILENCE AN OWL HOOTS. GORDON MAKES A QUICKLY STIFLED NOISE)

Only the owl, the watchman of the night. Wonder if there's anyone at home. Doesn't look like it. No lights.

(OWL HOOTS AGAIN)

Stupid bird. Hop off and catch yourself a mouse.

(IN THE MIDDLE DISTANCE – i.e. ABOUT 60 YARDS AWAY, BUT BLANKETED BY TREES, A CAR STARTS UP AND DRIVES OFF)

Is that a light. No. It's the fire. He must be coming back if he's lit a fire. I wonder if he's left the door open.

(CLICK OF LATCH, AND DOOR OPENING. IT IS A HEAVY OLD DOOR AND CREAKS A GOOD DEAL)

(Clearing his throat) Hullo! Mr Bannister! Anyone at home? (In friendly tones) Well there! Hullo, hullo. You're not a very good watch dog, are you, old boy. Suppose I'd been a burglar. (A pause) (Then, in quite a different tone of voice) He's dead!

(THE WHIRRING CLICK OF THE GRANDFATHER CLOCK GRINDING OUT THE FIRST QUARTER AFTER NINE)

GORDON: (Trying to be reasonable) Take a grip of yourself, Loftus. There's some quite simple explanation. The dog was dying. Old age. Had a fit. Bannister's gone to fetch help. That was probably him I heard driving away just now. He'll be back quite soon. I don't suppose he'd mind if I lit that lamp for a start. Matches.

(STRIKES MATCH. SHORT INTERVAL WHILST WE IMAGINE THE OIL LAMP BEING LIT. CLICK OF GLASS SHADE GOING BACK)

That's better. Now we can see. Now – (Voice trails off) we can see. Mr Bannister – (A panicky note creeping in again) Mr Bannister – oh God – (Whispering) He's dead, too. Get out of here quick. (A spark of commonsense)

Don't be such a damned fool. He may not *be* dead. He may need help. (<u>Self-interest intruding</u>) Anyway, it's no good running away. That policeman knows you were coming here. You're involved whether you like it or not.

(<u>PAUSE. FOOTSTEPS AUDIBLE</u>)

Someone coming.

(<u>LOUDER FOOTSTEPS</u>)

Suppose it's the killer coming back.

(<u>DOOR OPENS, AS LAURIE BANNISTER COMES IN</u>)

LAURIE:	Oh! Who are you?
GORDON:	I might ask you the same.
LAURIE:	This is Daddy's cottage.
GORDON:	Oh!
LAURIE:	Where is he?
GORDON:	Are you Miss Bannister?
LAURIE:	Who *are* you?
GORDON:	My name's Loftus. Gordon Loftus. I work for the Daily News. They sent me down here to ask about your father's book.
LAURIE:	Is that your car in the drive outside the Manor House? (<u>She is becoming easier now that the first shock has gone</u>)
GORDON:	That's right. I parked it there and walked down the path.
LAURIE:	Where's Daddy?
GORDON:	I....
LAURIE:	(<u>Coming forward and seeing the dog</u>) What on earth's wrong with the dog?
GORDON:	I'm afraid this is going to be a terrible shock for you.
LAURIE:	What....
GORDON:	I don't think you ought to look.
LAURIE:	(<u>Viciously</u>) Get out of the way. (<u>There is a moment of silence broken only by the heavy breathing of Laurie</u>).
GORDON:	What – what are we going to do?
LAURIE:	(<u>Quite calm now. Rather hard</u>) There's a telephone up at the house. Get hold of the Police.
GORDON:	What about....

LAURIE:	I'll stay here with him.
GORDON:	Are you sure?
LAURIE:	I shall be all right. Go on.

(FADE OUT. FADE UP FOOTSTEPS APPROACHING
COTTAGE. TWO PAIRS. WALKING SLOWLY)

GORDON:	I don't think Miss Bannister was very happy about that verdict, Inspector.
INSPECTOR VIGARS:	Oh, why was that, Sir?
GORDON:	Obviously, because she didn't believe it was suicide.

(COMING THROUGH THE DOOR)

VIGARS:	This is where you found him isn't it?
GORDON:	I saw the dog first on the floor. Mouth open, showing all it's teeth. And then Bannister. Slumped in the chair, with the same sort of ghastly smile on his face. I shan't forget it in a hurry.
VIGARS:	That's the way cyanide works. Mercifully, it's quick.
GORDON:	You're very certain it was suicide.
VIGARS:	That's what I think. That's what the jury thought.
GORDON:	Hum.
VIGARS:	(Softer) *You* don't think different by any chance do you, Mr Loftus?
GORDON:	I'm not sure.
VIGARS:	Look, we know he was worried and depressed. His neighbours said so. The doctor said so. In bad health *and* worried about it. He'd been to see his doctor three times in the last month. Right?
GORDON:	Lots of men over sixty start worrying about their health. But they don't commit suicide.
VIGARS:	Some of them do.
GORDON:	(Doubtfully) It's a bit thin isn't it?
VIGARS:	If that was the only thing, I'd agree. But you heard the evidence. 'Cyanide.' That's what killed him, and his dog, too. Cyanide's a thing which agents used to carry when they were parachuted into occupied France, I believe.
GORDON:	I believe they did. Yes.
VIGARS:	And if it was kept in an air-tight capsule, it could keep its potency for twenty – thirty – forty years.

GORDON:	That's what they said.
VIGARS:	And *if* he did it himself, that old dog makes sense. He was very attached to that dog. It's understandable he wouldn't want anyone else to have him. He'd take the dog along with him.
GORDON:	It's a pagan idea, but all right, yes, it's feasible.
VIGARS:	And, if you're thinking someone *else* killed him – why should they kill the dog?
LAURIE:	(From the open door-way) Obviously because if they hadn't, Corporal would have killed them.
VIGARS:	(Swinging round) I'm sorry Miss Bannister. I didn't see you there. What was that you said?
LAURIE:	I said that anyone who wanted to kill my father would have had to kill Corporal first. He was a guard dog. Trained to protect my father. If he'd seen him lying on the floor dead, or dying in agony, he would have gone for the murderer. Even if he hadn't killed him, he'd never have allowed him out of the room.
VIGARS:	(Tolerantly) Well, Miss, it's a theory.
LAURIE:	(Without any tolerance at all) And because it doesn't fit in with your idea of suicide, I suppose that's all it is. Just – (mimicking him) – a theory.
VIGARS:	I'm quite prepared to keep an open mind about it, Miss.
LAURIE:	Oh no you're not. That's the very last thing you're prepared to do. Once the police have adopted an official theory and have persuaded a coroner's jury to endorse it, that theory gets promoted. It becomes the truth. Which is convenient, because it allows the police to stop worrying about it and get on with their real work of persecuting motorists who drive without rear lights.
VIGARS:	I can quite understand your being upset, Miss.
LAURIE:	(Losing her temper) Ach, stop fathering me. Go away. Go and chivvy motorists. You've finished, haven't you? The case is closed. Then you've no more business here at all.
VIGARS:	(Still maddeningly refusing to lose his temper) That's quite all right. I'll wish you good morning.

(DOOR OPENS AND SHUTS)

GORDON:	(As Vigars goes) Poor man. You weren't very nice to him.
LAURIE:	I suppose not. I don't like dishonest policemen.
GORDON:	(Mildly) Dishonest?

LAURIE:	You heard the way the evidence was rigged at the inquest.
GORDON:	I thought most of it was pretty factual. The Squire saw your father walking down to the cottage around half past seven. I found him at a quarter past nine. And the doctor put the time of death between eight and nine which fitted in with both times.
LAURIE:	Oh, beautifully....
GORDON:	And nobody else had been seen near the cottage.
LAURIE:	They'd been heard though.
GORDON:	Heard?
LAURIE:	By you.
GORDON:	By me? Oh, that car you mean. I did mention that, you know.
LAURIE:	You did, and when the coroner asked the Inspector about it, what did *he* say? He said it was probably a car on the back road which had slowed down and was picking up speed again. You see? It didn't fit in with the suicide theory to have a car actually parked in the lay-by fifty yards from the cottage. So, it became a *passing* car. That's what I mean by being dishonest.
GORDON:	(Puzzled) Look here, Miss Bannister—
LAURIE:	Laurie.
GORDON:	Laurie. Do you really think – I mean – if it wasn't suicide – it could hardly have been an accident—
LAURIE:	Stop hedging. I think it was murder. I think Daddy was killed and poor Old Corporal at the same time.
GORDON:	But why?
LAURIE:	Because someone was afraid of what Daddy had written in the last chapter of his book.
GORDON:	*Had* written.
LAURIE:	Oh yes. It was finished all right. He told me so when I 'phoned him that day. I was coming down for the weekend.
GORDON:	You're sure? Sure he really had finished it?
LAURIE:	Daddy wouldn't lie to me. Why should he? He hadn't liked writing that chapter. It had upset him badly. I could tell that when I talked to him. He actually tried to stop me from coming down. So you see.
GORDON:	I'm not sure ...
LAURIE:	But it's perfectly obvious.

(WALKS ACROSS TO DESK AND TAKES OUT A

FOLDER OF TYPESCRIPT)

Here's the book, all except the last chapter. Right up to
the moment when he was betrayed to the Gestapo and
taken to their headquarters at Rouen and some of the
things they did to him. It makes you sick to read about it.
And to my mother. They cut off three of the fingers of her
right hand. One by one. To try and make her talk. It was
because of the things they did to her, I think, that she died
before she was thirty and if it hadn't been for the R.A.F.
they'd both have been finished off. The fighter-bombers
came in that night at roof top level and tore the place
apart. Almost the only people who survived were the
prisoners because they were down in the cellars. Daddy
carried my mother out of the ruins and they hobbled off
into the countryside and stayed hidden up till our armies
arrived.

GORDON: My God, what a story.

LAURIE: Yes, it's quite a story but it's a story without a finish,
because whilst they were in that foul prison, they must
have found out who the traitor was and that's what the
last chapter's about.

GORDON: Mmm....

LAURIE: Whatever you do, *don't* say 'It's a theory'. If you do I shall
hit you. It isn't a theory. It's the truth and if you don't
think it is the truth, answer me one question: *What's
happened to that chapter?*
No, it isn't there. I've turned the place upside down. I
thought Daddy might have posted it to me or the agent
or publisher. But he hadn't. It wasn't even burnt. You
can't burn twenty or thirty pages of manuscript without
leaving *some* trace.

GORDON: (Slowly) Do you know – I'm beginning to think that
perhaps there might be something in it.

LAURIE: It's so easy. Drive up by the back road. Park the car out
of sight. Walk up here. Knock on the door.

GORDON: But in the circumstances wouldn't your father have been
a bit embarrassed to see him?

LAURIE: Possibly. But knowing Daddy I'm quite certain he
wouldn't have allowed any degree of embarrassment to
stop him from offering him a drink. He'd offer the devil
a drink if he turned up unexpectedly. He'd have a capsule

ready to slip in Daddy's drink and a poisoned lump of meat for old Corporal. Drive off with the chapter in your pocket and your reputation safe. The reputation you've been carefully building up for a quarter of a century. A reputation which was going to be shown up as a rotten sham based on lies and cowardice and the torture and death of men and women who'd trusted you. There are people who'd kill for that.

GORDON: What are you going to do?

LAURIE: Find out who did it. If I can.

GORDON: What then?

LAURIE: I haven't thought as far as that. Maybe I'll tell him that I know, and watch him squirm. Then, if he's got a spare cyanide pill he'll swallow it himself rather than face what's coming.

GORDON: Nice girl.

LAURIE: And you're going to help me, aren't you?

GORDON: Am I?

LAURIE: It's your assignment. You've taken it on. The paper wouldn't like you to back out.

GORDON: I suppose they wouldn't really. Just how do you propose to start?

LAURIE: That's easy. The first thing we want to find out is who was involved in Daddy's war-time schemes and is still alive now. And we can start right here with Squire Naylor-Smith. He was in the same outfit.

GORDON: Right now, you mean?

LAURIE: Why not. He's at home. I saw his car outside the door when I came past. By the way, I wonder where *he* was that evening.

GORDON: What do you mean?

LAURIE: When you parked your car in the drive, did you see his car?

GORDON: No. And come to think of it, the house was dark too.

LAURIE: But when you went up to telephone. He was back then, wasn't he?

GORDON: What's so odd about that. He'd been out somewhere, and got back that's all—

(FADE OUT. FADE UP)

NAYLOR-SMITH: (His voice is so genuinely, authentically and absolutely county that one has a sneaking feeling that, like false teeth, the perfection is too absolute to be natural) Don't know that I can tell you much more, Laurie. Told it all to the Police. I saw your father when I was going out – had this County Agricultural nonsense in Halsfield. I told the police a quarter to eight. Only a guess, might have been five minutes either side, you know.

LAURIE:	Did Daddy say anything to you when you saw him?
N-SMITH:	Say anything? No. I don't think he *said* anything. Just waved. He was walking down to the cottage.
LAURIE:	You told the police he'd been depressed lately.
N-SMITH:	(<u>Vaguely</u>) Did I?
LAURIE:	That's what you said at the inquest.
N-SMITH:	At the inquest. Yes. Terrible acoustics in that hall. Half the time I couldn't hear what that coroner chap was saying.
LAURIE:	But you *did* think he'd been depressed.
N-SMITH:	Yes. (<u>Pause</u>) Yes. He had. (<u>Pause while he seeks the mot juste</u>) Down in the mouth.
LAURIE:	Did he say why?
N-SMITH:	I think it was the war. He never really got over it, you know. I think writing that book was a mistake.
LAURIE:	(<u>Sharply</u>) Oh. Why?
N-SMITH:	Brought it all back.
LAURIE:	But did he give any *particular* reason for being especially depressed lately?
N-SMITH:	No. Can't say he did. Matter of fact, we didn't see a great deal of each other at all. When I offered him the cottage I remember him saying 'all right, Tony. As long as we don't live in each other's laps'. All the time he lived there I don't suppose he came up to dinner twice.
LAURIE:	Did he talk to you about his book?
N-SMITH:	I knew he was writing it. Between you and me (<u>Pause</u>) I thought he was dragging his feet a bit.
LAURIE:	Oh?
N-SMITH:	Well, I mean to say, he'd been two or three years on the job. He ought to have been able to finish it in that time. I knew a man – well, he's a friend of a friend of mine – who writes six books a year. Been doing it for years. Of course, he's a professional.
LAURIE:	He didn't say anything about being in difficulties over the last chapter?

(SMITH WALKS AWAY TOWARDS DRINKS TABLE)
(APPEARS NOT TO HAVE HEARD LAST QUESTION)

N-SMITH:	Sun's over the yardarm. Like something to wet your whistle, Laurie?
LAURIE:	No thank you. I was asking if he said anything....
N-SMITH:	What about your friend?
GORDON:	Oh – well—
N-SMITH:	I usually take a whisky about now.
GORDON:	Thanks very much.
N-SMITH:	Soda or water? By the way, I didn't quite catch your name when Laurie introduced us.
GORDON:	Water please. Loftus. Gordon Loftus.
N-SMITH:	You knew Ben?
GORDON:	I knew of him. Everyone did. I never met him.

(ALL THIS WHILST DRINKS ARE BEING POURED OUT AND HANDED)

N-SMITH:	Really. Then you're a friend of Laurie's I imagine.
LAURIE:	Mr Loftus is a journalist. He works for the paper that was going to serialize daddy's book.
N-SMITH:	(Coldly) Oh. I see. I suppose you'll be able to cash in on this – this development. Can't say I approve of that sort of publicity. Seems wrong to me. But perhaps I'm old-fashioned.
LAURIE:	You've got this quite wrong. No one's cashing in on anything. At the moment the book's incomplete. The last chapter's missing.
N-SMITH:	Oh? Sad. Never had time to finish it. But still, I shouldn't think it'd matter too much, the paper'll find someone to – what's the word you chaps use when someone writes someone else's book for them?
GORDON:	Ghost.
N-SMITH:	Ghost. That's right, ghost. (The word seems to fascinate him. He says it again, almost to himself) Ghosts.
LAURIE:	A ghost-writer could only operate if he knew what he was meant to write. In this case it wouldn't be possible. The facts are missing.
N-SMITH:	(Casually) How's that? (Finishing drink)
LAURIE:	Daddy knew the name of the person who'd given them all

	away to the Germans. That was what was going in the last bit.
N-SMITH:	Are you sure of that? (<u>Back to her, by window – looking out</u>)
LAURIE:	Yes.
N-SMITH:	Did he ever tell *you* who it was?
LAURIE:	He never talked about the war at all. When Mummy was alive it would have hurt. After she died he seemed to want to forget it. All I knew I found out by reading his books. And that's full of hints and riddles.
N-SMITH:	And you think the answer would have been in the last chapter.
LAURIE:	Yes.
N-SMITH:	*If* he'd written it.
LAURIE:	He wrote it all right.
N-SMITH:	Then what happened to it?
LAURIE:	(<u>They now face each other</u>) It was stolen by the man who killed him.
N-SMITH:	Then I should think it's been destroyed by now. Wouldn't you?
LAURIE:	Possibly. (<u>Pause</u>) Or possibly not.
N-SMITH:	(<u>Breaking out of the clinch</u>) What do you want me to do?
LAURIE:	To help.
N-SMITH:	How?
LAURIE:	You were in the same – what did you call it – department, outfit, gang?
N-SMITH:	We called it the Circus actually.
LAURIE:	You knew what was going on, you knew who *could* have given things away to the Germans. There wouldn't have been many people involved I imagine – and a lot of them would be dead by now—
N-SMITH:	(<u>Softly</u>) Ghosts.
LAURIE:	What's that?
N-SMITH:	That's what you're asking me to do, Laurie, raise a lot of ghosts who've lain quiet in their graves for twenty-five years.
LAURIE:	Yes, I suppose I am.
N-SMITH:	(<u>He speaks clearly, but rather dreamily</u>) As you probably know, I was in charge of a section – it had some official name or number – I really forget what. *We* called it the Circus. We were the English terminal of a

bigger French outfit called 'Equipe Max', which operated in the Seine–Maritime area. Not a very healthy part
of the world in May 1944, crawling with Gestapo.
Vichy French militia, 'agents', double agents, plain trai-
tors – the lot. Equipe Max was about thirty Frenchmen
– and a woman. It had one single vital job. On D-day it
had to disrupt the whole German communications
centre in the Rouen area. Blow up wireless masts, cut
wires, wreck teleprinters. It had been preparing for it for
months. The Germans had come to suspect it existed
but they hadn't been able to penetrate it. Our job was to
supply the French team with anything they wanted –
and send two or three men over when the time came.
Co-ordinate the military side of the operation. Do you
get the picture?

GORDON: (Impressed) Yes Sir. That's quite clear. Who was involved
at this end?

N-SMITH: Just the three of us – four if you count Jessica.

GORDON: Jessica?

N-SMITH: Second Lieutenant Jessica Wrayburn, our wireless operator.

GORDON: Who were the other three.

N-SMITH: I was in charge. I was a temporary Major. Then there was
Captain Applin. Randolph Applin. And, of course, your
father. He'd actually been over in France for the last six
months. Six months was a hell of a long time to last at
that game. You needed luck and judgment.

(POURS HIMSELF OUT ANOTHER DRINK)

(To Gordon) Have another?

GORDON: Well – thank you. A small one.

N-SMITH: (To Laurie) You're sure you won't, Laurie?

LAURIE: No thanks.

N-SMITH: We operated from a small reception centre – just a couple
of rooms in a Nissan hut really – on the outskirts of an
airfield North of London. Jessica was the operator who
handled our confidential signals traffic:

(FADE OUT. FADE UP RAPID MORSE CODE. FIRST AS
HEARD THROUGH A RECEIVER. HIGH-PITCHED
BEEP-PEEP. FROM OUTSIDE THE HUT, THE NOISE OF

THE AIR-RAID ALERT SIRENS STARTING TO WAIL
OUT THEIR DISMAL WARNING)

JESSICA: Damn.

(WINDOW SHUT, WHILE MORSE CONTINUES. AIR-
RAID WARNING CONTINUES, BUT CONSIDERABLY
MUTED BY THE CLOSED WINDOW)
(DOOR OPENING LETS IN MIXTURE OF SOUND. AIR
RAID SIRENS LOUDER. SOMEONE SHOUTING
ORDERS. CAR BEING REVVED UP)

JESSICA: *Please*. Would you mind shutting the door.

BANNISTER: Parfaitement, mademoiselle.

JESSICA: Ben! Wait, wait. When did you get back?

BANNISTER: In the early hours of the morning. They've been debriefing
me ever since. Wouldn't even allow me time to shave.

JESSICA: It's lovely to see you. (Rattle of keys) Over and out.

BANNISTER: Venez-ici, mademoiselle.

(SOUND OF A COMPREHENSIVE EMBRACE)

JESSICA: Mmm. You haven't shaved, have you.

BANNISTER: It's lucky your Gerard isn't in England. If he caught me
doing that, it'd be pistols for two, at ten yards.

JESSICA: You're quite safe. That *was* Gerard.

BANNISTER: Who was?

JESSICA: Sending that message.

BANNISTER: Did he announce himself then? Bad security.

JESSICA: Of course not. But I knew.

BANNISTER: How?

JESSICA: When you've been taking down morse from someone for
six months you can tell his touch. It's like handwriting.
Quite unmistakeable.

BANNISTER: Handwriting! Nonsense! It's love.

JESSICA: Silly.

BANNISTER: There's Gerard sitting at his little transmitter in a hayloft
in Normandy. He touches the key, it's not a morse
message he sends, it's a message of the heart. A subtle
transmission to one recipient alone.

JESSICA: Six months in France hasn't cured you of talking
nonsense, I see.

BANNISTER:	(More seriously) It's cured me of a lot of other things.
JESSICA:	Such as?
BANNISTER:	Illusions, Jessica.
	(From the way they talk it is clear that these two, though not in love, are very much 'en rapport')
	I've seen men and women stripped down to the bone. I've seen that when it comes to the point, the only thing that counts with anyone is self-interest.
JESSICA:	With most people, Ben. Not all.
BANNISTER:	With all men. And most women. The north of France just now is a sweet little slice of hell. The French know we're coming – but they don't know when – so they're playing it off both ends of the pack. The Germans know – in their hearts – that when we do come, they'll be booted out of France. So the last phoney pair of kid-gloves has come off. They're playing it really rough now. Two weeks ago they strung up twelve workmen outside the power plant at Rennes because a dynamo broke down. They thought it was sabotage. It turned out to be a dud part from Germany. But it was too late to cut the twelve men down.
JESSICA:	Poor Ben. You must be glad to be out of it.
BANNISTER:	I'd be a lot happier if I could have brought my wife with me.
JESSICA:	Ben!! You didn't!! Marianne?
BANNISTER:	Yes.
JESSICA:	When?
BANNISTER:	On Easter Sunday actually.
JESSICA:	Oh Ben. I am glad for you. For both of you.
BANNISTER:	It wasn't exactly a white wedding. We were married by the curé in a small village outside Bayeux. Half the villagers turned up to watch, the other half were lying out round the village watching for Germans. We spent our honeymoon in a hut in the Maquis, specially built for us by the resistance. There was an alarm on the second night and we had to run for it.
JESSICA:	I'm glad it was the second night.
BANNISTER:	You've got a very nice mind, Jessica. I don't think we'll tell the others about it. Not just yet. Where is Randy anyway?
JESSICA:	Captain Applin's somewhere about nursing a hangover. I haven't seen Major Smith this morning.
BANNISTER:	They don't hit it off very well together, do they?

JESSICA:	I'm afraid they don't.
BANNISTER:	They'll have to make an effort – if they're going to work together in the field.
JESSICA:	*Are* they going over? How soon?
BANNISTER:	No one knows exactly when D-Day's going to be. But I wager we'll be over there before the end of next month.

(<u>DOOR OPENS</u>)

	Hullo Randy.
APPLIN:	By God, it's Ben. Well that's one cheerful sight in a bloody awful morning and whilst I think of it, congratulations.
JESSICA:	(<u>Thinking he is talking about marriage</u>) So you've heard.
APPLIN:	Of course I've heard. It was gazetted last week.
BANNISTER:	Oh, that!
APPLIN:	The modest hero on being informed that he had been awarded a second bar to his Military Cross, remarked 'Oh, that?'
JESSICA:	How splendid. I missed it.
APPLIN:	The snag is, it's making our Commanding Officer bloody jealous. *He'd* give anything in the world for a gong. And here's Ben got *three* – it's not fair.
BANNISTER:	(<u>Amused</u>) How is Tony?
APPLIN:	His normal bright bloody little self, what else.
BANNISTER:	Have you cured him of saying 'pardon' yet?
APPLIN:	Lord, yes. We've progressed well beyond that stage. He's a quick learner, is our Tony. When he was on leave he saw a film called 'Wings over the Reich'. Now everything's 'wizard prang' and 'shot down in flames'. Next thing he'll be telling Jessica she's got a trim little undercarriage.

(<u>SMACKS HER BOTTOM</u>)

JESSICA:	I think you're very unkind to Major Smith.
APPLIN:	You don't have to live with him, my poppet.
BANNISTER:	I should hope not.
APPLIN:	I wasn't referring to Tony's sex life. Always supposing he has one. If he got into bed with a girl, do you think he'd have a hand-book with him called 'Hints for the Upper-Class Lover'? Talking about sex life I hope you've been keeping an eye on Gerard, Ben. You know what these fiery Frenchmen are like.

BANNISTER:	Gerard has been behaving himself like a perfect gentleman.
APPLIN:	Not a single glance for les belles jeunes filles?
BANNISTER:	Not a glance. All his thoughts are for Jessica. They regularly tap out tender messages to each other.
APPLIN:	I've never tried making love by morse code. It must be quite an experience.
JESSICA:	Now you're both talking nonsense.

(DOOR OPENS)

APPLIN:	(With pseudo heartiness) Good morning, Major. How's the war going this morning.
SMITH:	(His tones are a good deal less County than when we heard them last) Were you aware that there is an air-raid alert in progress?
APPLIN:	The song of the sirens did penetrate my drink-sodden old eardrums some ten minutes ago.
SMITH:	It lays down quite clearly in Station Standing Orders, that *when* an alert is sounded *all* officers will carry steel helmets and respirators. If you don't do it, how can you expect the men to?
APPLIN:	I don't expect 'em to. It's a damn silly order and if I saw anyone not obeying it, I'd look the other way.
SMITH:	Hullo Ben. I heard you'd got back.
BANNISTER:	Oh? How?
SMITH:	I was pow-wowing with the DDA to the DDMI this morning and he told me you'd arrived.
APPLIN:	Touched down.
SMITH:	Come again?
APPLIN:	Touched down. In the Air Force we don't say 'arrived', Major. We say 'touched down'.
SMITH:	I was not aware that we'd been seconded to the Air Force.
APPLIN:	Let it go.
BANNISTER:	(Interested) Do you chaps spend *all* your time quarrelling?
APPLIN:	There isn't much else to do at the moment.
BANNISTER:	There soon will be.
APPLIN:	Ah!
SMITH:	Oh! (There is a shade more anxiety in Smith's reaction than in Applin's)

BANNISTER:	Didn't the DDA to the DDMI tell you?
SMITH:	No. He didn't say anything.
BANNISTER:	I gather that Mission Zero is to be placed on twenty-four hours notice to leave for France. That'll be you, Tony and Randy, plus a signaller. I expect Sergeant Truman will be told off for that job.
SMITH:	Is this just a a latrinogram, or is it true gen?
BANNISTER:	Top quality gen.
SMITH:	Then I think he might have told me first. Between you and I....
APPLIN:	You and me.
SMITH:	(To Ben) How do you know this is official?
BANNISTER:	Because I've been told to put you both in the picture as quickly as possible.
SMITH:	(Uneasily) I see.
APPLIN:	(Who has been watching him closely) No good wriggling, Tony. Zero hour is on us.
SMITH:	I don't find that remark funny.
APPLIN:	Actually, it wasn't meant to be.
BANNISTER:	You two should make a wonderful team in the field.
SMITH:	I don't imagine we shall see a great deal of each other. I shall be organising the base.
BANNISTER:	It's clear to me from that remark, Tony, that you've no idea what's really going on. When you talk about a base it pre-supposes an orderly arrangement with the enemy in front of you and your own troops behind you. It's not like that with the Equipe Max. The enemy is all round you. He's also in the middle of you.
SMITH:	Do you mean that the Equipe Max has been penetrated?
BANNISTER:	*That's* something we'd all like to know. The next door outfit, the Equipe Domodossola was broken up last month. No one knows where the leak occurred. Some say it was a girl who was not in the Equipe but knew a member of it and knew the work he was doing. She was indiscreet. The Gestapo forced her to reveal his name. He was taken secretly after dark and tortured all that night. They had to break him down quick, you see, because all these teams are organised in the same way. One man only knows three other names. Those three will know three different names. And those in turn, three others. If you work it out, you can see that in this way a team of 27 men can be covered in three rings.

SMITH: (<u>Speaking as if reluctantly</u>) What happened to him – to the man they – (<u>he cannot say 'tortured'</u>) to the man they caught?

BANNISTER: I know what they did to him, but it'd only upset you if I told you. He was dead by morning but he'd spoken the three names that mattered. They, too, were taken. From that point the disintegration of the ring was certain. It took a month.

SMITH: Does *no-one* know *all* the names in a team?

BANNISTER: No one who can be made to talk. Only the top-brass in London.

SMITH   But....

APPLIN: Go on, Tony, say it.

SMITH: I was only going to point out that we here know *all* the names and details of the Equipe Max. In the circumstances, might it be rather dangerous to allow us to go into the field. (<u>Conscious that the others are looking at him</u>) I agree, of course, that the military side of the operation has got to *be* organised. It occurred to me to wonder whether it couldn't be – well – just as efficiently organised from here.

BANNISTER: (<u>Quite gently</u>) The Equipe Max has been set up to undertake one, very important, very dangerous task. Every man and woman in it will be risking their lives. When troops are asked to do that, they like to see their officers alongside them.

APPLIN: Do you think the sight of Tony will *really* improve their morale.

SMITH: (<u>Really angry</u>) You've gone too far.

BANNISTER: Easy, Tony. He's only pulling your leg. The answer to your first question is this little gadget. There! You can wear it quite comfortably attached to your back teeth. I don't wear one because I'm always afraid I might chew it up by accident. But a lot of our chaps do.

SMITH: What's in it?

BANNISTER: It's cyanide. It'll kill you in six seconds.

(<u>THE ALL CLEAR SIGNAL STARTS FAINTLY,
CRESCENDO, TILL WE SEEM TO BE SITTING RIGHT
UP AGAINST THE SIREN, DIMINUENDO, FADING
RIGHT AWAY TO SILENCE. IN THE SILENCE RATTLE
OF A MORSE KEY AND ANSWERING PEEP-PEEP.</u>)

(DOOR OPENS AND HEAVY MALE FOOTSTEPS CROSS THE HUT AND STOP. RADIO OPERATOR SIGNS OFF WITH A FLOURISH)

BANNISTER:	What is it, Jessica? Another routine message, with love and kisses from Gerard.
JESSICA:	It was from Gerard. But it's not routine. I know that. I can't tell you *what* it is until I've decoded it.
BANNISTER:	Do you never get tired?
JESSICA:	X repeat X.... What can he mean by that?.... Oh, I see. What did you say?
BANNISTER:	I've been watching you do this for ten days. You seem to work a twenty-four day. You must get tired sometimes.
JESSICA:	(Working as she speaks) I'm sure that the people in the field get a lot tireder than I do. I can tell exactly what sort of day Gerard's been having from the way he transmits. I can tell whether he's fresh, or tired. Or cheerful because things are going well. Or depressed – or scared.
BANNISTER:	That's permanent, believe me. You're scared *all* the time.
JESSICA:	Once, I even knew he'd been drinking too much.
BANNISTER:	Don't tell me you could smell his breath over the air.
JESSICA:	There was a sort of flourish – a panache – about his sending.
BANNISTER:	He'd better watch out for it when you're married. (Change of tone as he looks at Jessica) What is it?
JESSICA:	You'd better read it.
BANNISTER:	Oh. (Pause) Oh, not too good.

(DOOR OPENS)

APPLIN:	You've both got faces like a wet Monday. Something wrong?
BANNISTER:	Read this.
JESSICA:	The Major ought to see this message at once.
APPLIN:	Do you think Gerard may be exaggerating, lost his nerve or something.
BANNISTER:	Gerard's not given to panicking. If he says the Gestapo is sniffing round the Equipe Max – they're sniffing. It's May 25th. No moon. Something tells me you'll be off tonight.
APPLIN:	Then you must let *me* have the pleasure of telling Tony.
BANNISTER:	You don't think he'll like it?

APPLIN: (<u>Viciously</u>) Like it? He'll love it. He'll love it so much he'll wet his pants.

BANNISTER: When it comes to the point, he'll probably be as good as any of us.

APPLIN: Care to bet on it? I'll give you long odds. I've been studying Tony's running form. Joined up in 1940. In 1942 his regiment was ordered to North Africa. A week before it went, Tony transfers to Five Corps. In England. 1943, Five Corps goes to Italy. Tony transfers to this outfit. Two *very* neat pieces of evasive action. Do you realize he's sat out four years of this war without hearing a shot fired in anger?

(<u>DURING THE END OF THIS TONY SMITH HAS COME INTO THE ROOM QUIETLY, HE MUST HAVE HEARD AT LEAST THE LAST SENTENCES, POSSIBLY MORE</u>)

APPLIN: (<u>A momentary loss of assurance</u>) Oh – hello Tony. We've got some news for you.

BANNISTER: I'll tell him. We've had this from Equipe Max. Some bad trouble is blowing up.

SMITH: (<u>Expressionless</u>) Oh?

BANNISTER: It looks as if they're going to want your help.

SMITH: Mmm.... When?

BANNISTER: We're in the middle of the no-moon period. Jessica could send a message now. If we get a positive response you could go tonight.

SMITH: Can the RAF be ready in time?

BANNISTER: They've had a plane standing by for the last three days.

SMITH: (<u>After a pause</u>) Then I'd better warn Sergeant Truman.

(<u>DOOR CLOSES WITH A BANG</u>)

BANNISTER: Well, he took that on the chin.

APPLIN: He's gone off to pack and you know what his kit will consist of? One cyanide capsule on each tooth and a box of spares in his pocket.

BANNISTER: Hadn't you better be getting your own stuff together?

APPLIN: I suppose I had. (<u>Going</u>) Next time you're chatting on that machine of yours to Gerard, darling, tell him to put a hot water bottle in my bed.

(<u>DOOR CLOSES</u>)

BANNISTER: (<u>Sighs</u>) I don't know which of them I find least attractive. But I can tell you this, Jessie. If they keep up this feuding when they get to France, they'll be written off pretty fast. All right. That's their look-out. But they may get a lot of other people killed too. In which case, I think they'd better *not* come back.

(<u>FADE OUT. FADE UP DEAFENING ROAR OF A LIBER-ATOR TAKING OFF DOWN THE FLIGHT PATH. SAME NOISE MUCH FAINTER HEARD FROM INSIDE OF THE HUT FADES UP. FADE RIGHT OUT TILL ALL THAT CAN BE HEARD IS TICKING OF THE CLOCK</u>).

BANNISTER: (<u>Yawning prodigiously</u>) What time is it, Jessie?
JESSICA: Five to one. They should be there by now, shouldn't they?
BANNISTER: *If* everything's gone according to plan. Which it never does. Yes. They should be dropping now.
JESSICA: What's it like? I've often wondered.
BANNISTER: It's a wonderful sensation when the parachute opens. A feeling of complete release. For a whole minute you don't belong to earth or air. There's no sensation of falling. Actually, it's more like flying—

(<u>THE RADIO GIVES A WARNING 'PEEP'</u>)

JESSICA: That'll be them now.

(<u>SHORT MORSE MESSAGE</u>)

BANNISTER: What is it? (<u>Reading</u>) 'Party arrived. Reception safely completed'. What's that?
JESSICA: (<u>In a strangled voice</u>) That's Gerard's call sign.
BANNISTER: Well, that's all right then. (<u>Pause</u>) Jessie – what's wrong?
JESSICA: It's Gerard's call sign. But it wasn't Gerard transmitting. It was someone pretending to be him.
BANNISTER: God! The Gestapo's moved in.

(<u>FADE RIGHT OUT. FADE UP</u>)

N-SMITH:	(<u>It is noticeable how much his accent and intonation have improved in the intervening 25 years</u>) Of course, you understand I didn't hear about a lot of that until much later – some of it only after the war – when I got the full picture of what was happening whilst the three of us were floating down into occupied France.
GORDON:	Floating down into the outstretched hands of the Gestapo I imagine, Sir.
N-SMITH:	If it hadn't been for an extraordinary stroke of luck, that's exactly what we should have done. They'd located Gerard with their direction finders – caught him actually transmitting – extracted the details of our rendezvous from him – poor devil.
GORDON:	You called that luck?
N-SMITH:	No. The luck came when our pilot made a nonsense of his map reading and put us down in the wrong place. It wasn't exactly a comfortable landing. We came down among a lot of brickstacks. Sergeant Truman hit the top of a chimney. He was killed. Applin broke an ankle. I landed a little further on. I was only winded. I managed to get to a farm.
GORDON:	What happened to Applin?
N-SMITH:	When he could move, he made his way back towards Cherbourg. He was picked up soon after the D-Day Landings.
GORDON:	He didn't try to get in touch with you?
N-SMITH:	(<u>Coldly</u>) He may have tried – all I can say is that he didn't succeed.
GORDON:	So you were on your own?
N-SMITH:	Yes. A day or two later Max got through to me. That's when I heard about Gerard being captured. Max wasn't too worried. Gerard didn't know any names. His job was simply to transmit.
GORDON:	That meant you were in a position to pick up the pieces and get on with the job?
N-SMITH:	No doubt I should have been – but there was a further – and I must say, somewhat unfortunate – development. It was your father, Laurie. He arrived in France. He came over against the wishes of our superiors. I'm not at all sure that it wasn't against orders.
LAURIE:	(<u>Sharply back on the scene again, from over by the window</u>). He was never a great one for taking orders.

N-SMITH:	In this case – if you'll excuse me saying so – de mortuis and so on – it might have been a good thing if he had.
LAURIE:	(<u>Very sharp. Her next five speeches are barked out like prosecuting counsel</u>) You can say what you like. It won't hurt him now.
N-SMITH:	It's *your* feelings I was thinking about, Laurie.
LAURIE:	Don't fuss yourself about my feelings. What we want are facts.
N-SMITH:	Of course, of course.
LAURIE:	After all, most of the people concerned are dead, aren't they?
N-SMITH:	(<u>Uncomfortably</u>) Yes. They are.
LAURIE:	And what we say won't worry them.
N-SMITH:	No – naturally—
LAURIE:	And you needn't worry about *my* feelings. So say what you like.
N-SMITH:	(<u>Somewhat thrown by this savage interruption</u>) Well – as I was saying – your father insisted on coming over. It was quite natural – no doubt he was worried about your mother – (<u>Waits for some reaction but gets none</u>) – But there was no time to make proper arrangements for his reception. Gerard had been taken. Sergeant Truman was dead. There wasn't even a reliable signaller. Ben landed blind. And he was caught almost immediately. And taken off to their Gestapo prison at Rouen.
GORDON:	Did you see him – before he was captured?
N-SMITH:	No. I was – (<u>Pause</u>) – I was lying doggo at this farm. As soon as the news of Ben's capture came through *everyone* went to ground. It wasn't that they thought that he would talk. They knew him too well – but there comes a time – even the bravest man—
LAURIE:	(<u>Harshly</u>) I know what they did to him. It's in his book. I know what they did to my mother, too. *They* didn't talk. Neither of them talked.
N-SMITH:	No.
LAURIE:	Do you mean no. Or are you saying it to please me?
N-SMITH:	(<u>After a slight pause</u>) I mean No. They would neither of them have talked. They weren't that sort of person.
LAURIE:	(<u>Gently</u>) But someone talked, didn't they?
N-SMITH:	Yes.
GORDON:	How can you be sure of that, Laurie?
LAURIE:	Obviously, because in one night, about a week later, every

man and woman working for Equipe Max was pulled out of their beds and shot. (<u>To Naylor-Smith</u>) That's right, isn't it? That's what happened.

N-SMITH: (<u>Unhappily</u>) Yes.

GORDON: Good God! Who – I mean – did anyone ever find out— (<u>Pause</u>)

N-SMITH: Several people were suspected. French collaborators – no one ever knew for certain.

LAURIE: That's where you're wrong – (<u>Murmur from the other two</u>) Daddy knew.

GORDON: How could he have known if he was in prison?

LAURIE: He knew because the Gestapo told him. It was their technique. They enjoyed gloating over him and demonstrating their power and omniscience. It was part of the process of breaking him down. And, of course, they didn't mind *him* knowing. They were going to liquidate him anyway. And they would have done if the RAF hadn't laid on this raid and blasted the whole vile place out of existence.

N-SMITH: (<u>A bit too casually</u>) Did he tell you all this, Laurie?

LAURIE: (<u>Smilingly</u>) He told me that he knew. But he wouldn't tell even me who it was – (<u>Pause</u>) You were saying that during all this time you were – lying doggo?

N-SMITH: We all kept our heads down for a bit. Then I managed to get out and about, and do a spot of organisation behind the lines. The Equipe Max was gone but there were other teams doing useful work – disrupting communications – sabotage – that sort of thing. We carried on like that for three months until the final break out.

LAURIE: Which teams?

N-SMITH: Pardon? (<u>Correcting himself</u>) What did you say?

LAURIE: You said – there were other teams. They all had code names didn't they?

N-SMITH: Well – yes. There was – let me think – there was the Croix de Lorraine team and the Hercules Organisation in the Amiens area. Those were the main ones.

LAURIE: And you worked with them?

N-SMITH: Yes.

LAURIE: What did you actually do?

N-SMITH: Well – it's a difficult question to answer – in a few words. I suppose you might say that I co-ordinated their efforts—

LAURIE:	Successfully?
N-SMITH:	(<u>Smilingly</u>) I think we had a fair degree of success – yes.
LAURIE:	Then why didn't the French give you a medal?
N-SMITH:	My dear Laurie, the answer to that is quite simple. When General de Gaulle assumed charge, it didn't suit his book to emphasise the efforts of his allies. What medals there were went to the French.
LAURIE:	I see.
N-SMITH:	(<u>Smugly</u>) However, the English were apparently not dissatisfied with my efforts.
LAURIE:	You mean they gave you a Military Cross?
GORDON:	(<u>Who evidently considers they have been straying from the point</u>) Just a minute. I've been trying to think this out. If the Gestapo suddenly swooped down and pulled in everyone, it can't have been a process of gradual breaking down. They must have had an actual list – all the names—
LAURIE:	Obviously.
GORDON:	How many people *knew* all the names – apart from your father?
LAURIE:	It's a fair question.
N-SMITH:	Two or three people in London. High-ups.
GORDON:	But the Germans couldn't have brought pressure on people like that. Who both knew and was in reach of the Gestapo?
N-SMITH:	Well – really – I suppose the only person – actually – was Applin.
LAURIE:	(<u>Sweetly</u>) Oh, but, there was *one* other person wasn't there?
N-SMITH:	If you're implying—
LAURIE:	I wasn't implying anything. I was stating a fact. There *was* at least one other person who knew *all* the names.
N-SMITH:	(<u>Rather pompous</u>) Ever since you came in here you've been making hints and suggestions. If you have any accusation to make, I suggest you make it in plain terms.
LAURIE:	Of course.
N-SMITH:	Well, then?
LAURIE:	I was thinking of Second Lieutenant Jessica Wrayburn.
N-SMITH:	(<u>This is obviously a facer</u>) Jessica? But she wasn't in France at all.
LAURIE:	No, but Gerard was. The Gestapo were holding him. And she was in love with him.

N-SMITH: (<u>Thinking it out</u>) But – how – I don't see.

LAURIE: You're not trying very hard, are you? The Germans had a private line of communication over the wireless directly to her and no one else. All they had to say was – give us the names – and we'll treat Gerard gently and you can have him back in one piece after the war.

N-SMITH: Good God!

LAURIE: Of course they broke their word. They always did. But she wasn't to know that.

GORDON: What actually happened to her?

N-SMITH: Jessica? After the war? I didn't see a lot of her. When she heard about Gerard's death she seemed to – freeze up. She became very detached – almost inhuman. It's difficult to describe it.

LAURIE: As far as I'm concerned you don't have to describe it. I knew the lady well.

N-SMITH: You know her?

LAURIE: I spent four unhappy years at St. Monica's School for girls – I beg your pardon – for young ladies – at Ashford. Miss Jessica Wrayburn, C.B.E. was the headmistress and one of the principal causes of my unhappiness.

(<u>FADE OUT. FADE UP</u>)

BATSON: (<u>On telephone, talking to his superior, the Editor, shade more respect in his voice than previously – one-sided conversation</u>) Oh, good morning, Sir. I agree. It could be big. Very big indeed. (<u>Pause</u>) The suicide verdict killed the Inquest, but if we could prove that the verdict was wrong. Get it re-opened. We shouldn't be sitting on half a story then. We should have a story and a half. (<u>Pause</u>) I've got Loftus here with me now. (<u>Pause</u>) I'll warn him about that. (<u>Pause</u>) I couldn't agree more. We've got to be damned careful. All the people involved are pretty important. One's a Deputy Lieutenant of the County, and a J.P. One's the headmistress of a large girls' school and, I understand, next in line for the headship of an Oxford College. And the third – well, that's Randolph Applin. If not the biggest fish, certainly the richest. (<u>Pause</u>) Yes, I'll impress that on him.

(<u>TELEPHONE RECEIVER DOWN</u>)

GORDON:	You've located Applin then?
BATSON:	Randy didn't take a lot of locating. He's not the shrinking violet type who hides his light under a bushel. He owns at least three very successful gambling clubs. Officially, they're members' clubs, but the only real qualification for membership is a full wallet.
GORDON:	Are they crooked?
BATSON:	The police say no. The play's straight. It's the debt-collecting that's a bit rough. Suppose you had a bad evening and wrote out a cheque for your losses. And suppose it occurred to you, in the cold light of morning, to stop the cheque. A bit later on you might receive a visitor who would – persuade you to change your mind.
GORDON:	You mean he employs a lot of thugs who'd come and beat you up.
BATSON:	Right.
GORDON:	He sounds rather a rough character himself.
BATSON:	Ye-e-es. You'll have to be pretty careful when you interview him.
GORDON:	When I—?
BATSON:	We could hardly expect Miss Bannister to do it, could we?
GORDON:	But surely – the Police—
BATSON:	Unofficially, I gather the Police are very interested in Randolph Applin. Officially – they haven't got enough evidence, yet, to justify an inquiry. On the other hand, it would seem quite natural for you – with this story to follow up – to go and have a word with him. Wouldn't it?
GORDON:	(Unhappily) I suppose so. Yes.
BATSON:	Right – well – the Riverboat Club is the one the Major uses as his headquarters. It's on the Thames, above Staines. It's got the extra advantage – from his point of view – that it's on an island. A private island. That means he can carry on his operations with the minimum of interference.
GORDON:	(Still more unhappily) With the minimum of interference. I see. Charming.
BATSON:	I suggest you go along this evening. Got in as an ordinary gambler. You can draw twenty pounds out of the petty cash float. Right?
GORDON:	(Moving to door) All right. I – (Changes his mind about what he was going to say) – Yes, all right.

(DOOR CLOSES. RECEIVER PICKED UP. DIALLING)

BATSON: (As the thought has struck him) Miss Ponsonby. You might check up that we've got the normal accident insurance on Loftus, would you. Gordon Loftus. That's right.

(FADE OUT. FADE UP SOUNDS OF GAMBLING CLUB. ROULETTE WHEELS.)
(FADE OUT. FADE UP SOUNDS OF PRIVATE GAMBLING CLUBS. ROULETTE WHEELS CLICKING)

CROUPIERS'
VOICES: (Bit short on accent) Rouge et pair/Rien ne va plus, etc.

(BACKGROUND HELD FOR A SECOND. DOOR SHUTS FADE OUT BACKGROUND, FADE UP FOOTSTEPS ON BOARD. PAUSE. NERVOUS COUGH. TIMID KNOCK AT A DOOR. RATHER FIRMER KNOCK. NO RESPONSE. CREAK OF DOOR OPENING AND SHUTTING. MORE FOOTSTEPS ON LINOLEUM. PAUSE)

GORDON: Oh, Private. Well let's try in here.
LESLIE: (From behind) Hey!
GORDON: (Startled) What – I didn't see you there.
LESLIE: (Cockney) No? Can't you read? P'raps you're blind or something. (Anxiously) You aren't blind, are you?
GORDON: No.
LESLIE: What that notice says is 'Private'. Strictly Private. That means – Keep out. Admission by appointment only. See?
GORDON: Yes – I – I can see that.
LESLIE: (Coming closer) What d'you want anyway?
GORDON: I – um. I had a complaint to make.
LESLIE: A complaint, eh.
GORDON: It seemd to me to be odd that zero should come up three times running – particularly with so much money on the board.
LESLIE: You think the wheel's bent, or something.
GORDON: I thought it needed looking into.
LESLIE: Which table?
GORDON: (Who obviously hasn't thought it out) Which table?
LESLIE: That's right. Which table was it zero came up on three times.

GORDON: Oh – the one in the middle. The main one.

(<u>CLICK OF HOUSE TELEPHONE RECEIVER BEING LIFTED</u>)

LESLIE: Harry? Leslie here. I've got a geezer here complaining you've been having too much zero. (<u>Pause</u>) Ah. (<u>Pause</u>) I just wondered. (<u>Pause</u>) No bother. I can handle it. (<u>A menacing note creeps into his voice</u>) You've been telling fibs mister. The big table hasn't had a zero all evening. What's the game?

GORDON: I'll tell Major Applin, when I see him.

LESLIE: But *will* you see him? That's the point, lad. Who are you?

GORDON: Nothing to do with you. Now, kindly step out of the way.

LESLIE: You're not a Policeman, are you?

GORDON: I'm—

LESLIE: No. I thought not. You look stupid. But not quite that stupid. Wait! I got it! You're a private eye. Like on the films, with all them lovely girls. What I can't make out is, if they've got all them lovely girls, why they waste their time detecting. You ever think of that?

GORDON: Will you get out of the way.

LESLIE: We had a private detective here last winter. He fell in the river. Laugh! Mind you, it wasn't too funny, because it was Christmas Eve and the river was full of sodding great lumps of ice.

GORDON: Look here—

LESLIE: The water's a bit warmer tonight. All the same. It's a hundred yard swim, best part of. Won't do that sharp suit of yours much good. So if I was you, lad—

GORDON: (<u>With more firmness than he feels</u>) Get out of my way.

(<u>FEET STAMPING, A BLOW, AND A SHARP RATHER STARTLED CRY FROM GORDON AS LESLIE CATCHES HIM A CHOP ON THE FOREARM</u>)

LESLIE: (<u>Slightly breathless</u>) You know something, I changed my mind about you. I don't think you can be a private detective. You wouldn't lay yourself open like that if you was. Give you a tip. When you're aiming to hit someone, don't signal your intentions. Let it come out of the blue.

(THUD)

Like that.

(SOUND OF DOOR OPENING)

APPLIN:	Leslie!
LESLIE:	Yes, Major.
APPLIN:	Who is it?
LESLIE:	There's been a number of different theories about that, Major.
APPLIN:	Who are you? What do you want?
GORDON:	(Just able to speak). Newspaper man.
APPLIN:	Which paper?
GORDON:	Daily News.
APPLIN:	Got anything to prove it?
GORDON:	Wallet.
APPLIN:	(After a pause) Daily News. Second largest circulation in Great Britain. That's no way to handle our public relations, Leslie. Come inside, Mr Loftus.

(DOOR SHUTTING)

	Have a drink.
GORDON:	Well—
APPLIN:	That's right.

(POURS OUT A DRINK)

	You don't want to take too much notice of Leslie. He's just a natural delinquent. Here you are. Unhappy home background I wouldn't wonder.
GORDON:	Thanks.
APPLIN:	Now – what can I do for you, Mr – (Pause, while he looks at card) – Loftus? We're not afraid of publicity here. Nothing to hide. Everything's fair, square and above board. Nothing to shock the vicar. We had a vicar in here the other night. Took a packet off us at chemmy, too.
GORDON:	As a matter of fact, it wasn't your club I wanted to talk about, Major Applin.
APPLIN:	Oh?
GORDON:	It was about your war-time experiences.

APPLIN: (More cagily) Oh?

GORDON: I don't know if you read in the papers about Ben Bannister.

APPLIN: (Thoughtfully between drinks) Poor old Ben. Yes. I read about it. I did hear he'd been going a bit queer lately. Not to be wondered at really, when you think of what the bastards did to him—

GORDON: The thing is, some people had a sort of idea that it mightn't have been suicide.

APPLIN: No? (Pause) Odd sort of accident.

GORDON: Not an accident.

APPLIN: No? (Brief silence) Perhaps you'd better tell me what this is all in aid of. For a start, just how do you come into it?

GORDON: I was sent down by my paper to see about a book he was writing—

APPLIN: You the chap who found the body?

GORDON: I found it. Miss Bannister turned up a few minutes later.

APPLIN: Laurie, oh? Quite a girl. (Chuckles) Mind of her own. I bet it's her idea someone knocked off her old man. Am I right?

GORDON: In a way – yes.

APPLIN: And *she* thinks it's something to do with what happened in the War? Someone who didn't want her Dad to blow the gaff in that book of his?

GORDON: As a matter of fact, he *had* blown the gaff. He'd finished the book. But someone seems to have walked off with the last chapter.

APPLIN: How do you know he'd finished it?

GORDON: He told his daughter so.

APPLIN: Did he *show* her the finished job?

GORDON: No. But he said he'd done it.

APPLIN: Ah. Well I'll tell you what I think, Loftus. I think Laurie's got a bee in her bonnet. Odd girl. Odd upbringing. Wasn't spanked enough when she was young.

GORDON: She's certainly a very – determined – girl.

APPLIN: I mean, let's get the thing into perspective. Agreed, none of us came very well out of that last show – except Ben and his missus, of course. But the War's been over a bloody long time. It's ancient history.

GORDON: I wonder if you could tell me what actually happened to you?

APPLIN: (Pause) You won't get much copy out of *my* story son. I broke my ankle coming down and had to be ferried back to safety. Mostly in the backs of carts. Once I travelled under a load of turnips and I can tell you, it's a bloody uncomfortable way of travelling. (<u>Guffaws</u>) No. I'd had my belly-full of cloak-and-dagger. I got back to a nice safe job in the Sappers and finished the War helping to run the docks at Hamburg. And was *that* a place for piling up the crackle. If I could have got home half the stuff I laid my hands on, I could have filled a ship. On second thoughts, you'd better leave that out of your report. It might be misunderstood.

GORDON: One thing I couldn't understand was how you came to miss Major Smith. I mean – you both jumped out of the same 'plane.

APPLIN: I jumped. He was pushed. And it took a bloody long time to push him.

GORDON: How do you know that?

APPLIN: I talked to the despatcher who kicked him out. Mind you, I wasn't surprised. Tony was one great big bluff. Well – he got away with it. So good luck to him. (<u>Drinks</u>) It's funny when you come to think of it, Loftus. In the Kaiser's War the people who did best, so I've heard, were the hard faced businessmen who stayed at home. The losers were the poor bastards who went out to the trenches and got killed. Hitler's War, it was just the other way round. The people who really *made* something out of the war were the Tony Smiths. (<u>Unconsciously the light touch goes, and venom begins to creep in</u>). Look what his M.C. and his phoney war record did for him. It got him a seat on the Board. Before the war, he was a salesman. Then it hoisted him up to be Chairman *and* it got him a rich wife and that's when plain Mr Smith became Naylor-bloody-Smith. She had the tact to break her neck out hunting two years after they were married. So now he's got an estate in the country and every letter after his name you can think of from J.P. to B.F.

GORDON: You seem to have kept in pretty close touch with his career, Major.

APPLIN: (<u>Change of tone. He seems to realise he has blown off more steam than he meant to</u>) I haven't seen him for years. You can't help reading about him in the glossies.

GORDON:	You said his war record was phoney.
APPLIN:	That's right.
GORDON:	Your theory is that during those three months he was behind the lines he simply lay low. Saved his own skin. And all that organising resistance groups was lies.
APPLIN:	That's roughly it.
GORDON:	Did it occur to you that he might have been picked up by the Gestapo and *bought* his safety by giving away the whole Equipe Max?
APPLIN:	And?
GORDON:	And Ben found out about it. And was going to tell the truth in his book. Wouldn't Squire Naylor-Smith D.L., J.P., have gone to *any* lengths to stop that?
APPLIN:	(Half to himself) I don't believe he'd have the guts. (To Gordon) Anyway, you'll never prove it now. All the German records at Rouen were destroyed. All the Frenchmen who might have known are dead. And most of the English too.
GORDON:	But not all.
APPLIN:	(Ugly) Thinking of anyone in particular?
GORDON:	I was thinking of your wireless operator. Second Lieutenant Jessica Wrayburn.
APPLIN:	Jessica. Good Lord. I haven't seen her or thought about her for twenty-five years. She was a nice girl. I wonder what's become of her?

(FADE OUT. FADE UP KNOCK ON DOOR)

JESSICA:	(25 years of increasing authority has changed her voice almost as radically as his ascent in the social scale has changed Tony Smith's) Come in.

(DOOR OPENS)

Good gracious! It's Laurie. What a nice surprise. Come in.

(DOOR CLOSES)

	Do sit down.
LAURIE:	Thank you Miss Wrayburn.
JESSICA:	Mmm. You haven't changed, I see.
LAURIE:	Oh?

191

JESSICA:	You always were an – extremist.
LAURIE:	(<u>Puzzled</u>) An extremist? Oh, I see. You mean my skirt. (<u>Scrape of chair as she hitches it forwards a fraction</u>)
JESSICA:	It is a bit – abbreviated.
LAURIE:	Just the relic of a natural revolt against school clothes. Do the girls still wear those hideous uniforms?
JESSICA:	(<u>Sighs</u>) Last year the Governors decided that the Sixth Form could wear what they liked. When we saw the clothes they came back in, we rather wished they hadn't.
LAURIE:	At least it shows you're moving with the times.
JESSICA:	Not *with* the times, Laurie. No school moves *with* the times. Ten years behind them. Like the House of Lords. I read about your father, I'm sorry.
LAURIE:	(<u>Shortly</u>) Yes. Do you mind if I smoke?
JESSICA:	Please do. Did he ever talk to you about the War?
LAURIE:	Hardly ever. It was only the other day that I happened to find out – from someone else – that you were colleagues.
JESSICA:	Colleague – rather too grand a word. I was the maid-of-all-work in his outfit.
LAURIE:	I suppose that's why he sent me to school here. It seemed most unsuitable in every other way.
JESSICA:	*You* wouldn't have fitted comfortably into any school, Laurie.
LAURIE:	What makes you think that?
JESSICA:	You're a natural non-conformist. St Monica's happens to be a Conservative school. We follow traditional patterns—
LAURIE:	I know. Cricket, the Classics and Confirmation before the age of consent.
JESSICA:	—So, naturally you adopted an ultra-modern left-wing pose.
LAURIE:	What makes you think it was a pose?
JESSICA:	My dear Laurie, of course it was a pose. If your father had sent you to a progressive school – one of those tiresome places where girls are encouraged to call the mistresses by their christian names and smoke and drink between classes – you'd have come out as a true blue conservative reactionary.
LAURIE:	Well, it's a theory. That's what a policeman I know says when he thinks you're talking nonsense. By the way, I met Miss Crofts on my way in.

JESSICA:	Oh yes?
LAURIE:	I'm glad she's still here. I liked her. She was faintly human.
JESSICA:	I must tell her.
LAURIE:	She said that St Monica's might have to be looking for a new headmistress soon. Is that true?
JESSICA:	(Slightly put out) It's true. But I wasn't aware that it was public knowledge.
LAURIE:	These things get out. Is it right that you're in line for Oxford?
JESSICA:	Unofficially, I believe that the decision has already been made.
LAURIE:	In your favour?
JESSICA:	I understand so.
LAURIE:	I wonder how you will make out with the students.
JESSICA:	(Grimly) You think we shall come into conflict?
LAURIE:	Sure to, I know what I'm talking about.
JESSICA:	You may be right.
LAURIE:	There's one topic I *am* an expert on. I took part in more student demonstrations than any other girl in my year. The high point was when I was arrested for assault on a Police Inspector. You don't approve?
JESSICA:	It's not the sort of item I should include in our 'News of Old Girls' Activities'. I suppose that a certain amount of dissent is a healthy symptom.
LAURIE:	That sounds fine. But you wait till they start throwing tomatoes.
JESSICA:	One must learn to dodge.
LAURIE:	And fill the petrol tank of your car with treacle.
JESSICA:	Goodness! Do they still do that nowadays? It was nice of you to come and warn me. I must have a lock fitted to the petrol cap. (Gets up) I have so enjoyed our talk.
LAURIE:	Er—
JESSICA:	Yes?
LAURIE:	There was something else I wanted to talk about.
JESSICA:	(Sitting again) Yes?
LAURIE:	It was about Daddy's death.
JESSICA:	Oh?
LAURIE:	You read about the inquest?
JESSICA:	I think I've read every account that was published. I cut out the best ones. (Takes a book from a drawer). The News was much the fullest.

(PAPER RUSTLE)

Why will they always put that in – about the balance of the mind being disturbed? It's upsetting – and usually meaningless.

LAURIE: It means even less in this case.

JESSICA: Oh?

LAURIE: Since he didn't commit suicide at all.

JESSICA: (After a pause) Is that your idea? Or is it official?

LAURIE: Unofficial. The police think it was suicide. They managed to force their ideas on the inquest.

JESSICA: Really? I should have said that it was the only possible verdict. But then – the newspapers may not have had all the facts.

LAURIE: They didn't mention the most important fact. That Daddy was writing a book about his war-time experiences.

JESSICA: Oh?

LAURIE: But that the last chapter – the one he had just finished – was missing.

JESSICA: (Speaking for the first time roughly and sharply) And you think someone stole it? Is that your idea?

LAURIE: Yes.

JESSICA: And killed your father to get it?

LAURIE: Yes.

JESSICA: And poisoned his dog?

LAURIE: (Sharply) How did you know his dog was poisoned?

JESSICA: (Contemptuously) It's in half the newspaper accounts. Here – read them if you don't believe me.

LAURIE: (Taken aback by Jessica's manner) Oh!

JESSICA: (Very sharp) Laurie, you've got to stop this nonsense at once.

LAURIE: It's not nonsense.

JESSICA: (Overriding the interruption) You've been telling yourself stories. Making up mysteries where no sort of mystery exists.

LAURIE: If there's no mystery, where's the last chapter?

JESSICA: I should think the likeliest explanation is that he never wrote it.

LAURIE: I know that he wrote it. He told me he had. Why should he lie to me?

JESSICA: Very well! Then *he* destroyed it.

LAURIE:	How?
JESSICA:	Burned it.
LAURIE:	In that tiny grate. Twenty or thirty pages without leaving a sign?
JESSICA:	Or threw it away.
LAURIE:	Where?
JESSICA:	I—
LAURIE:	Next suggestion. He gave it to the dog to eat and that's what killed him.
JESSICA:	Laurie, for the last time. Will you listen to me. You've got to stop this. If you don't, someone's going to get hurt. Badly hurt.
LAURIE:	I'll stop when I'm convinced that it was suicide. Not before.

(LONGISH PAUSE)

JESSICA:	I once wrote on your report – 'Laurie has a good and tenacious brain. She is as yet incapable of that logical and disciplined thought which is the hallmark of a scholar'.
LAURIE:	Do you remember all your reports?
JESSICA:	I remember that one because I thought very deeply before I wrote it. (Gets up) Let me give you some advice. Before you take any further steps in the matter do some thinking. Think about the dog.
LAURIE:	About Corporal?
JESSICA:	Was that his name? Yes. About Corporal.

(DOOR OPENS)

LAURIE:	By the way, there *was* one other thing.
JESSICA:	Yes?
LAURIE:	When I was talking to Miss Crofts just now, *she* was saying how sorry she was about my father, and when had it happened, and when I mentioned the date, she said, 'Oh, yes,' she remembered that evening particularly. She remembered it because you'd cancelled a staff meeting at the last moment.
JESSICA:	(Indifferently) Yes?
LAURIE:	(Persevering) They saw you drive off in your car, and wondered what could have called you away so suddenly.

| JESSICA: | Private business, Laurie. Private business. Well, goodbye for now. And remember what I said. Think about the dog. |
| LAURIE: | Goodbye. |

(DOOR SHUTS)
(SLOWISH FADE OUT. FADE UP)

BATSON:	Here you are, Loftus. That one – that's from our man in Paris. Yes, you can keep it. It's a copy of what he found in the Archives of the War Ministry.
GORDON:	The Croix de Lorraine?
BATSON:	Yes. They were operating in the hills south of Rouen. The other one is the Hercules Organisation from Amiens. Interesting reading, don't you think?

(PAPERS BEING TURNED OVER. SLIGHT PAUSE)

GORDON:	Very.
BATSON:	They *were* the two names Naylor-Smith mentioned.
GORDON:	I'm sure they were. I wrote them down.
BATSON:	Yes. Well. You can see for yourself. Nothing about Naylor-Smith in either of them – not a word.
GORDON:	What he said was that De Gaulle was so keen on making it an all-French liberation that he suppressed the names of English helpers as far as possible.
BATSON:	He stopped 'em getting medals and public recognition. But this isn't a public document. It's a war diary. A day-by-day account of what went on. And what's more, when English people *did* help, they got mentioned all right. There's an English Liaison Officer in the Hercules Group. Man called Cowper. He features on almost every page.
GORDON:	Might *he* be able to help us?
BATSON:	He might have, only he was killed a week before the Liberation.
GORDON:	Oh.
BATSON:	O.K. It's only negative evidence, I agree. Naylor-Smith may have been working away in the background like a beaver. A pretty invisible beaver. But, as it happens, we've just unearthed another bit of evidence – something a lot more – up-to-date – and more definite.
GORDON:	Yes, Sir?

BATSON:	Simmons has been down at Halsfield, ferreting about. Talking to the locals. He's found two characters who actually saw Naylor-Smith's car come out of the drive around 7.30. They were in the hedge opposite, and I think they may have been setting snares – they're a bit coy about that bit.
GORDON:	But – but that confirms what he told us. He drove into Halsfield, for a Farmers' Union Meeting.
BATSON:	Quite so. And to get to Halsfield you turn left out of the gate. He didn't. He turned right. They're quite definite about that. On the other hand, *if* you turn right it takes you to the back way which leads to the cottage.
GORDON:	I suppose he might have had some other job he wanted to do before the meeting.
BATSON:	There was no meeting.
GORDON:	What!
BATSON:	There was to have been. But *he* put it off.
GORDON:	(Pause) Oughtn't we to tell the police?
BATSON:	All in good time, Loftus. All in good time. They could have found out themselves, if they'd done their job properly. At the moment, it's *our* information. Exclusive. But I think we might ask Naylor-Smith to – comment on it – don't you?

(FADE OUT. FADE UP)

HOUSEKEEPER:	Would there be anything more, Sir?
N-SMITH:	(Deep in his own thoughts, says nothing. Throughout the following scene he is clearly distrait)
HOUSEKEEPER:	Would there be anything more, Sir?
N-SMITH:	Sorry, Mrs Buck. No, nothing more.
HOUSEKEEPER:	There now. You haven't drunk your coffee and you've let it get cold.
N-SMITH:	Sorry. I was just thinking about something else. Did I hear a car drive up just now?
HOUSEKEEPER:	It's that young man – the one from the newspaper. The one that was here that night when poor Mr Bannister – you remember.
N-SMITH:	Yes, I remember. Where is he?
HOUSEKEEPER:	He went off down the path. I expect he was going to the cottage to have a word with Miss Bannister.
N-SMITH:	Oh, yes. I suppose he would be.

(SLIGHT PAUSE)

HOUSEKEEPER: If there isn't anything else, Sir, I was thinking of slipping down to the village to see my daughter. She's not been too well lately.

N-SMITH: That's quite all right, Mrs Buck. Off you go.

(RATTLE OF COFFEE THINGS BEING COLLECTED)

I can look after myself.

HOUSEKEEPER: Thank you, Sir. Then I'll run along. (Off) I put the brandy out on the sideboard.

N-SMITH: Have to be the 12-bore.

(N-SMITH GETS UP OPENS THE CUPBOARD DOOR. NOISE OF 12-BORE SHOT-GUN BEING BROKEN – AND SNAPPED SHUT)
(FADE OUT. FADE UP)

LAURIE: (Low, she and Gordon sitting quite close together) So he was lying?

GORDON: Not just lying about there being a meeting. He cancelled it himself.

LAURIE: When?

GORDON: At the last moment. He telephoned the other committee members.

LAURIE: Did he give any reason?

GORDON: He said he was feeling under the weather. The doctor had advised him to stay indoors.

LAURIE: And that was a lie, too?

GORDON: I think so.

LAURIE: There didn't seem to be anything wrong with him.

GORDON: And anyway, he did go out.

LAURIE: But not to Halsfield.

GORDON: No. (Pause)

LAURIE: So it's pretty clear where he did go. He drove round, parked his car in the lay-by, and walked up here.

GORDON: You told me that although your father and he were neighbours, they didn't visit much.

LAURIE: No.

GORDON: So, to put it mildly, your father would be a bit surprised

	to see Naylor-Smith walk in unannounced at that time of night. What'd he do?
LAURIE:	Knowing Daddy – offer him a drink.
GORDON:	Exactly. And when your father's out of the room – fetching water for the whisky or whatever – nothing easier than to drop a capsule of cyanide in the glass. *And* a piece of poisoned meat into poor old Corporal's dish.
LAURIE:	Why take the car? He could just as easily have walked down.
GORDON:	I fancy we shall find that he was setting up some sort of alibi. He couldn't fake the N.F.U. Committee Meeting. It involved too many people. That's why he had to put it off—
LAURIE:	Then who's the alibi?
GORDON:	We don't know – yet. *Because he hasn't had to use it.* But I don't mind betting that if suspicion swings in his direction, he'll trot it out fast enough. 'I had to put the meeting off', he'll say, 'because I was meeting – someone or other – at some place miles away on the other side of Halsfield – at eight o'clock.'
LAURIE:	You sound pretty sure about this.
GORDON:	I *am* sure. Quite sure. (Pause) Theoretically sure.
LAURIE:	Meaning?
GORDON:	Meaning, Laurie, that I believe it with my head, but not with my heart. He's the obvious person. He had the means *and* the motive *and* the opportunity and what's more, he's been telling lies.
LAURIE:	Well?
GORDON:	I just don't think he's the type.
LAURIE:	You mean he hasn't got the guts.
GORDON:	He hasn't the shape of a killer.
LAURIE:	(Scornfully) To save his precious, phoney, reputation, he'd kill for that.
GORDON:	*If* you're right—
LAURIE:	I know I'm right.
GORDON:	—what are we going to do about? Tell the police what we think? Would they act on it?
LAURIE:	I'm damned certain they wouldn't. Squire Naylor-Smith! A Pillar of the County! If he wrote out a confession *and* swore it in front of a Notary Public they wouldn't believe it.

GORDON: So we do nothing?

LAURIE: Couldn't you get your paper to publish what we've found out. Not make any definite accusations – but sort of – let the facts speak for themselves.

GORDON: They'd never do it. Too scared of libel.

LAURIE: Then suppose *we* tell him.

GORDON: What good would that do?

LAURIE: It'd provoke some sort of reaction, don't you think?

GORDON: (<u>Softly</u>) Did it occur to you that it might provoke a reaction that was altogether too violent for our comfort.

LAURIE: Too violent?

GORDON: If he's killed once to protect himself – has it occurred to you that he might kill again?

LAURIE: (<u>Unconsciously dropping her voice still further</u>) He's not that sort of man – you said so yourself.

GORDON: We were wrong about him once – we could be wrong again.

LAURIE: Talk sense. He was able to kill Daddy because Daddy trusted him. We don't trust him. We'd be on our guard. If he offered us a drink – what is it?

GORDON: It's all right. I thought I heard something. Go on. If he offered us a drink—

LAURIE: We'd refuse it. That's all.

GORDON: I wasn't thinking about poison. I was thinking of something – more direct. He's got plenty of guns in that room of his. Suppose he decided to come down here and stage a little accident.

LAURIE: He'd never dare.

GORDON: (<u>Half joking</u>) Or a suicide scene perhaps – love nest in game-keeper's cottage.

LAURIE: (<u>Jumping up and knocking chair over</u>) You may be enjoying this. I'm not.

GORDON: What's up?

LAURIE: I'm getting out of here.

GORDON: Where are you going?

LAURIE: Back to London. Somewhere where there are plenty of people.

GORDON: I shouldn't.

LAURIE: (<u>Irresolutely</u>) Shouldn't what?

GORDON: Go outside. I thought I heard someone moving a moment ago. I heard it again just now. There *is* someone out there.

LAURIE: (<u>Whispering</u>) Are you sure?

GORDON: Don't whisper. Talk in a natural voice. Yes, I'm quite sure. What I heard was a foot hitting that scraper thing. I nearly fell over it myself the first time I came here. Someone's standing quite quietly outside that door. He's listening to us. He can't hear what we're saying and as long as we go on talking naturally there's a chance he won't come in. There's only one thing for it. We've got to rush him. Can you reach that poker – careful—

(<u>SLIGHT NOISE OF METAL ON STONE</u>)

Good. Now, as soon as I'm in position, you've got to get up quietly, go across and open the door. *But until then keep talking*!

LAURIE: (<u>Conversationally</u>) Oh, God. I can't think of anything to say. One two three. Three blind mice. They all ran after the farmer's wife. She cut off their tails with a carving knife. God, but I'm scared.

GORDON: (<u>Gently</u>) Now.

(<u>A RAPID AND NOISY SEQUENCE. DOOR FLUNG OPEN. CRASH OF POKER HITTING DOOR POST, AND THEN BEING DROPPED WITH A CLANG ON STONE FLOOR. A FLURRY OF FOOTSTEPS. THEN MOMEN-TARY SILENCE</u>)

VIGARS: Hold it. Something bothering you, Mr Loftus. Sorry to startle you, Miss Bannister.

GORDON: (<u>Breathless</u>) Inspector. That man behind you. Watch out for him.

VIGARS: Oh?

GORDON: He's dangerous.

VIGARS: I'm sorry to hear that. Have you two met before?

GORDON: We've met all right. He's called Leslie. I don't know his other name. He works for Major Applin – the night club owner. He's a – he's a criminal.

VIGARS: There now. It just shows how easy it is to jump to conclu-sions, doesn't it, Miss Bannister?

LAURIE: (<u>Angry, because she has been frightened</u>) What's going on Inspector? Who is this man? What are you two doing here?

VIGARS:	One question at a time, eh? This young man is Detective Constable Locke of the Criminal Investigation Department. Seconded, as of now, to the Kent Constabulary to assist them in their investigations.
GORDON:	Leslie!
LESLIE:	Sorry I had to be a bit rough with you, Mr Loftus. Since I was acting as Major Applin's bodyguard – well – I had to act the part, see.
GORDON:	Did you have to be quite so enthusiastic?
LESLIE:	Took me six months to work my way into that job. Couldn't spoil the ship for a ha'porth of tar.
VIGARS:	Next question. You were wondering why we were listening outside your door. The answer to that's quite simple, too. We heard a man's voice but we couldn't quite make out who it was. And we wanted to be sure it *wasn't* Mr Naylor-Smith.
LAURIE:	Oh? Why?
VIGARS:	I thought the time had come for a frank exchange of views, Miss. Last time I spoke to you here, you expressed dissatisfaction about the verdict at the inquest on your father.
LAURIE:	I was dissatisfied then. And I'm a great deal more dissatisfied now.
VIGARS:	Why would that be?
LAURIE:	Because Mr Naylor-Smith lied about his movements that night. He said he was going to a Farmers' Union Meeting at Halsfield. There was no meeting. And he didn't go to Halsfield. Did you know *that*?
VIGARS:	Oh yes. We knew that.
LAURIE:	How—?
VIGARS:	You carry on, Miss. Finish your side of it first. Then I'll give you ours and we'll see how they fit.
LAURIE:	We've found out – not for certain, but almost for certain – that he was guilty of a piece of despicable cowardice during the War. We think my father knew this and had decided – at last – that the truth ought to be told.
VIGARS:	And that would have been in the last chapter of that book he was writing?
LAURIE:	Yes.
VIGARS:	The chapter that disappeared.
LAURIE:	Yes.

VIGARS:	Pity.
LAURIE:	What's a pity?
VIGARS:	It's neat. It's logical. It's convincing. But it isn't true. Naylor-Smith wasn't down here that evening between eight and nine. He wasn't anywhere near here. He was twenty miles away in a pub at Latchingford called the White Hart.
GORDON:	Ah! Didn't I say he'd dream up a phoney alibi.
LAURIE:	Who says he was there?
LESLIE:	I do, Miss.
LAURIE:	*You?*
LESLIE:	One of my jobs, you see, was driving the Major – particularly when he was out on a dodgy trip – something he didn't want other people to know too much about, see?
LAURIE:	Do you mean to say—
LESLIE:	That's right, Miss. It was the Major who was meeting Mr poor-old-sucker Smith at the White Hart. By appointment. And not for the first time either, I gather.
VIGARS:	The fact is, Applin had been blackmailing him for years. What you found out, about his war-time career was true. Not that he betrayed his comrades. I don't think that came into it. But the fact that he didn't really *do* anything at all – the story he told when he got back – it was a lot of wish-wash. He ought never to have had that medal. That's for sure.
LESLIE:	From what I gathered from the Major – he used to laugh about it a good deal – Smithy hid up in a farm. Trouble was, all the young men on the farm had been conscripted by the Germans for forced labour. So, they dressed him up – as a woman.
GORDON:	What—!
LESLIE:	Makes you smile doesn't it. Applin went back to the farm afterwards, got the whole story *and* a photograph of Smithy. *In* a skirt. That was one of the things he was going to circulate. If Smithy didn't cough up.
GORDON:	Good God!
LESLIE:	It wasn't as if Applin actually needed the money. He didn't. But he hated Smithy's guts. Squire Naylor-Smith, D.L., J.P., M.C. The big county magnate. What Applin really enjoyed was watching him squirm.
LAURIE:	The sadistic beast.
VIGARS:	Don't worry, Miss. He'll soon be laughing on the other

side of his face. With what Locke here has picked up about his business methods, we reckon we can put him away safe enough.

GORDON: The only thing is – if he goes down – won't he take damn good care that Squire Naylor-Smith goes down with him? After all, he'll have nothing to lose.

VIGARS: I'm afraid that's a risk we'll have to take. (He breaks off)

(DISTANT SOUND OF 12-BORE SHOT GUN BEING FIRED)

That sounded like a shot. Come on!

(FADE OUT. FADE UP. DISTANT HAMMERING ON FRONT DOOR. DOOR FLUNG OPEN & TWO PAIRS OF FEET POUND ALONG THE PASSAGE. ROOM DOOR FLUNG OPEN. MOMENTARY SILENCE)

VIGARS: (Breathless) What happened, Sir?
N-SMITH: (Indistinctly) What—
VIGARS: We heard a shot.
N-SMITH: Sorry. Terribly sorry.
VIGARS: (More insistent) What happened?
N-SMITH: Cleaning the gun. Must have been loaded. Went off.
VIGARS: I see.
N-SMITH: No harm done, Inspector. Damaged that wall a bit.
VIGARS: That was lucky for you, Sir, wasn't it?

(FURTHER FOOTSTEPS IN PASSAGE)

N-SMITH: Oh, hullo Laurie. Loftus. Silly thing to do. Gun went off.
VIGARS: You'll excuse me saying so, but I should have thought you'd have had enough experience with guns not to do a thing like that.
N-SMITH: Can't account for it.
VIGARS: Perhaps your mind was on other things.
N-SMITH: Yes.
VIGARS: Like Major Applin.

(PAUSE)

N-SMITH:	Major – who? Sorry, I didn't quite get the name.
VIGARS:	Applin. You spent quite a bit of time together in 1944.
N-SMITH:	Oh, *Applin*. Randy Applin. Yes. (<u>Moves off</u>) Would you care for a drink, Inspector?
VIGARS:	Not just now, Sir.
N-SMITH:	Loftus. No? Er – I'm afraid I don't know your name.
VIGARS:	This is Detective Constable Locke, (<u>Firmly</u>) and he won't have a drink either.
N-SMITH:	Oh, well, perhaps you'll excuse me if I do. I'm still feeling a bit shaken. (<u>More comfortably</u>) Applin. Yes, of course I remember Applin. Quite a character, Randy Applin.
VIGARS:	I thought you *might* remember him particularly as you met him so recently.
N-SMITH:	(<u>Vaguely</u>) Met him?
VIGARS:	Ten days ago. At the White Hart at Latchingford. I don't know if you happened to catch sight of the man who was driving his car on that occasion.
N-SMITH:	Was it—?
LESLIE:	That's right, Sir. Of course I had a cap on then. Makes a difference, a cap.
N-SMITH:	(<u>Slowly</u>) Why are you telling me this?
VIGARS:	Because, Sir, I think you can help us. And we can help you.
N-SMITH:	Help me?
VIGARS:	If you'll let us.
N-SMITH:	How?
VIGARS:	It's come to our knowledge that Applin was extorting money from you. Considerable sums. Has been for some time. Well – he's going down. Not for that alone. Other things too. But this is one thing that will come out, that's for certain.
N-SMITH:	I see.
VIGARS:	And it seems to me that the best thing for you to do – in a manner of speaking – is to take the bull by the horns.
N-SMITH:	(<u>Softly</u>) Not sure that I follow you.
VIGARS:	*If* you were willing to give evidence against Applin, on the charge of extortion, it seems to me that you'd come very well out of it, Sir. The Court would protect you. No names. No photographs. In fact, no identification at all. Mr X. You know the form.
N-SMITH:	You're being very frank, Inspector.
VIGARS:	Then you'll help us?

N-SMITH:	Must I give you my answer now?
VIGARS:	We'd like to move in on Applin tomorrow.
N-SMITH:	Then I'll give you my answer tomorrow.
VIGARS:	Fair enough. (<u>Move off</u>) We shall be at Ashford Police Station. I'm going back there now.
N-SMITH:	Don't go, Laurie. Or you, Loftus. There's something I want to say to you. Hang on whilst I show these gentlemen out.

(<u>AGAINST THE BACKGROUND OF THEIR RECEDING STEPS, A MURMUR OF DISTANT CONVERSATION AND FRONT DOOR BANGING</u>)

GORDON:	The gun, Laurie. Pass it over here, quick.

(<u>SOUND OF GUN BEING BROKEN</u>)

Both barrels loaded. (<u>Sniffs</u>) Only one fired. I think we'll have the other cartridge out. Safer like that.

LAURIE:	He couldn't be going to—
GORDON:	Maybe not. All the same, better take no chances. (As he closes the gun and replaces it, Naylor-Smith comes back).
N-SMITH:	Won't you sit down. You're sure you won't have a drink?
GORDON:	Not as sure as I was.

(<u>NAYLOR-SMITH POURS TWO DRINKS</u>)

N-SMITH:	I asked you to stay behind because there was something I had to say to you. I'd judge from what the Inspector said that you know *why* Applin was blackmailing me.
LAURIE:	He was blackmailing you because he hated you.
N-SMITH:	(<u>Surprised</u>) Did he? Yes. I suppose he did. (<u>Pause</u>) I certainly hated him. Because he knew the truth about me. And that's very simple. I'm a coward. Always have been. Expect I always will be. (<u>Drinks – and continues in a conversational tone</u>) In the ordinary way you know, it's a thing a man conceals easily enough. Not from himself, perhaps, but from other people. If you don't hunt and you go to a good dentist and keep clear of bar-room brawls. You can build up a very convincing model of a man. It's only a dummy. But with a bit of luck the truth need never come out. But you can't do it in

	Wartime. Not entirely. You can dodge and duck, but it catches up with you in the end. It caught up with me in France. The alternatives were plain enough. I could lie low and do nothing. Or I could take an active part in the Resistance. With an odds-on chance of getting captured. And I can tell you this, if I *had* been captured, I'd have told the Gestapo anything they wanted to know right away.
GORDON:	So would Applin probably.
N-SMITH:	Probably. He'd have held out a bit longer. Because he had less imagination than I had. What makes you really afraid is the pictures you see inside your own mind. I could *see* that Gestapo whip shining with blood cutting into a naked back, then pulling away with little bits of flesh and skin sticking to it.
LAURIE:	Don't.
N-SMITH:	Do you know, that's why, when it came to the point, I couldn't even shoot myself. At the last moment, I saw my own head with the jaw blown away and the blood running out of the empty eye sockets.
LAURIE:	That's horrible. Stop it.
N-SMITH:	If you understand that, you'll understand what I've been living with for the last twenty-five years. And, you may begin to understand my admiration for your father, who was the bravest man I ever knew. *He* wasn't stupid, like Applin. He had plenty of imagination. But he had it under control and he was modest with it. Do you know what he said when I offered him the cottage to live in? 'As long as we don't see *too* much of each other,' he said, 'We should get on comfortably enough. Two old paper tigers.'
LAURIE:	He said *that*?
N-SMITH:	Yes. (<u>Pause</u>) Of course he was joking.

(<u>TELEPHONE RINGS</u>)

Hullo. (<u>Listens for a moment then pushes 'phone across to Laurie</u>) It's Inspector Vigars. He seems to want to talk to you, Laurie.

LAURIE:	Yes. (<u>Longish pause</u>) Who? (<u>Pause</u>) Are you absolutely sure? (<u>Pause</u>) I see. Well, thank you for telling me.

(<u>RECEIVER REPLACED</u>)

GORDON:	Well?
LAURIE:	That was Inspector Vigars.
GORDON:	We gathered as much. What did he want?
LAURIE:	I think he wanted to apologise for disbelieving you.
GORDON:	Me?
LAURIE:	Remember you said you heard a car starting up and moving away from behind the cottage – that night?
GORDON:	Well?
LAURIE:	They found someone who saw it. And they've got the number. KKJ 116E.
GORDON:	So they'll be able to trace the owner.
LAURIE:	Oh, I *know* who the owner is. That's Miss Wrayburn's car. (Pause) I did wonder why she cut that staff meeting.
N-SMITH:	Jessica, but what on earth could she be doing here.
LAURIE:	I did wonder why she cut that staff meeting.

(FADE OUT. FADE UP WHEEZY OLD GRANDFATHER CLOCK IN GAMEKEEPER'S COTTAGE COUGHING OUT THE HALF-HOUR)

GORDON:	Do you think she'll come?
LAURIE:	She'll come.
GORDON:	When you telephoned her, what did you say?
LAURIE:	I just said, there'd been some important developments about Daddy's death, and could she come over as quickly as possible.
GORDON:	What did she say?
LAURIE:	First she said, 'Oh!'. Then she said, 'All right. I'll be there at half past eight'.
GORDON:	I still can't believe it.
LAURIE:	Why not.
GORDON:	A woman—
LAURIE:	I don't find that difficult. When it comes to the point, women are a lot more ruthless than men. And she'd got most to lose.
GORDON:	More than Squire Naylor-Smith?
LAURIE:	For him, it was loss of face. For her, it meant losing the one job she'd set her mind on.
GORDON:	Would she have lost it?
LAURIE:	You know what College authorities are like. One breath of scandal – even old scandal – and they'd pull down the shutters.

GORDON:	How do you suppose she found out – about the book being finished?
LAURIE:	No difficulty. Daddy would have told her. He wouldn't spring it on her – he was much too fair.
GORDON:	Had she been here before?
LAURIE:	Yes. When I was at school. I thought she came over to discuss my bad character. It was probably to talk about old times.
GORDON:	So she'd know where to put the car. And the back way in.
LAURIE:	Yes. And Corporal knew her. And trusted her. In fact, they both did—
GORDON:	Listen.

(DISTANT CAR PULLING UP. DOOR SLAMMING)

LAURIE:	That's her. You still don't believe it, do you?
GORDON:	It's such a – such a – cold-blooded thing.
LAURIE:	She's a cold-blooded person.
GORDON:	What do you think she'll do – when she knows we know—?

(CRUNCH OF FOOTSTEPS ON THE PATH OUTSIDE)

LAURIE:	I've no idea.

(DOOR CREAKS OPEN. MOMENTARY SILENCE)

JESSICA:	Well, Laurie?
LAURIE:	Won't you come in.
JESSICA:	Ah, and—?
GORDON:	My name is Gordon Loftus.
JESSICA:	I gather there's something you want to tell me?

(DOOR CLOSES)

	Something urgent.
LAURIE:	Yes.
JESSICA:	Well?
LAURIE:	(With nervous determination) I want to know – why you killed my father.
JESSICA:	(Grimly) Aren't you telescoping two questions? First. Did I kill your father? Second. If I killed him, why did I do it?

LAURIE: We know you did it. You put off your meeting that night. And you drove over and left your car; exactly where you left it just now, then you came up here and—

JESSICA: Go on—

LAURIE: You killed him. Both of them. You poisoned Corporal to prevent him attacking you – and you poisoned Daddy.

JESSICA: Do you mind if I sit down.

(SCRAPE OF CHAIR)

I warned you once before, Laurie, that although you have plenty of imagination, you lack the faculty of disciplined reasoning. If you'd thought about this – if you'd thought about it clearly – for even ten seconds – you'd see that what you're suggesting is completely impossible.

LAURIE: Oh?

JESSICA: Which of them am I supposed to have poisoned *first*? Your father or the dog?

(PAUSE)

Cyanide acts instantaneously. If the dog was lying dead, do you imagine your father would have quietly accepted a drink—?

LAURIE: In that case—

JESSICA: But – if your father had died first the dog wouldn't have eaten his food. He'd have attacked *me*. You said so yourself.

(LAURIE IS STILL TRYING TO GRAPPLE WITH THIS)

Or do you perhaps suggest that I stage-managed the affair with such exquisite precision that the dog consumed a slice of poisoned meat *and* your father drank a poisoned drink at precisely the same moment? (Pause) It won't work, Laurie. Think again.

LAURIE: It's no good. Whatever you say. I *know* you did it.

JESSICA: I see. Credo quia impossibile. Then perhaps we can move on to the second part of your proposition. Why should I kill your father – who was, incidentally, one of my oldest friends.

LAURIE: You killed him because he told you what he'd put in the last chapter of his book.

JESSICA: Which was—?

LAURIE: The name of the person who betrayed Max and his helpers to the Gestapo.

JESSICA: And that was supposed to be me, was it?

LAURIE: Yes.

JESSICA: Although I never left England.

LAURIE: We know all about that. You sent the names over the air to the Gestapo man who'd taken Gerard's place. You did it because you thought you could save Gerard's life.

JESSICA: (<u>After a pause</u>) I wonder. Really, I do wonder.

LAURIE: What?

JESSICA: If it *had* been put to me – just like that – I wonder whether I should have done it. In the light of after knowledge, of course, the answer's 'No'. You could never trust the Gestapo. But at the time – I was very fond of Gerard. Yes I might have been tempted. (<u>With a brisk return to the present</u>). But since it *wasn't* put to me, the question doesn't arise. I think you'd better know what happened that night.

LAURIE: (<u>Grimly</u>) I think I had.

JESSICA: But I think I should tell you alone.

GORDON: Er – no – I'm afraid I can't agree to that.

JESSICA: What I have to tell Laurie is for her alone. (<u>Pause</u>) Well? What are you afraid of? Do you think I shall try to poison her too?

GORDON: I think she might feel more comfortable if I stayed.

JESSICA: I can assure you that she won't.

(<u>PAUSE</u>)

LAURIE: I shall be all right, Gordon.

JESSICA: (<u>Sardonic</u>) You can stay quite close, Mr Loftus. In the garden. If you hear her scream you can come rushing in. I'm sure you'd enjoy *that*.

GORDON: Laurie – are you sure—?

LAURIE: I'll be all right. Really.

(<u>DOOR OPENS AND CLOSES</u>)

(<u>To Jessica</u>) Well?

JESSICA:	I came here that night in answer to a telephone call from your father. He was obviously upset, almost incoherent. But one thing was clear. He wanted me. So I put off my meeting and I drove over. When I came into this room the first thing I saw was the dog lying dead on the floor. And the next thing I saw was your father. In that chair you're sitting in. He was dead too.
LAURIE:	(<u>Fiercely</u>) It's a lie. You're making it up.
JESSICA:	(<u>Unperturbed</u>) I'm afraid it's the truth. And I know who killed him. There's not the least mystery about it. There never has been.
LAURIE:	Go on.
JESSICA:	Are you sure you want to know?
LAURIE:	Of course I do.
JESSICA:	You don't think, perhaps that after twenty-five years, one should let the dead bury their dead.
LAURIE:	I'm going to know. And I'm going to see that everyone else knows.
JESSICA:	Youth, youth. So clear sighted. Black or white. Right or wrong. No half-truths. *No compromising*. Let justice be done though the sky fall. Never mind how uncomfortable it may be for the people it falls on.
LAURIE:	It's no use. You can't talk your way out of this.
JESSICA:	So I see. Actions not words.

(<u>DOCUMENT CASE UNZIPPED</u>)

LAURIE:	What's that?
JESSICA:	The last chapter of your father's book.
LAURIE:	So it *was* you who stole it.
JESSICA:	Stole, Laurie? Since it was lying on the table, in this envelope addressed to me, in your father's own handwriting, I hardly think we can call it stealing.

(<u>LAURIE HAS GASPED AT THE SIGHT OF THE ENVE-
LOPE. TURNS PAGES OF MANUSCRIPT</u>)

You'll find what you're looking for on page eight. I've marked the place.

(<u>MORE PAGES TURNED OVER</u>)

LAURIE:	But's it not true – it can't be true.
JESSICA:	(<u>Slowly</u>) Truth, as the ancient pointed out, is a lady. She lives at the bottom of a well. She comes up very rarely, but when she does appear, there is no mistaking her face.

(<u>CONTINUING TURNING OF PAGES</u>)

LAURIE:	Then it was *him*. It was Daddy himself – who betrayed Max, and all his people.
JESSICA:	Yes.
LAURIE:	I don't believe it.
JESSICA:	Nothing the Gestapo could do to him would have made him utter a single word. I'm as sure of that as you are. But they had one weapon that even he couldn't face. They tortured his wife – in front of him. They went on – until *he* broke down. That's the secret he's been carrying with him all these years. In the end, he couldn't live with it any longer. So he wrote it all down, in these last few pages, to let the world know. Maybe, also, to clear anyone else who might be under suspicion. That'd be like him too. And when he'd done it – when he'd written the last word, he ended a life which had become a burden to him. And he took old Corporal along with him – for company.
LAURIE:	Oh – (<u>It is a cry of pain</u>)

(<u>DOOR OPENS</u>)

GORDON:	Laurie, what is it?
LAURIE:	(<u>Fiercely</u>) Go away.
GORDON:	I heard you call out. What's she done to you?
LAURIE:	Please go away.

(<u>DOOR CLOSES</u>)

GORDON:	Very well, if that's what you want.
JESSICA:	Poor young man. He'll never know how near he was to the scoop of a lifetime. Well, Laurie. Do we observe your father's wishes? Do we tell the truth? Hurt who it may. Do we tell the world?
LAURIE:	(<u>She is crying</u>) No – no.
JESSICA:	Let justice be done, though the sky fall.
LAURIE:	(<u>Recovering some of her spirit</u>) This is *quite* different.

JESSICA: Then might I suggest we have a good fire here – if we tore the sheets up, and fed them in.

(<u>SOUND OF PAPER BEING TORN ACROSS</u>)

—one at a time.

LAURIE: (<u>Against a background of roaring flames</u>) Poor old Daddy.

APPENDIX A

The Casebook of Henry Montacute Bohun

The following includes all known short stories and plays as well as the full length novel in which Henry Bohun features. All the stories had their first publication in a variety of newspapers and magazines, mainly in the 1950s. In later publications, some of the stories were given alternative titles.

Novels

'Smallbone Deceased' (United Kingdom, Hodder and Stoughton, 1950; United States, Harper, 1950)

Short Story Collections

'Stay of Execution' (U.K., Hodder and Stoughton, 1971)
    Xinia Florata
    The System
    Weekend at Wapentake

'The Man Who Hated Banks and Other Mysteries' (U.S., Crippen and Landru, 1997)
    Every Monday, a New Letter
    Money is Honey
    After All These Years
    The Craven Case
    An Appealing Pair Of Legs

'A Pity About The Girl and Other Stories' (U.K., Robert Hale, 2008)
    What Happened At Castelbonato?

Plays

'The Man Who Could Not Sleep' (U.K., Robert Hale, 2010)

    The Man Who Could Not Sleep – A serial thriller in six parts

    The Hampstead Flat

    The Early Hours of the Morning

    Miss Tappett and Her Tortoises

    Trouble at the Law Society

    Closing the Gap

    The Traveller's Rest

APPENDIX B

Radio plays by Michael Gilbert with dates of broadcast

Plays especially written for radio

The Man Who Could Not Sleep – A serial thriller in six parts on the light programme.

21/07/1955	The Hampstead Flat
28/07/1955	The Early Hours of the Morning
04/08/1955	Miss Tappett and Her Tortoises
11/08/1955	Trouble at the Law Society
18/08/1955	Closing The Gap
25/08/1955	The Traveller's Rest
20/03/1956	Unnatural Causes (No.1 in the series 'Doctor at Law') broadcast on Home Service
30/11/1957	The Waterloo Table – Home Service (H.S.)
19/07/1958	You Must Take Things Easy – Light Programme (L.P.)
10/01/1970	The Last Chapter – Radio 4 (repeated 12/01/70)
01/04/1972	Black Light – Radio 4
14/07/1979	In the Nick of Time – Radio 4

Adaptations of novels and short stories for radio

08/06/1953	Death in Captivity (adapted by Wolf Rilla) H.S.
25/09/1954	Blackmail Is So Difficult (adapted by Michael Gilbert) H.S.
13/11/1954	Fear To Tread (adapted by C.E. Webber) H.S.
28/05/1955	Death Has Deep Roots (adapted by Antony Brown) H.S.

Crime Report – A series of four episodes based on Gilbert's short story The Murder of Diana Devon broadcast on L.P.

03/07/1956	The Body of a Girl
10/07/1956	The Fingers of a Hand
17/07/1956	The Missing Fortnight
24/07/1956	The Final Question

25/08/1956   Sky High (adapted by Wolf Rilla) H.S.

16/11/1963   After The Fine Weather (adapted by Cynthia Pughe) H.S.

03/10/1965 to 07/11/1965 Stay of Execution – A series of six untitled episodes. L.P.

Game Without Rules – A series in twenty parts. Radio 2

28/10/1968	In Which Mr. Calder Acquires A Dog
31/10/1968	The Peaceful People
04/11/1968 and 07/11/1968 The Spoilers
11/11/1968	The Road To Damascus
14/11/1968	Cat Cracker
18/11/1968 and 21/11/1968 Double, Double
25/11/1968	One-to-Ten
28/11/1968	The African Tree Beavers
02/12/1968 and 05/12/1968 Cross-Over
09/12/1968	The Lion and the Virgin
12/12/1968	Ahmed and Ego
16/12/1968	The Mercenaries
19/12/1968	Churchill's Men
23/12/1968 and 26/12/1968 Heilige Nacht
30/12/1968	Signal Tresham
02/01/1969	St. Ethelburga and the Angel of Death

10/07/1971   Smallbone Deceased (adapted by Nesta Pain) Radio 4 (repeated 28/12/1987)

19/10/1974   Flash Point Radio 4

Petrella – A series of fifteen plays based on the short stories. The last nine episodes were adapted by Michael Butt.

09/09/1976	The Elusive Baby – Radio 4
16/09/1976	The Death of Mrs Key – Radio 4

23/09/1976	The Banting Street Fire – Radio 4
30/09/1976	Why Tarry The Wheels Of His Chariot – Radio 4
09/06/1979	The Last Tenant Radio – 4
06/04/1983	The Oyster Catcher – Radio 4
19/11/1997	The Phantom Billboard – Radio 4
10/08/1999	Good Fences Make Good Neighbours (repeated 02/11/2009 and 03/11/2009)
17/08/1999	The Myth Of Return (repeated 03/11/2009 and 04/11/2009)
24/08/1999	Vengeance Foreseen (repeated 04/11/2009 and 05/11/2009)
31/08/1999	Outpacing The Fiend (repeated 05/11/2009 and 06/11/2009)
25/06/2001	Heroes and Villains (repeated 12/11/2009 and 13/11/2009)
02/07/2001	Missionary Position (repeated 13/11/2009 and 14/11/2009)
09/07/2001	Death Watch (repeated 16/11/2009 and 17/11/2009)
16/07/2001	Original Sin (repeated 17/11/2009 and 18/11/2009)

Adaptations of stage plays for radio

| 29/09/1962 | A Clean Kill (adapted by Cynthia Pughe) H.S. |
| 30/03/1964 | The Bargain (adapted by Peggy Wells) H.S. |

APPENDIX C

Television plays and serials written by Michael Gilbert with date of broadcast.

Date	Series	Episode
01/12/1956	Crime of the Century	The Death of a Canary
08/12/1956	Crime of the Century	Abbie
15/12/1956	Crime of the Century	Taffy
22/12/1956	Crime of the Century	Major Trump
29/12/1956	Crime of the Century	The Century Opens
05/01/1957	Crime of the Century	The Century Closes
15/06/1957	Wideawake	Trouble Near Lincoln's Inn
22/06/1957	Wideawake	Digging for Evidence
29/06/1957	Wideawake	Cork is Drawn
06/07/1957	Wideawake	In Search of Wideawake
13/07/1957	Wideawake	Visitors to the British Museum
20/07/1957	Wideawake	All Ends Meet at Watersmeet
27/04/1958	Saturday Night Theatre	The Body of a Girl
05/07/1958	Fair Game	Bull and Bear
12/07/1958	Fair Game	St Asaph's School for Boys
19/07/1958	Fair Game	The Black Cat
26/07/1958	Fair Game	The Carleon Country Club
02/08/1958	Fair Game	The House in Warren Square
09/08/1958	Fair Game	The Golden Oriole
14/08/1958	Crime Report (Dramatised Documentary)	
07/04/1959	Blackmail is so Difficult	
14/08/1959	Dangerous Ice	
02/11/1959	The Men From Room 13	The Man Who Stole Cameos Pt 1
09/11/1959	The Men From Room 13	The Man Who Stole Cameos Pt 2
16/11/1959	The Men From Room 13	The Man Who Made Keys Pt 1
23/11/1959	The Men From Room 13	The Man Who Made Keys Pt 2
30/11/1959	The Men From Room 13	The Man Who Sold Romances Pt 1

07/11/1959	The Men From Room 13	The Man Who Sold Romances Pt 2
11/11/1950	No Hiding Place, one episode, The Man Who Left His Coat	
14/11/1959	The Men From Room 13	The Man Who Watched Birds Pt 1
21/12/1959	The Men From Room 13	The Man Who Watched Birds Pt 2
28/12/1959	The Men From Room 13	The Man Who Lost His Trousers Pt 1
04/01/1960	The Men From Room 13	The Man Who Lost His Trousers Pt 2
11/01/1960	The Men From Room 13	The Man Who Tried Too Hard Pt 1
18/01/1960	The Men From Room 13	The Man Who Tried Too Hard Pt 2
16/03/1960	A Clean Kill – A scene from the Duchess Theatre production	
29/04/1961	The Men From Room 13	The Man Who Made Fires Pt 1
30/04/1961	The Sunday Night Play	Scene of the Accident
06/05/1961	The Men From Room 13	The Man Who Made Fires Pt 2
13/05/1961	The Men From Room 13	The Man Who Made a List Pt 1
20/05/1961	The Men From Room 13	The Man Who Made a List Pt 2
27/05/1961	The Men From Room 13	The Man Who Made Careful Arrangements Pt 1
03/06/1961	The Men From Room 13	The Man Who Made Careful Arrangements Pt 2
10/06/1961	The Men From Room 13	The Man Who Made Money Pt 1
17/06/1961	The Men From Room 13	The Man Who Made Money Pt 2
24/06/1961	The Men From Room 13	The Man Who Made Things Go Pt 1
01/07/1961	The Men From Room 13	The Man Who Made Things Go Pt 2
08/07/1961	The Men From Room 13	The Men Who Made Trouble Pt 1
15/07/1961	The Men From Room 13	The Men Who Made Trouble Pt 2
22/07/1961	The Men From Room 13	The Men Who Made Trouble Pt 3
01/10/1961	The Sunday Night Play	A Clean Kill
16/12/1962	ITV Drama 62	The Betrayers
09/06/1963	Sunday Play	Trial Run
14/08/1963	BBC Zero One	Louder Than Nightingales
26/07/1964	Armchair Mystery Theatre	The Blackmailing of Mr S
14/06/1965	The Mind of the Enemy	The New Member
21/06/1965	The Mind of the Enemy	The Trap
28/06/1965	The Mind of the Enemy	A Forcing Bid
05/07/1965	The Mind of the Enemy	Process of Elimination
12/07/1965	The Mind of the Enemy	The Fatal Slip
16/07/1965	The Third Man	The Trial of Harry Lime
03/06/1966	The Man In Room 17	Undue Influence
19/03/1971	ITV Hadleigh	The Sealed Offer

30/07/1971	AP Herbert's Misleading Cases	The Usual Channel (adapted with Christopher Bond)
06/08/1971	AP Herbert's Misleading Cases	What is a Snail? (adapted with Christopher Bond)
20/08/1971	AP Herbert's Misleading Cases	The Sitting Bird (adapted with Christopher Bond)
27/08/1971	AP Herbert's Misleading Cases	A Tiger in Your Bank
03/09/1971	AP Herbert's Misleading Cases	How Free is a Freeman? (adapted with Christopher Bond)
10/09/1971	AP Herbert's Misleading Cases	Regina vs Sagitarrius (adapted with Christopher Bond)
10/08/1974	Orson Welles Great Mysteries	Money To Burn (from the short story The Psychologist by Margery Allingham)
13/11/1975	Orson Welles Great Mysteries	Where There's a Will